The Quest

Book One: A Tale of Revenge

The Quest

Book One: A Tale of Revenge

S E Wilson

Birch Tree Publishing

Birch Tree Publishing

originally published by Sumner Wilson 2012

Bought to you by the Publishers of Birch Tree Publishing
ISBN: 978-1-990089-07-7

Chapter Listings

The Quest

Book One: A Tale of Revenge

SWEET HOME, KANSAS, 1880

For Linda

1

It'd been an especially slow night for a Saturday. Jack Mahan had closed the doors of his saloon early. He and Carla Daws, his barmaid, sat at their table and talked over their day as she counted out the take. At length, he scraped back his chair, and stood up to await the end of her tally. He loved to watch as she concentrated on the count. Her brows knitted in deep thought, and then the muscles involved in this activity slowly relaxed, which allowed her face to flower once more with the soft, golden sway of the honesty and goodness of the woman's spirit.

Carla smiled up at him when she finished, then handed him the sturdy canvas sack that held today's meager receipts. In the bright glow of the overhead lamplight, her eyes sparkled and glinted with an extraordinary sense of humor—one of the outstanding characteristics of her personality.

She tossed her hair back out of her eyes and smiled up at him.

"Think you can tote so much money, mister?" she said. "I hope you don't strain your back."

Jack laughed. "Probably, but you can help. Come on out back with me. Be my guard."

"Get out of here." She shooed him with the dainty fingers of one hand. Her tender palm flashed white as the bloom of a lily in the silky glow of the lamplight.

"Never know but what I might run into trouble."

"Yes, but you'd run into greater trouble if I stepped inside your bedroom with you." She wrinkled her brow in mock displeasure.

He turned and crossed the floor to the door that led into the storage room.

He clutched the moneybag beneath an arm, took up a lamp off a small table alongside the door, located a match in a pocket of his brocaded vest, and swiped it in a swift motion down the door face. The match flared to life from the quick swipe, and the sharp, unpleasant sulfur odor of the match stung his nostrils. He removed the globe, touched the flame to the wick, which sputtered in an aggressive protest. He placed the globe back on the lamp, and when the flame brightened, he twisted the doorknob.

With the door in hand, he paused and peered back once more at Carla. She smiled. He returned the smile and stepped down into his storage room to go to his bedroom to stash the money in his floor safe.

He planned to keep the money in the safe in his bedroom until Monday when he would deposit it in the bank. The sputter of the lamp grew sinister when he shut the door, and its eerie, pale yellow light threw his humpbacked shadow along the east wall. A keen sensation of doom fired up in his mind then. He sensed trouble, and it grew even stronger as he drew nearer his bedroom.

The soles of his feet tingled. His breath caught in his chest, and his heart pounded loud against his inner chest. The pressure grew until he felt his ears were about to explode.

Then, standing at his bedroom door, he experienced a powerful urge to turn, flee back inside the saloon, and return with his Colt .44.

But what would Carla think? Would she laugh at him? Would she think he'd been foolish to flee from shadows? He thought so, and she would be right, too. He shrugged, aware that he couldn't follow his instincts this time, and decided there were worse things than grim thoughts and gut-fear.

He tossed aside his instincts, opened the door, and stepped up into his bedroom, leaving the door open. Just then, his intuitive sense of anxiety nearly knocked him down, and he felt he could smell danger.

The room held a chifforobe for his duds and boots, a small round table on which to place his lamp, and two plain, straight-backed chairs, one on a side, and the cot he slept in. As a bachelor, he required little room, and owned no luxuries. In fact, Jack lived a life of austerity that would put to shame the strictest religious monastic order.

He set the lamp atop the table, turned around, and caught a whiff of sour sweat, of horseflesh. The sense of unease he'd felt erupted then in full-fledged fright, and he fought to control his breath, which threatened to explode inside his lungs.

"Hell," he muttered.

A man sat on the edge of his cot with a pistol in hand.

"Take it," Jack said. He tossed the moneybag toward the man. "Knocked the lock off my back door, didn't you?"

The intruder caught the bag neatly out of the air, glanced at it with little interest, then put it inside a jacket pocket. He smiled smugly from beneath his wide mustache, put his feet beneath him, stood up, and trained his pistol on Mahan's broad chest.

Jack exhaled a slow bitter breath, and just as he did so, Carla Daws cried out from inside the saloon.

"Jack, look out!" Her voice sounded mute and far off through the wall that separated them.

He took a step forward to go to her.

The man with the gun had different ideas. He stuck the barrel of his pistol into Mahan's gut, and this put the quietus to that notion.

The man stood about five-eight, short, but strongly built.

Jack noted the small tuft of hair beneath his lower lip, known as a barbula. It looked to Jack as if he'd spent considerable time with it, for he'd sculpted it in the exact shape of an upside down spade-spot straight off a gaming card, which revealed the man's conceit.

"On outside," he said, and stepped to the side to allow Jack enough room to pass.

Jack stepped forward, but stopped as he drew alongside him. The notion to take the gun from him caught fire in his mind.

The robber must've been a mind reader, saw the intent in his eyes, or possessed an extraordinary instinct for trouble.

He popped Jack with the barrel of his pistol, flush against his thickly ridged brow. Jack's stumbled backward as if he'd stepped unaware on a sheet of glare-ice. He performed a couple of nifty dance steps and stayed on his feet. When he hit the floor safe, he latched on to it, and this saved him from a fall.

He shook his head in sidelong arcs and prevented the blinds of darkness from falling down inside his mind. Blood flew in a misty spray, and he seemed to gaze at the sun through a thin screen of red clay dust.

He touched his benumbed nose where the gun barrel had skidded downward off his brow onto it. Broken.

Jack had been a prizefighter in his youth and had a keen knowledge of the unique sensation of broken bones. His nose had been broken several times. He also knew how an opponent's nasal bones felt as they snapped beneath his own fists.

"That's so you'll know I'm not asleep," the man said.

Jack's vision returned slowly. The headshaking prevented him from going under. But he knew he could shake his head all day long, and this cocky little strong-armed man would still be there when he finally stopped. He figured he'd go along with him until he found a way out of the trap he'd fallen into.

"What do you want, mister?"

The man should be after money. But when he ordered Jack out of the room without looting the safe, this generated a troublesome notion the intruder wanted something else. All he had in the world worth much, besides his Sweet Home friends, was Carla Daws. She was his lady friend and close companion, and he would hate himself if she got hurt.

He swiped a backhand across his nose. The flow of blood decreased.

The bad man flagged him toward the doorway again, and Jack did as ordered.

2

Jack stepped back again into the gloomy storage room.

"Inside," the man commanded.

He nudged him in the back with the barrel of his pistol and pushed him on inside the saloon.

Someone had snuffed out every lamp inside the saloon, except for a small one behind the bar. The room looked haunted to Jack. Dismal, sinister shadows stood everywhere. The weak glow of the lamp cast just enough light to show the bright glimmer of the recently polished bar. He cast his eyes down its length, spying another cutthroat at the far end.

This man held Carla Daws around the neck by a thick forearm across her windpipe, which forced her eyes to bulge and roll in fright. Jack heard her pitiful, snubbing attempts to weep, for the man's thick arm restricted her air.

"What the hell's going on here?" Jack said. "Turn her loose. Take all the money and leave us be."

"Shut up, barkeep. Your racket'll bring the whole town."

"Everyone's home in bed at this hour," Jack said. "Turn Carla loose.
What is she to you?"

The man behind him struck him in the back of the head with the heavy barrel of his pistol. The blow dropped Jack's eyelids. His knees buckled. His head knelled like a rung bell. "I told you to shut up. If you bring somebody on the run, you'll be the first to die."

Jack hated the sound of the man's voice. He looked at Carla. Her eyes screamed for mercy, and for him to go along with them, no matter what they were after.

Jess Jordan, the sheriff of McDonald County, had been in earlier to look in on them, then left to check on the other three saloons in town. Jess wouldn't be back tonight, Jack figured.

All the other merchants along High Street had long ago blown out their lamps and hit the hay. He and Carla were on their own in this. It fell so silent in the room Jack could hear the individual intake and release of breath from all there. He also heard the soft whisper of clothing whenever someone moved.

He did not know what the men were after and realized they were in no hurry.

Just then, he heard the soft snuffle of a horse out front, and a few seconds later, a huge troll of a man appeared.

It hadn't snowed yet, but was plenty cold enough to wear a coat outdoors.

The man who entered the room wore a heavy dark wool overcoat, the bottom hem of which struck his boot tops.

He paused at the table nearest the door, removed his coat, tossed it over the back of a chair, and placed his low-crowned beaver hat atop the coat, as if he planned to stay awhile.

The man turned to him. Jack saw just how huge he really was. Not tall, but possessing enormous shoulders that rippled with muscles beneath his shirt, and with a chest the size of Jack's safe. The man strutted to the center of the room. His booted feet struck the floorboards in a loud ring, and he stared about him in a grave assessment. When he swiveled on his toes, his eyes struck Jack first, then moved on to Carla Daws.

"Jack!" she cried out.

Her guard stifled her with an arm wedged across her windpipe.

Tears brimmed at the edge of her eyes, ready to burst forth and cascade down her face.

Carla sounded tormented, filled with revulsion for the man who'd just entered the saloon.

"I'll get to you in a moment, Lenore," the man said.

He stepped toward Jack, stopped, and stared up at him, for Jack stood several inches taller.

His face and not only his face, but his entire baldhead, were covered in long dry runnels of twisted, raised scars like where the flow of a volcano had sliced up the earth in deep ditches, creating high and serrated ridges.

Jack figured the man had spent a long term in hell, but had somehow fought his way out. A chill raced throughout his system. He shivered as if he'd just avoided stepping on a snake.

Years ago, as a young man in his uncle's saloon in St. Louis, his uncle warned Jack of just such men. He referred to them as mentally unhinged—degenerates.

He'd run up against a few of the type his uncle Hank had warned him about.

This man, though, looked to be a breed apart—one upon a more dangerous level.

He spun a finger in the air. The guard whirled Jack around.

"Put your hands behind you, Mahan."

Jack heard the heavy clank of chains and felt cold iron manacles bind his arms behind him. When he finished the task, the man spun him back around.

"I've searched for your lady friend there for a good long time," he said. He nodded toward Carla and shoved in closer.

"In case you don't know who you've been sleeping with, Mahan … Lenore's my wife."

Jack felt that Carla would have nothing to do with such a man, but locked the lid to his trap shut.
"This woman, who now calls herself Carla Daws, is an impostor and a thief. She's so devious I doubt she even has a soul."
"Look, I don't know or care what she was in the past. All I know is she works for me now and is an excellent employee…"
The man raised a hand to silence Jack. "I know all that, Mahan."
Jack was still shocked at the man's outlandish claim.
The repulsively ugly man laughed, although he was the only one to do so.
"This demon who now calls herself Carla Daws loves to burn people. It's a miracle she hasn't set fire to you while you were asleep."
He pushed away from Jack, strode over to Carla and raised her chin from her chest.
"I take you home, Lenore," he said in a soft voice, which sounded as if it held genuine affection for her, and this revealed his softer side. "Mother has missed you. I've missed you. We've all missed you."
She attempted to withstand his cold, pierce-eyed gaze for a time, lost out, then dropped her face from his.
"You know this man, Carla?"
His guard struck him in the back of the skull. He mumbled curses at his tormentor. The man busted him again.
The big man forced Carla's head upward toward the ceiling, presenting her fragile neck. "You've given me quite a chase. This is the longest you've hidden from me."
She sobbed freely then, and this pained Jack.
The big man stared over his shoulder at Jack, then added, "Lenore has a habit of running away from home. I believe this is the fourth time, isn't it, Lenore?"
Carla didn't answer, and he said, "She won't cooperate right now, but take it from me. This is the fourth time. She takes a peculiar delight in frustrating me. It's become her little game. A small game she enjoys.
"So far, I've gone along with it since I love her so. But, now, well—I've grown weary of it all."
He leaned in closer, peering deeper into her face. "You hear me, Lenore? I'm plenty fed up with this little amusement of yours."
The degenerate applied pressure to her chin, squeezed hard, forced her to cry out, and Jack felt her fear. When it seemed she'd cried out sufficiently, he released her.
"If you fly again, I'll clip your wings. That way I'll be sure you stay in your cage."
Carla dropped her head.

The scarred man swung about, moved back toward Jack, calling out to the man who held Carla. "You and Billy Bolt take her on ahead in the buggy, Withers. We'll catch up when we're done with Mahan."

The saloonkeeper figured they would beat him to a pulp now. This wouldn't be the first time, of course, but at thirty-three, he was no longer a young man. The wonderful resiliency of his youth had already begun its retreat.

Just then, the big man drew over his head a razor on a thin chain, kept hidden under his shirt. In a sharp flash of reflected light, the blade sprang open from between handles of tan bone.

Withers escorted Carla out the front door. Jack drew up a knee and kicked the big man in the groin.

Carla's child-like sobbing disturbed him even more and lingered long after she left the building.

The man folded inward.

Jack kicked him again and watched him crash in a heap like waste rags. He wouldn't allow the man to slice him up with the razor. Not until after the fight, at least.

The man behind him rapped him with his pistol barrel again.

Jack's head expanded and then exploded. He fell to his knees. In the darkness brought about by the blow, he saw the approach of the cold, corkscrewing black tunnel that always precedes unconsciousness. Somehow, he turned it aside.

"Hold," roared the big man.

He stirred to life from the pile of rags Jack's knee made of him.

"Hold back. If you knock him out, you'll answer for it. I want him alert for what I have in mind."

Jack heard a buggy outside get up in the wind, heard it pound on up High Street like Satan's personal coach-and-four.

The deviant stood with the razor held firmly in hand.

Jack Mahan watched his every move with a wary eye. With a deft twist of the man's wrist, the razor rolled until the blade caught and turned the lamplight. Its brilliance dimmed Jack's vision for an instant, like sunlight upon the surface of a swift, rippling stream.

He attempted to warn him. "Mister..." But he got no further. The blade shot forward in a swift blur. Jack felt only the slightest touch, as if a butterfly had just brushed him.The man then stepped back to wait.

He wondered briefly if the strike had even drawn blood. No sooner had he thought this, though, than he felt a warm, lazy trickle of liquid wend down his eyebrow. The man's face brightened with the raptness of a child promised a bright red apple. Jack realized beyond a doubt now that the talk he'd heard in his uncle's saloon years ago had been true. How certain men for some no-good reason derived pleasure from wounding a man, then watching with joy as the stricken one suffered worlds of agony.

3

The swift movements of the man's hand blurred Jack's vision. The lamplight flashed off the blade. Again, he experienced the soft brush of tiny wings against his face—the ridge of his left eye, this time. He felt the warm spread of blood oozing over his brow into both eyes.

He blinked against the blood to free his vision, and it worked for a second.

For he had no trouble seeing the incredible glow of elation lighting up the man's face.

The big man struck him with the razor again, on the right side, and then set up a soft, repetitious murmur like a contented infant at the breast of its mother, which sounded perverse, arising from the chest of an adult.

The man's breath grew ragged.

"I don't intend to kill you, Mahan. After all, you had no way to know Lenore belonged to me. But you'll soon discover sometimes death would be best."

He made it seem as if Jack were getting a bargain.

The razor sprang alive in his hand again. This time, Jack heard and felt the strike.

The blade raked his jawbone, his jaw teeth, and he was shocked to discover it'd penetrated the flesh of his cheek … all the way through.

He raised a leg to kick at him, but the man by now had grown as wary as a spooked horse. He kicked at him anyway, but missed. The man's eyes grew wider with twisted pleasure.

"I'll take both your eyes, Mahan," he said. "Or should I leave one? I'll soon make you cry for mercy. If you cry enough to suit me … if it pleases me, maybe I'll leave you one."

The thick wrist rolled once more, and once again, the blade turned the lamplight like the sun.

Jack expected the next strike and jerked his head to the side.

The silky blade caromed off his jawbone, and plunged downward, traversed the side of his neck to the collarbone, skidded to the left and missed the carotid artery by less than an inch.

"You have to hold still. I said I wouldn't kill you, but if you continue to flounder about your apt to cause your own death.

"Now hold still while I fix your face so Carla won't be attracted to you."

Blood flowed freely down Jack's shirtfront. He felt the cloth of his shirt cling to his chest like an extra layer of skin. He smelled his own blood, rank, acidic, hot.

Jack muttered a long string of obscenities then and tried again to kick him.

This served only to set the man off again. He cooed like a pleased pigeon. His pupils grew enormous, and he twisted about like a wormy dog.

Jack discovered by this, the man expected him to react in this way. So he decided it best to remain silent in hopes this would cool his fire. Maybe if the man grew bored, he might light out, and leave him enough time to go down to Dr. Caron's residence before he bled to death.

Both of Jack's cheeks stung from his wounds. Blood flowed down his brow and mingled with his sweat. Hungry for diversion, he locked his eyes upon a large painting on the far wall, a reproduction of the recent battle between U. S. Cavalrymen and Plains Indians, which a brewery in St. Louis sent him in an advertising campaign.

The big man said, "A man can get by with only one eye." He extended the razor, and passed it before Jack's face, as if attempting to decide which eyeball to take.

"Does it matter," he continued, "which eye I pluck?"

To subdue his growing panic, Jack forced himself to think of Carla Daws. Of how they'd become noble friends. Somehow, the thing he'd once vowed never to allow happen to him had indeed happened.

He fell in love with her and asked her several times to marry him. She'd turned him down every time. Occasionally, she did so with a quick, humorous brush-off, at other times with a nearly violent dismissal, leaving him with the suspicion there was something dark and tragic in her past preventing her from giving her full love to him.

He decided now he'd discovered her secret. Carla Daws had been married all along. But truthfully, he would believe that only when he heard the admission from her lips.

Suddenly he felt the longer he lived, the more he learned, the more he discovered affairs and events hiding from him, which allowed occasional flashes of the truth, but never in full.

Here he stood, face-to-face with a man who'd just asked him to choose which eye he should pluck from his skull. His mother had died giving birth to Jack's brother, who died with her. His father, with a ranch to run, handed Jack over to Aunt Anne and her husband, Uncle Hank.

They took him from his father, his last anchor to the harbor of love found only in the close ties of family. He went off to live in St. Louis with them.

By and by, he grew of an age to earn his keep. Uncle Hank took him into the saloon to learn the business. He'd attempted to make it clear to the boy that it hadn't been his father's fault they'd taken him from his home and all he knew and loved.

Uncle Hank figured Jack must feel some aversion, or at least harbor animosity toward his own father.

Uncle Hank had been right. Jack realized he hadn't learned the natural way of the strong family ties that accompany growing up in a house with a child's true parents. He'd experienced the sensation of being lost, of being an outcast, of being cast-off. This, he coupled with a feeling of abandonment, and the notion burrowed deep within his mind, hard to uproot.

He took up boxing later, when almost grown, on a quest for the missing ingredient he felt lacking in his life. It'd not been until his return to Sweet Home Kansas, that he found the warmth and camaraderie—the deep fondness he'd searched for all his life. After this discovery, he set out on the road to recovery, one that was still occurring.

Jack jerked back from those long-ago mental images to confront his present danger.

"You have a preference, don't you?" said the degenerate.

His eyes were dancing elatedly in their scarred sockets. "Make your choice. Or would you rather I did so for you?"

Jack kicked at him again. He missed. The man had grown too cautious for Jack to strike him with a sudden kick. But he continued to try. This was all he could do. The man behind him bounced his knotty fist off Jack's head.

"Damn you, Bobby Sikh. You'll pay for it, if you knock him out."

Bobby Sikh, his identity revealed now, grumbled under his breath, and tightened his grip on Jack.

The ugly, corrupt man moved his hand. The razor hovered just above the bridge of Jack's nose. Sweat from his armpits inched down his sides like worms. The mingling of blood and sweat upon his shirt was hot, clinging tightly to his skin, smelling even ranker than earlier.

Again, he tried, "Mister…" but wasted his breath. Nothing would turn the man now, except a bullet to the brain. All Jack could do was squirm about, resist, and give him as much grief as possible.

"What have I ever done to you, mister?"

"You took my wife. That's enough. No one takes from Axel Twelvetrees."

"I didn't know Carla was your wife."

"I told you before. That's the only reason I haven't already killed you. Be thankful and hold yourself still. Your flopping around could cause me a bum aim. This razor could slice right into your brain."

Jack pushed back with all the strength of his legs. He drove Bobby Sikh up against the bar, then followed this by aiming a kick at the man who'd just given his name as Axel Twelvetrees.

Again, Twelvetrees sprang to the side, out of the range of Jack's foot strike.
"The sooner you cooperate, the sooner this will all be over, and we'll cut out. You're bleeding like a stuck pig already. Keep resisting and you might not have the energy to hunt up a doctor when we leave."
"Go to hell," Jack said. He continued the struggle with Bobby Sikh.
Bobby Sikh stuck the barrel of his pistol into Jack's ear.
"Axel promised not to kill you, barkeep," he said, and his breath was labored from wrestling the much larger man, "but I didn't. Now, by god, hold still or I'll blow your brains out."
Jack felt he would rather die than be carved up like a beef, and blind to boot. He continued his battle. He lunged forward with the faint hope he could catch Twelvetree's nose between his teeth and bite it off. He missed, and Twelvetrees grabbed him by the hair of the head. He twisted Jack's face toward the ceiling as he'd done to Carla Daws.
"You've worn out my patience," Twelvetrees said.
He set his teeth so tight they grated together. Jack could hear them grinding away like a gristmill. Spittle foamed from his mouth, spraying hot on Jack's face.
Jack attempted to drop his head, but the man's fingers were entangled in his hair. He had no choice but to succumb. He fell limp.
"That's better," Twelvetrees huffed. "Hold it, just like that. This minor operation will soon be over, and we'll leave."
The will to resist soon sparked hot in Jack once more. He flailed about wildly, knowing to give in was to die.
His arms, pinned to his sides, were too much of a disadvantage to overcome though, and his resistance crumbled. Slowly, Twelvetrees was conquering him, like castrating a horse.
Just as he was close to the absolute end of his will to survive, he heard a strong, familiar voice strike up, loud, determined and angry.
A vengeful angel had just alit in the center of Jack Mahan's saloon.
Old Ben Short, the man Jack had bought the saloon from, had entered unnoticed. He stood there growling like a mistreated bulldog with his weapon aimed at Twelvetrees. "Dump that razor, mister," he demanded.
Ben Short had made it a habit to drop in on Jack every day. He even helped him occasionally when the saloon overflowed with customers. So Jack felt no surprise to see him now, only deep gratitude. Ben's big, rolling, gravel encrusted voice was the sweetest sound Jack had ever heard.

He sensed freedom, cut up like rags for a quilt, for sure, but alive, and with his full sight intact.

"I said, drop it!" Short said. "If you don't, I'll blow your black heart out of your unholy body.

"See then how much weight you have to throw around."

Axel Twelvetrees turned to face Short.

"This could become a stalemate. My man has his gun barrel stuck in the bartender's ear."

"Who gives a donkey's ass?" Short countered. "It's you I got the drop on. You're the old boy who'll die first. Damned soon, too, if you don't drop that razor.

"If you got good sense, you'll tell your bully ruffian to shed his rusty pistol, and be quick at it."

Jack Mahan felt Bobby Sikh tense up when he heard Short's nonnegotiable command, as if this had given him second thoughts about being a paid hard man.

The next move belonged to Twelvetrees. He still held his razor. Jack hoped though the man would make an agreement with himself that he'd be better off to comply with Short's demand.

The scarred man lost the debate with himself and folded the razor.

"Drop it, Bobby," he said. "Looks like this man means business. I know you, don't I old-timer?"

Short didn't mumble a word in answer, but kept his revolver trained on the big man.

Jack was trembling to his feet when Bobby Sikh unscrewed the gun barrel from his ear.

He stood and watched, uneasy on his feet.

He looked to Ben Short again, and his blood pressure dove into his boots. For just behind Short stood a newcomer with a pistol aimed at the old man.

Ben Short wasn't even aware of this man's existence, and the man stood near enough to him that a single shot would drop him like a side-dump railcar freeing a load of ballast stone.

When Short finally sensed the man's presence, he spun and lifted his gun against the man.

He was too late.

Two shots rang out. One chased the other and boomed loud in the room. The first shot erupted from the newcomer's gun, the second from Short's.

Ben Short caught a slug mid-chest. Short's own slug tore into the far wall, gouged out wood chips that sailed into the air as if struck from a log by the blade of an axe.

His bones and muscles seemed to have dissolved on him. His legs buckled, and he fell straight down, thumping sadly as he struck the floorboards, blood flowing freely onto the floor of the barroom.

"It's about time," said Twelvetrees to the newcomer. "Just how damned long did you propose to wait, anyway?"

The hard case didn't reply, ignoring the big man's sarcasm.

The newcomer's eyes held that same cold evil Jack had witnessed burning in Twelvetrees's eyes. The two men seemed strongly united in cruelty.

The face of this Johnny-come-lately was pinched keenly. Sharp bony ridges, thin ledges and rough shelves dominated his face. A wide, military mustache, black as chimney soot, covered his upper lip.

Twelvetrees moved first.

"We better get out of here," he said. "The entire town will be here in a matter of minutes, hearing those shots."

He swung to Jack with the look on his face of a fisherman who, until then, had had a good day, and was reluctant to give it up.

"You're one lucky sonofabitch," he said. "Looks like I don't have time to finish what I started."

Twelvetrees strode toward the door, paused at the table, donned his hat, drew on his coat, and headed toward the entrance.

Over his shoulder, he said, "Knock him cold, Bobby. We'll see if we can catch up to Billy Bolt and Withers. Damned if I ride horseback all the way home."

Jack Mahan knew his hide was about to be tossed in the loft.

He tried to avoid the blow, but wasn't fast enough.

He didn't feel Sikh's gun butt crash against his skull, but heard instead, a tremendous rending sound like a mountain being severed in two. A blinding white light followed. A dozen suns swung in the same sky inside his brain.

4

Jack Mahan lived through several centuries in a state of unconsciousness.
He felt no pain, but floated above it all.
When he finally awoke, he continued to hold his eyes shut, favoring the darkness.
When he gathered the courage to open his eyes, the incredible brightness of the lamp-lit room struck him a tremendous blow. Quickly, he shut his eyes. By this time, it didn't matter. The pain was there to stay, eyes open or shut. He tried to sit up.
Strong hands, wide, and female, held him in a gentle restraint.
They eased him back down.
"Just keep still, Mr. Mahan," stated a harsh voice. "Lay quiet now and no bully shenanigans while I change your bandages."
The owner of those wide hands and harsh voice, he discovered, belonged to Mrs. McWorthy, the woman who ran his eatery next door to the saloon. She was a rough-and-tumble lady, and was the best cook in McDonald County. Jack counted himself lucky to have her running his eatery. They had come to an agreement the day she took over the dining room. She was satisfied to cook and thought it proper for him to pour whiskey next door. They split the profits from the dining room right down the middle. At times, Jack felt he was cheating on her when he took his half. But he was the one who'd put up the money for the eatery, after all.
Mrs. McWorthy, a large woman, heavy of bone and ham-handed, wore her hair in a beehive atop the back of her skull.
If someone forced him to venture a guess, Jack would have guessed her to be fifty, or maybe a little more than that.
Her husband had died five years ago. They'd had no children of their own, but she had one niece. Back then, Mrs. McWorthy had had a great deal of time on her hands. When Jack bought the dining hall, a friend referred him to her. She had the reputation of being a superb cook, and since her husband had weighed nearly two-hundred and fifty pounds, he figured she must be some fine cook. He hired her right away.
Soon, he found that there were so many entanglements and traps in her unwritten contract it would've spun the head of a shrewd lawyer. He found it best to keep quiet and let her just go at it. Mrs. McWorthy had stamped the place as her own, and by this time, he suspected it belonged more to her than to him.
Mrs. McWorthy unwound the bandages from his head, and did so as gently as possible, he figured, but despite her care, his head felt as if it would blow apart at any moment.
He felt faint. His head spun like a top. His memory was flighty.
"Where's Carla?" he said.

"Carla's gone, Mr. Mahan. Good lord," she announced involuntarily, removing the bandages. "I don't see how Dr. Caron saved you … sweet Jesus, if your face ain't cut up, now!"

She drew in her breath suddenly, realizing her mistake. In an attempt to cover up, she added, "But, he did a fine job with these here stitches."

Jack lifted his hands to his face on an exploratory mission.

Mrs. McWorthy slapped them down, as if he had no business inspecting his own face.

"Keep them hands off," she grumbled. "It'll be a month or six weeks before your face heals. Now just keep them hands off. If you keep messing around, you'll infect them wounds, and they're already plenty bad enough."

He pressed her until she told him the story.

Jess Jordan, the sheriff, had heard gunshots in Jack's saloon. He dressed and rushed over. Just as he reached the saloon, he caught a quick glimpse of three riders passing over the railroad tracks at the north end of town.

Jordan found Jack sprawled out face down, still manacled, bleeding like an artesian well. Old Ben Short lay a few feet from him, in a bad way from a gunshot wound to the chest, clinging feebly to life.

Jordan surmised Ben Short had come up on the gang, got the drop on the cutthroats, but somehow—maybe they'd had a man staked outside for just such an emergency, and this man had shot Ben Short for his troubles.

At first, Jordan figured Short interrupted a robbery, since it was Saturday night, and the take for the entire day would be on hand until Monday morning. But when he saw Jack's face cut up so savagely, and because Carla Daws was gone, he ruled out robbery. He further figured it was Carla they'd come for, which puzzled him.

Later on, everyone in town was baffled that the intruders had taken the time to carve Jack up as they had. It was as if they did it as an act of vengeance.

For what, none could dare a guess. This, and the fact they carried Carla off with them, led everyone in Sweet Home to conclude they accomplished exactly what they came for.

"Where's Carla?" he tried again.

"I told you already," she replied, and applied a heavy, gooey black salve to the cuts, which pulsated with pain.

"She's gone, Mr. Mahan. Them men carried her off. The same ones sliced up your face this away and shot poor old Ben Short."

"Has anyone looked in her apartment?" he continued, unaware of the great length of time that'd passed since the ordeal in the saloon had taken place.

Mrs. McWorthy sighed. She sat down on the edge of his cot. "It's four o'clock in the morning, Mr. Mahan. Monday morning. You were out since sometime after midnight, Saturday night. You were out for over twenty-four hours. They ain't no need asking for Carla. They've been folks done looked for her. Now shut up about it. It won't help none asking."

"How can a man sleep that long?" he said. He felt Mrs. McWorthy was mistaken. She had to be wrong. "How's Ben?"

"Oh, lord, he ain't doing no good. I don't see how he can ever make it. He's a tough old man, though, and just might fool me, fool all of us."

Years ago, after the death of his aunt Anne, and the later death of his uncle Hank Colter in St. Louis, Jack packed up and moved back to his father's ranch twenty miles outside of Sweet Home. He hoped somehow to be of service to his father.

He was not, though and found he was the perfect example of how not to be a good ranch hand.

He'd been too long in the city, too long behind the bar in Uncle Hank's saloon, too long in the prize ring where he'd attempted to wipe away the feelings of inadequacy brought on by the death of his mother. As well as from being trundled off from home at such an early age to his aunt and uncle's place.

Jack first felt he'd gone into boxing for the love of the sport and had cherished everything about it. By the time he realized just what he was really trying to accomplish by plunging his fists into the flesh of a fellow human being, the sport fled the game.

He dropped it in a snap, even though he had built up quite a handsome record, and had become well known in boxing circles. So he gave up seeking salvation in this manner.

Shortly after he returned to his father's ranch, his father followed Aunt Anne and Uncle Hank in death. Jack sold the ranch, moved to Sweet Home, and hired out to Ben Short as a barkeep. He then discovered the warmth and closeness of Sweet Home was the very thing he had sought, the ingredient to make his life complete.

The community became family to him, and he learned to treasure the compassion and love it offered. He was still discovering what the true meaning of "family" meant.

A few years later, Ben Short's wife persuaded the old man to retire—even though he really hadn't wanted to. Jack bought the place with the money he received from the sale of his father's ranch. But although he'd retired, Ben Short couldn't shake the habit of showing up for work every day. The saloon could be ready to take a dive to the bottom in a sea of Saturday, court-day or holiday business, and Jack would glance up to see Ben there, sleeves pulled up off the wrists, and tied back with butcher twine. He always pitched in and fought as hard as Jack and Carla to prevent the saloon from going down in a sea of chaos.

Lying upon his bed, he felt a deep sense of regret. He realized what he'd lost in the old man. Maybe he'd been wrong to allow Ben to spend so much time in the saloon. His wife had tried her best to break Ben of the habit, but failed. Maybe, if he'd run him off a time or two, Ben might have found something else to occupy his time.

If he had, the old man wouldn't be laid up right now, knocking at death's door.

But Jack knew there was no way he could've run Ben off. The saloon was his whole reason for existing. He couldn't have been that cruel in a million years. Besides, Ben had been invaluable to him. When he ran up against a problem, he could find no answer to, Ben was sure to have gone through the same thing in the past, and had long since discovered its solution.

After she changed his bloody bandages, Mrs. McWorthy left his bedroom. Later, she returned with a bowl of beef stew.

He tried his best to eat, but in the end, he managed to put away less than half of it before he wore himself out. He sighed and sank back down in bed.

"You rest now," she said. "I'll be in later to check on you."

Lying there, he tried to recall what'd taken place in the saloon on Saturday night. But he fell asleep, unable to remember anything.

The next time he awoke, the sheriff, Jess Jordan, sat at the small table in the room. He had his legs crossed at the ankles, boot heels hooked on the edge of the table, and all thrust back in a straight-backed chair, asleep. The chair itself stood on its two hind legs.

Jordan's deep snores shook the walls. It seemed a shame to wake him, but Jack felt the need to talk. Finally, his need over-powered him. He cleared his throat. "Jess."

Jordan jumped, startled. His booted feet fell in a loud clatter to the floor. He sprang to his feet and upset the chair.

Jack attempted to laugh, but ended up scarcely able to prevent choking, and experienced a searing pain in his head.

"Caught you asleep, didn't I?"

"Damned if you didn't," said Jordan. The sheriff stretched, lifted his arms toward the ceiling, and then allowed them to drop to his sides. "I thought you were fixing to sleep all day again."

"What time is it?"

"Nearly noon."

"It was around four o'clock when Mrs. McWorthy was here. I've slept almost eight hours."

Jordan laughed. "Nope. Today's Tuesday, Jack. You've slept over thirty hours this go 'round."

Jordan squatted on his heels alongside the bed and rolled a cigarette.

Finished, he rocked from heels to toes, found a match in a pocket of his trousers, and lit up.

"You hold the belt in the sleeping division, I reckon."

They talked for a time. Jordan asked a few questions about Saturday night.

Did he remember what they looked like? How many of them were there?

But Jack couldn't remember much at all.

"My face must be pretty well cut up, ain't it?" he said.

Jordan attempted to rise. Jack put out a hand and stopped him.

"It ain't your face that's got everybody worried, Jack. Dr. Caron says you might have a fractured skull. One of them fellers rapped you a right, damn good lick with a pistol butt, or something just as heavy."

He let his hand slide from Jordan's shoulder, and the sheriff stood up.

"Doc's worried you might get some kind of brain infection. He said that wouldn't be a damned bit good." Jess drew on his cigarette and then turned to leave. "Be in to check on you later."

He left Jack there to stare at the slow dispersal of cigarette smoke, to roll when it rolled, and rise when it rose. This carried him off on the gentle swell and billow.

By and by, he fell asleep.

The next time he awoke, Mrs. McWorthy stood above him, hands on hips, brow furrowed in thought, face twisted. Behind her, on the table, set a bowl from which he saw steam rising in a slow curl. The sheriff stood beside the table, one hand at rest on its top.

"Thought you said he was awake," said Mrs. McWorthy in her harrying voice.

"He was when I left," Jess Jordan said. His voice betrayed no emotion, and he was not put-off by her bluster.

She reached then and shook Jack, and said, "You wake up now, Mr. Mahan."
Her voice mellowed a trifle, but still sounded as if she were shouting out every word. "It's time you ate some stew."
He attempted to sit up on the pillows to comply with her demand, even though he wasn't in the least hungry. He found he couldn't sit up by himself.
But with Mrs. McWorthy's help, he was soon propped up on the pillows.
He cast about the room, which slowly revolved, as if he were in the critical stages of a nasty drunk.
The gruff woman turned to Jordan. She nodded to him curtly. Jordan hefted the tray with the bowl and carried it to the bed. Mrs. McWorthy took it from him and sat on the edge of the bed tray on her wide lap. She used a large spoon to swirl the stew around in the bowl to cool it before raising it to Jack's lips.
Nausea from the spin of the room, and from the disagreeable odor of the soup, nearly conquered him. When he took his first sip, he thought he would heave up his guts. Finally, he subdued the reflex, and downed all the stew.
This thrilled Mrs. McWorthy.
She set aside the bowl and moved closer to inspect his bandages.
"The bleeding has stopped," she announced. "I must change these bandages though."
Several times, as she removed the bandages, he forced back cries of pain, and while at heart, he figured her to be of a compassionate nature; he felt certain she had no will to abide weakness in anyone.
"Fetch me that basin," she commanded Jordan.
Jess Jordan took the basin and held it before her.
"Hold it right there till I'm done."
She cleansed the dried blood from around the wounds, and for once, she became what he might term gentle. After a considerable time of daubing and patting, she dried the entire area with a soft towel, then sat back to admire her work.
Jack felt a strong desire to see the damage the razor had inflicted.
"Hand me a mirror."
"You don't need no mirror," she said.
"Pass me that mirror from atop my dresser, Jess."
She shot Jordan a quick, angry scowl. "I'll have to look sometime."
He spoke as gently as possible, but figured his face belonged to him, after all.
She sat with her gaze fallen onto her hands, which were at rest upon her lap.

Jordan thrust the mirror into his upraised hand, and Jack felt a great shock at what he witnessed in the mirror. Angry red welts reared up from the surface of his face like the upheaval of the earth in the act of mountain building. His face was swollen, fat and hot with fever. It bore so many stitches he realized it'd be a mistake to run a tally.

"So much of that is just swelling, Jack," Mrs. McWorthy said. Her voice sounded much softer than usual.

Jack had never considered himself handsome. His nose had been broken too many times in the fight ring for that. He realized sadly that the only looks he'd receive from women in the future would be those of morbid curiosity. He wondered what Carla Daws would think of his new face. By and by, he figured he shouldn't wonder about that since it was unlikely he'd ever see her again. This sent a wave of such painful loss throughout his system he briefly doubted he could master the emotion.

At last, he gained command again, grew thankful he still had such spiritual resiliency, and vowed to himself not to fall victim to self-pity.

He gazed into Jordan's face to gauge how others would react to his new face.

Jess just stood there, immobile, strong as a boulder, and gave up absolutely nothing. Jack wondered by this if perhaps his eyes had lied to him.

He turned to Mrs. McWorthy, and for the first time since he'd known her, she couldn't maintain his gaze. He felt sure, by this, that Jess Jordan possessed a remarkable poker face.

"It won't look so bad later," she said. She patted his hand. "It's still got a lot of fever, a lot of swelling, and when it heals some ... well, it'll look a lot better."

He knew what he'd seen, though, and it didn't look good.

"I was never a handsome man, Mrs. McWorthy. Now, if I looked like Jess there, handsome as a new Studebaker hack, well, maybe a few tears might be in order."

After this, he didn't ask for the mirror again.

5

Mahan slept a good deal in the next three weeks, but after a time he slept less and less, until, at last, he was sleeping but eight or ten hours, and this all of a nighttime. He grew stronger and started going outside to the jakes by himself. He got rid of the pot which had been a source of great embarrassment, and had demoralized him. He sat at rest on an upholstered chair Pete South brought him, and reached the point where he spent most of his days there, returning to bed only when an infrequent attack of nausea overwhelmed him. Dr. Caron told him these attacks were born of his fractured skull and predicted they'd persist for some time yet.

The dizzy spells he experienced grew more infrequent and lasted for shorter durations. The loud exaggeration of even the softest sounds fell away and became more normal. At length, he could stand to hear the sounds of footsteps without the need to clap his hands over his ears in defense. So he felt he was recovering more with each new day.

He received visitors. A. Ray Leavitt, the town lawyer who had been a great friend of Jack's father, came every afternoon, when not out of town on court business.

They passed time in discussions of politics and horse races, both of which were great passions of the lawyer's. As for Jack, he could take them or leave them, but still he enjoyed Leavitt's company.

Pete South, Jack's good friend, visited him every day. Pete had taken to running the saloon for him. He opened late in the afternoon when he finished his own work. Pete kept the saloon open until midnight, or until business fell off to nothing, depending on whichever came first. Jack first argued he should just leave the saloon set idle until he could resume the work himself. Pete wouldn't hear of it, being of the mind that if it set idle too long, Jack's old customers might not return when he did finally open his doors again.

When Pete visited, their talks revolved around carpentry. Jack learned so much about the proper use of wood planes, and of which type saw worked best, he figured he could build a fair cabinet himself. Jack decided Pete felt as passionate about his craft as Leavitt did about the law.

Jack learned Ben Short was still abed, and would have one good day followed by several bad ones. Everyone spoke of the old man as if he were already dead.

They felt he had but a short time left. Jack hoped they were wrong, because Ben had been like a father to him—not to mention the fact that he'd saved his hide. Ben knew almost everyone in McDonald County, knew their life situations as well, and was at heart a kind, humane person.

Dr. Caron came around twice a week, and while he still felt concerned about his condition, he assured the saloon owner he'd passed the most critical stage. If no setbacks occurred, he'd likely recover with few complications, except for occasional headaches.

One day Jack informed the doctor his strength had returned enough where he felt he could go back to work. Dr. Caron cautioned against this and warned him he should take it easy for a few more weeks.

Eventually, he felt well enough to walk the length of High Street. He'd go up one side and back down the other, and cross over when straight across from his saloon.

Jack hadn't used a razor since the close shave Twelvetrees had given him.

As a result, his beard took shape. He allowed it to grow, and to leave it on. He'd never been a vain man, but he discovered there was something to having what were already limited good looks, wrecked by a razor in the hands of a lunatic, to turn a person defensive. He was reluctant for anyone to see his scarred face and didn't want to frighten the children of Sweet Home by the awful display of his carved up mug.

So the beard was on to stay.

At last, he decided that when he could walk twice around all of High Street, he'd return to work, no matter what Dr. Caron said. On these strolls, he often wondered about Carla Daws, worried over where she was. Was she still alive and safe?

These gloomy thoughts haunted him daily, in particular since his memory still hid out from him.

Everyone he met on these walks treated him fine. They called out to him even from all the way across the street and stopped him often and shook his hand like a long-lost brother. All his friends were so warm and friendly he often found himself about to drip a few tears when he thought he could get away with it.

On these occasions, he felt such a strong devotion to the town he realized he'd do anything in the world for these special people. Sweet Home had become his life and passion. As to Carla Daws, he'd never completely felt certain about her. She'd always held back from him, even after he'd proposed to her. Carla hadn't turned him down flat, but had turned him aside. She claimed he was not quite ready for marriage.

Even in their most intimate moments, he felt she kept something hidden from him, which held her hostage, and this'd prevented her from giving herself to him in full.

Carla had been the one not ready for marriage, he now realized.

With all that'd happened to him, he wondered just what might come up next.

The more he worried over it, the more confused he became. So he resolved to get to the bottom of the entire sorry affair.

Two weeks later, he entered his saloon, but not yet to do business. This was just an attempt to set his senses aright. He lit the lamp behind the bar and drew up a stool he used at slack times. He sat there, staring down the length of the bar top, admiring its deep shine. The early morning sun slanted in through the east window and soon chased away the morning shadows as he sat there and pondered his situation.

Jack had always hated mornings, was a late riser, but the change in his schedule brought about by his head injury had taught him something new.

He found he enjoyed the early morning play of sunlight in the room, admired the display of the felt-topped pool tables, and with all the cue sticks at rest in their racks upon the wall. He acknowledged just how nice it was to watch the sunlight carom off the racked billiard balls, and how serene mornings were, and he a man known never to rise until eight o'clock in the morning. He felt there was something behind his new attitude. Through his brush with death, he discovered a new way to look at everyday commonplace events, and wondered if he'd ever fall again into the old habit of looking at everyday objects without really seeing them for what they truly were.

Perhaps he'd revert someday, but as for now, he liked the change, and welcomed it, if not for life, then for whatever amount of time it lasted.

But even though he enjoyed this fresh viewpoint, he felt something lacking. Without Carla, a special piece of his saloon and of himself had disappeared. Somehow, he had to fill up that space.

He snuffed out the lamp, took a .44 from a drawer along with its holster, strapped it on, and left the saloon. Later, he stopped by Emmit's store and bought a twist of tobacco for Ben Short. Ben's wife, Ellen, had long ago forbidden Ben to chew at home. But Jack felt it'd not do to visit him empty-handed. He entered the residential district through a cut-through street, which was an extension of High Street that ran through the housing area all the way on out of town. A few minutes later, he stood and rapped on Ben's front door.

Ellen Short answered his knock. She stood aside to allow him to enter.

"He's been asking for you, Mr. Mahan," she said.

Jack grew besieged by guilt for his reluctance to visit Ben. He'd dreaded the prospect of seeing him abed. For Ben Short was a man filled keenly with the strength of life's great energies. Jack then admitted his cowardice, which had assumed another name in his mind, but nevertheless, was just plain old-fashioned cowardice no matter what name he hung on it.

His conscience cracked the tough shell he'd built around his denials, and this forced the visit.

"Right this way," Ellen Short said.

He followed her, hat in hand, and paused when she stopped at the head of the hallway to pick up a basin of soapy water, a washcloth and towel from atop a small cabinet.

"It's time for his shave," she informed him. She walked down the hallway toward the bedroom while the keen scent of soap floated back in Jack's face.

When they reached the bedroom door, Jack saw determination flash brightly in her eyes. This, he knew, had been the same resolve that subdued Ben Short's will to the wild side, his willfulness, many years ago.

"One moment, please. I'll wake him and let him know you are here. He's not himself."

Jack nodded in agreement. She disappeared inside the room with a soft swish of the fabric of her dress.

A short time later, she opened the door. "Please come in."

He followed her, took a seat, and watched while Ellen shaved the old man, who had nodded weakly when Jack entered.

Ben looked as if he were a hundred years old to Jack. He clutched the blanket feebly with one hand like a child. His silvery hair stood awry in a way Jack had never seen it before. Being a saloonkeeper for most of his adult life, Short had made it his personal habit to be neat and well groomed.

After she shaved him, Ellen brushed his hair. When done, she hefted the basin, nodded to Jack and quietly left the room. Jack fought briefly against the biting odor of the sick room. Mrs. Short had probably just dumped the pot that Jack saw in one corner of the room.

"Hell, Jack," said the old man. His voice, normally deep and filled with power, squeaked pitifully. "I've worried some about you. Haul that chair up a little closer. Let's chaw the fat. Somebody said you was dying."

He moved his chair nearer to the bed, and sat back down, hat at rest upon a knee of a leg draped over the other one. "No, sir. Not yet, anyway."

"Malicious rumors abound." Ben chuckled with little strength.

"Sonsabitches dealt us a right stout lick, didn't they, barkeep?"

Jack Mahan could find no proper way to thank him for saving his life without getting downright sloppy about it. He made a stab at it though and knew he'd messed up just as it split his lips.

"I owe you an enormous debt, Ben…"

"That all you come to say, I 'spect you might as well just leave. Then when you get things properly sorted out, fetch me a pail of beer when you return."

"I'll do it."

"Ain't been able to keep much down these days. Leon Brown brought me a snifter of whiskey, but I got my taster fixed for a good sup of beer. Might just be able to keep it down. You ain't got a chaw of tobacco for me, do you?"

Jack reached into a coat pocket, withdrew the twist of tobacco he'd bought, and watched the magic return to Ben Short's eyes.

"Now, If you ain't just the very prize."

Right away, Ben attacked the twist and bit off a chaw with his yellowed, ancient teeth.

"How many men were there in my saloon that night, Ben?"

"Three," answered Short. He spat out the words like a rasp over metal. "That's all I saw. But someone carried off your barmaid. So there had to be at least one more. A right fine bunch of bully bastards, I'd call 'em."

"One of 'em beaned me with a gun butt," Jack said. He watched Ben's eyes brighten with enthusiasm for the conversation. "I have little memory of being cut up."

"Fetch me that peach can from beneath this here bed, would you?

My woman, Ellen's, a tiny thing, and couldn't hurt a flea. Her soul is immense, though, and she whipped me down long ago. I shouldn't be going again' her will like I sometimes do, but hell's fire, I'm dying, anyway. What's a little chaw going to hurt?"

Jack got down on all fours and cast about beneath the bed, found Ben's spit can, stood back up, and handed it to him.

Ben accepted the can. "A. Ray Leavitt fetched me a chaw a couple of days ago, but he's so blamed afraid of Ellen he didn't dare leave me any. It's good to see you up and around, son. Damned if it ain't."

"What did that gang look like? Like I said, I have little memory of it all."

"Like a perfect bunch of lowlife, scurrilous shit-heels. But I 'spect I know what you're fixing to do. You plan to run down that bunch, don't you, barkeep?"

"Passing it through my mind, yes."

"You out for revenge, or to get the girl back?"

"Maybe a little of both. I don't even know if Carla wants me to come for her. I've got a lost feeling about Carla, Ben … and we were really close, too."

"You'd be better served to forget it and stick to spilling beer and spirits. You might search from now on out and still not find 'em … and, personally, I'd call that a run of good luck."

"I need a good description of those men," Jack said. He placed a hand atop Short's free hand. "As a favor."

Ben replied, "Wouldn't be no favor, if I told you and you went off and got killed. Them fellers are heathenish, barkeep. I know that bunch of no-'count scum."

"I'm begging you, Ben." He dropped his hand from the old man's, and then leaned back in his chair. "And I can't recall there being much of anything else worth begging for in my life."

"That's what's got me worried, Jack, although risking your life over a woman would be a noble endeavor in my humble opinion. Especially a fine woman like Carla Daws."

Jack sat quietly to give the old man a short break and replayed in his mind what little he remembered of that night.

Vaguely, he recalled or imagined it, Ben Short, as he stood in the saloon, hip deep in a thick mist. He watched him train his revolver on a man just out of range of his vision, and just that quick, he dredged up the name, Twelvetrees. He'd heard the name spoken while Ben stood up against a man massively built, with enormous arms like the lower limbs of a tree.

"Twelvetrees," Mahan muttered. He leaned in to read Short's reaction, to see if he might be onto something.

"I remember you talking to a man," he added. "I thought I heard someone call him by that name. You had your gun on him. What's the rest, Ben?" "Damned determined, ain't you?"

"Yessir, I am. Damned."

Short squirted brown, sticky-appearing tobacco juice into the can. "The big man's name is Axel Twelvetrees," he said. "I knew him in Missouri, years ago … before ever I married. The man now looks like somebody held his head in a right good fire … held it there for a long spell. It was Axel, though. I recognized his voice. Proud as hell of it, he is. Plus, he ain't got no taller, nor a bit lighter. He weighed three hundred pounds back then, and I 'spect he'll go even more now. But he damned sure ain't soft.

"His ugly head was bald as an onion back then and still is. Except now, he has ridges of scar tissue on his skull. Makes him even uglier.

"Axel's as rank as a shitty-assed bull, barkeep. As pure a sonsabitch as you'll ever meet … in this lifetime, and hopefully in the next one.

Unless you run up against Satan hisself … not wishing you no bad luck."

"I'll take that as a fair warning."
"Well, you should."
Ben's breath escaped his lips like a soft breeze. "I ain't got but a couple of days left the way I figure.
"I lived 'bout as tough an old life as any man can. Never figured to die abed like some rich Tory bastard—as Pap used to say.
"Anyway, the man who shot me's named Tom Easy. Many claim he's a mute, but don't believe it. He speaks plenty with his gun, and with them black eyes of his.
One thing he ain't is deaf. He's put many a man in the ground trying to slip up on him.
"That other little feller—him, I don't know, but you'll recognize him by that tuft of hair beneath his lower lip trimmed in the shape of an upside down spade."
"Spade?"
"Like on a playing card. He looked damned sly. All in all, though, he can't be nearly as bad as Easy. Tom'll kill you dead, and you won't even see him do it. And, worse than all the rest, there's Twelvetrees, hisself. There's a woman, too, his mother. Axel has a sister as well. Fights with her fists. Both of them women are as cold-blooded as reptiles. The mother brought both of 'em up thinking wrongheaded.
She was depraved even before Axel's father found her in a dive in some town over in the land of Spain.
"She latched onto him for his money. The old man was a rich shit from England—many years older than her, but even for that, she wouldn't allow nature to take its course. She killed the demented old fool, so the story goes, for his money.
She brought up Axel and the girl, Lana, and filled their heads with all manner of decadence and filth … every sort of rot known to man."
"She still alive, Ben?"
"Can't say. But if she is, and if you happen up onto her, take all precautions to protect yourself. She'll kill you, barkeep."
"They thieves? How do they get by?"
Ben chuckled low, as if Mahan were a naïve country boy. "No. Twelvetrees don't have to resort to thievery. His old man fell heir to a full fortune like I told you.
He devoted his sorry life to the pursuit of pleasure. That is until he married that witch from Spain.

"When she killed the old man, well, she got all his money. Then, as with her kind, after a time, she found it more and more difficult to derive pleasure in the way any normal human does. The only pleasure she finds now is in inflicting pain.

"Course she might've mellowed some. But I doubt she's mellowed much.

I surely wouldn't count on it, Jack."

"Any idea where they call home?"

"No sir, I don't. I'd say they must've moved somewhere close by … or else they was just passing by when they paid you that little visit."

Jack got to his feet, placed the chair back in front of the dresser where he'd found it, and tried again to thank Ben for saving his bacon.

The old man waved off the saloonkeeper's awkward attempt with a pale, frail hand.

"Just don't forget that pail of beer you promised me, Mr. Barkeep."

"I won't. I'll bring it tomorrow."

As they say, though, tomorrow never comes. Ben Short died later that day, just as the sun was setting. He was more than Jack Mahan's loyal friend.

His death presented the saloonkeeper with a severe case of the blue-leg that lasted for several weeks.

6

A few days after they buried Ben Short, Jack stopped by the sheriff's office to visit Sheriff Jordan. He hoped to learn something about Axel Twelvetrees, Bobby Sikh and Tom Easy. For he needed a direction in which to point his horse.

Without one, it would be hopeless to start.

Jordan sat at his desk, with paper work cast out on top of it in disarray.

It looked as if he'd thrown in the towel.

He looked up when Jack stepped inside and shut the door behind him.

A smile brightened his face and replaced the look of boredom Jack had observed on his face through the windowpane.

Jordan shoved back from the desk and waved him toward a chair. Jack drew it up to the desk, while the sheriff rolled a cigarette.

Jordan had voiced his hatred for the sheriff's job many times, and had taken it only after he made a vow to do so to his dying boss, the rancher Double O. Arnold.

The promise had been to take the job until the county held another election.

The problem with that was so far no one had stepped up to run for the job.

So it looked like he was stuck with it until someone else claimed it. Jordan, a man natural-born to ranch, suffered daily from boredom as the sheriff of McDonald County.

"Got some information you might need, Jack," he said. "The sheriff in Green County wired me back and said that a troop of folks who fit the description of those hell raisers who hauled off Carla Daws passed through his county. Didn't catch on in time to stop and question 'em, though."

"Does the time fit?"

"Yeah, it fits. It's the same bunch. Few could fit the description, not with a woman along."

"Green County," said Mahan.

He stood up, stepped to the wall map. "Here it is."

He placed a finger on the spot on the map that represented Green County.

"It's in the north-central part of the state just north of Military Springs."

"Been over a month. It'll be hard finding them—cold trail like that."

"Seven weeks," Jack corrected, and walked back to his chair and sat down. Jess Jordan inhaled with a look of pleasure on his face, then blew smoke toward the ceiling in a gray plume. "That's even worse. You'll wind up baying at the moon. No telling where that bunch is by now."

"Yeah," agreed the saloon owner, "but I have to try."

"Well, you'll need help," Jordan said. He spat a flake of tobacco from his tongue. "I'll have one boy at the ranch go with you."

"Thanks, Jess. But I won't need any help."

"You'll step in a jackpot ... you'll need help, all right."

"You're probably right, I know, but I have to try it. I can't ask a man to risk his life on my account." "I think you know you don't need to ask," said Jordan.

"No," Jack said. "This is my job. I must do it myself."

Jordan shrugged, dragged deeply on his cigarette. "Have it your way. What'll you do with the saloon while you're gone?"

"Shut the doors until I return."

"If you return. Better find some help, or just stay home."

"Yeah, I know," Jack said. "But this is personal, if you know what I mean."

Jack slapped his knees, sending dust motes dancing in the sunlight streaming in through the east window. He got to his feet and headed for the door.

"I have to go, though," he said. "I won't be able to live with myself until I find out what happened to Carla. Sweet Home ain't quite the same place without her, and I don't intend to get anyone hurt on my account."

He left Jordan there, amid a big backlog of paperwork.

Jack had set his mind to take out in a rip to find that bunch of cutthroats, to see if he could square things with Twelvetrees, and to bring Carla home. He owed that man an enormous debt for his fractured skull and needed to repay Ben Short's killer.

But his calmer mind won out. He had to go at it slow, learn more than what he now knew. He couldn't just up and leave the saloon shut down as he'd just told the sheriff. He reopened the saloon, and this freed Pete South to go back to his full-time occupation as a carpenter.

After a few months, he found it hard work. He'd become so used to Carla's help, and now with Ben Short dead and buried, it became even worse. Mrs. McWorthy hinted daily for him to hire her niece, Bridget, since she was homeless and out of work. Lately, he hadn't even had time enough to exercise his horse. He needed help, for sure. When her father died, Bridget wound up on the street. She tried to live with her aunt, a firm conservative. Mrs. McWorthy took the girl in and expected to be paid room and board.

But Joan McWorthy's rough voice and abrasive manner became more than Bridget could bear. She'd bundled up her clothes and left. Afterward, she lived wherever she dropped, often under the sky. This became a source of embarrassment to Mrs. McWorthy. She went to her several times to make up with her, but Bridget could stomach no more of her harshness, and refused her proposal of peace.

"I'd hire her as my kitchen help, if not for Mrs. Black. Can't just turn her out," the cranky old woman said.

"Bridget lives with whoever'll feel sorry for her enough to take her in for a time. I fear if you don't take her on, she'll ruin her life … become one of them girl's of no-'count. She has her father's blood. She's a good worker, but backtalk from her ain't nothing out of the ordinary. I just felt I ought to warn you beforehand."

Jack felt guilty for even considering giving over Carla Daws's job so soon. For he still felt hopeful she'd show up again. Eventually, he relented and hired the girl.

He kept close tabs on Bridget for the first week to see that the cowhands who made up fifty-percent of his clientele didn't take advantage of her.

When some of them had imbibed too much alcohol, they lost their normal inhibitions and good manners, and fell back on the rough language used on the range.

But Bridget had been raised in a rough household of six boys—she the only girl—and had heard it all before. Her mother died before Bridget's father had, and soon after her death, the boys all left home and scattered out across the state. Bridget stayed home and tended to her father, who was in poor health, due mainly to alcohol abuse. He'd arrived in Sweet Home as a section hand when the railroad made it all the way to Sweet Home some years ago.

Jack learned soon enough that Bridget had a fine spirit of competition he found rare in a female. After a few weeks, he discovered she handled herself around a crowded bar with the ease and dignity he'd seen in no other woman except Carla Daws.

All the customers loved her. She faced each day with a smile, a sly wrinkle of nose and a vivid flash of eyes. He learned she was trustworthy enough to run the bar alone at slack times each day. He used the free time to exercise his horse.

The only drawback he discovered with Bridget was that her youthful good looks and smile brought in every tongue-tied young cowhand in the county, and more often than buying drinks, they were satisfied to stand and stare in awe at her bright red hair and freckled face. This was only a minor complication, because Bridget also brought in the crowds to drink and to stare at her. They arrived in droves a good bit larger than did the gangly young spectators.

When the rains stopped, the creeks dried up with the summer's heat, and the rivers dropped to dangerously low levels. He decided it time to go off on his search for Carla Daws.

He'd just opened the saloon one day, was standing behind the bar, reading an article in the Sweet Home Tribune. The Kansas state legislature was considering the prohibition of the sale of liquor, except for medical or scientific purposes.

If this came-to-pass, he knew it'd put him out of business. He folded the paper and set it aside when booted footsteps outside announced the first customer of the day.

It was Sheriff Jordan. Jordan rested his forearms on the bar top, smoking without removing the cigarette from his lips.

"Picked up a man early this morning," he said. He squinted tightly against the burn of tobacco smoke. "Talk to him. Leon Brown let him sleep last night in his hayloft at the stable. The man bummed the makings from Leon and promised not to smoke in the loft. But when he opened early this morning, he caught him on the nod with a lit cigarette between his fingers.

"Leon got hot. They had it out, and when they dropped their hands, Leon found himself in second place. He came to me, and I arrested the man for vagrancy.

He was after that all the time, I 'spect. We must feed him for a few days, then turn him loose. The old boy looks like he's been on starvation rations. He's poor as a whippoorwill. But, anyway, he says he wants to talk to you."

"About what?"

"That's your chore, Jack. Go talk to the man. Find out for yourself." At four o'clock, Jack turned the saloon over to Bridget, and crossed the street to the jailhouse.

He drew a chair up to the bars of the drifter's cell. The man was fast asleep, mouth open wide, catching flies. Jack rapped loud enough to wake him. He jumped up, stood in the middle of the cell, and looked about in confusion from wide, fearful eyes.

When he reacquainted himself with true east, he approached the bars.

He fired off a look of pure torment toward Jack from eyes, deep within the caverns of their sockets. Jack couldn't recall seeing a man so put upon by demons.

"Sheriff says you wanted to see me."

"Mahan?"

"That's what they call me."

The drifter's clothes were filthy and hung slack upon his stick-like frame.

Jack wondered how he'd been able to get the best of Leon Brown, a man well known in the area as the lover of a vigorous brawl, and good at it too. Desperation, he decided, as he studied those troubled eyes.

"Got the makings, Mahan?"
"Don't smoke." Jack watched the warmth of expectation fall from his eyes like a grudge.
"The sheriff'll give you a smoke later."
"Naw, I wore out my welcome with him in that respect."
"What do you want, mister? I got a business to run."
"I know where your lady friend is."
The vagrant then stared at Jack, as if he'd said too much.
The saloonkeeper allowed this information to stew inside him for a time, but when it caught fire and flared up, he leapt forward. The man didn't have time to jump backward.
Jack caught him by the shirtfront, dragged him snug up against the bars, and searched his tortured eyes as they bugged out in a full cry for mercy.
They stood nose to nose, separated only by the bars. Both men breathed hard, open-mouthed.
"Where is she?"
"Unhand me. I'll tell you, but you got to turn me loose." Jack relaxed, and his trapped breath seemed to explode from his lungs. He let go of the man, sat back down in the chair, removed his beaver hat, and ran his fingers through his hair, still wound up tight.
"Sorry, mister," he said.
He watched a fine relief spread across the sun-tortured face of this rolling stone.
"She's northwest of here. In Nebo County near a town called Scarlet. Ain't far from the Nebraska line."
"Can you take me there?"
"I could, but I damned sure ain't going to."
"Pay top dollar."
"They ain't that much money in the world would make me go back there … me just escaped by the bare skin of my bony ass.
"Damn, but I wish I had me a smoke." The man's name was Darnell Gage. He and a friend, Ed Ketch, had been gentling horses for hire in the northern part of the state. They hit on a round of bad luck, unable to rustle up work to bless their hard-luck souls. A barkeep in a tavern in Scarlet advised them of a rancher who needed a couple of hands. Given that it'd been over a month since they'd had work, they checked out the tip.

They reached the ranch and discovered a huge three-story house upon the windblown plain. The first story was built of stone. The two upper floors were constructed of pine logs. The house looked to Gage more like a fortress than any ranch house he'd ever seen. He thought it odd, since it sat precariously on the edge of a deep arroyo, upon an otherwise wide, treeless plain. So Gage felt by this the owner had gone to a good deal of effort and expense to transport the materials for such a grand house upon this secluded, bum site.

The two men rode up to the yard gate, dismounted, pushed through the gate, and walked up to the foot of a wide, extensive set of stone steps that led up to a huge broad porch. The front of the house faced the east. The porch lacked a front rail, and the side rails were of heavy, split pine logs.

A large dark woman met the two bronc'-peelers.

She looked to Gage to be a Mexican. She spoke fair English, but with a trace of an odd accent, he decided must be British. A silent fellow, with dark hair the color of black boots polished to a high gleam, stood alongside her, hand at rest on the grip of a .44. Off to their left, upon the deck of the porch, a man of colossal girth, sat upon a chair that looked built especially to accommodate his enormous bulk.

A young woman sat in a chair next to him, dressed in black, as if she were mourning. A laced veil covered her face.

The big man and the veiled woman sat in silence. The man watched them from engaged, hoggish eyes while the woman held her face downcast.

The bronc'-busters asked for work taming horses, and the "Mexican" lady told them there was no such work available. But as they turned to mount their horses, her deep, husky voice halted them. She told them there was other work there, if they were interested. Being near desperation, they were interested.

The silent man with the slick-backed hair escorted them to a small bunkhouse with a corral built alongside it. After they turned in their animals, the "big-talker" showed the door of the bunkhouse for them to enter. Enter, they did.

This turned out to be their first mistake, second, counting the one they'd made when they'd hunted up the ranch. No sooner had they stepped inside, noted three bunks, a stove and a small table, than the door banged shut, followed soon by the sound of a bar slamming into place.

They were trapped. This was no bunkhouse, they learned, for there were no windows in the structure.

After they wasted time and energy to beat down the heavy door, they resolved to face their situation calmly. Gage struck matches and explored their jail. He found a pail of rusty water and a dented dipper. So they knew they wouldn't die of thirst. Even though food shelves lined the walls, they were bare. Death from starvation was a definite threat.

There were no lamps to light the room. So they stumbled about in the dark until they'd gauged the dimensions of the lockup.

For days the two men were kept locked up in that dark, forced confinement.

At last, they smoked up all their tobacco, and with no sustenance other than water.

"You just don't realize what the light means to a man," Gage said. "Not until you're kept hidden off in the dark that way. Our nerves got frayed. Then, when our tobacco ran out, things went further to hell in a damned hurry. Me and Ed talked together for so long I come to hate the sound of his voice. I 'spect he wasn't too much in love with mine neither.

"We hid from each other for hours on end. Didn't speak for hell, it might've been days for all I knew.

"I don't think it'd been half so bad if we hadn't run out of tobacco.

"After we conquered the tobacco demon, our water ran out. I figured it'd only take a few days more of this old business till we died of thirst, and we didn't even know what the hell for. "When someone finally flung open the door, I felt like I ought to rush up and kiss the feet of the old boy that opened it. It turned out it was that dark, slick-haired feller. Some old man was with him, so frail he could scarce walk.

He lugged a pail of water I could smell same way a cow dying of thirst can.

When he set the pail down on the floor, we went at it hard, while the old-timer found our slop jar and carried it outside.

"Both them old boys was smoking, and the smell of them tobacco leaves on fire nearly started a stampede. But they didn't give us any, of course.

"We both demanded to know why in hell we was penned up and starved that away. Then, when they left, Ed caught the slick-haired sonsabitch by the shoulder, and demanded something to eat. He whipped Ed a sharp blow with a snout-whacker like a pig farmer uses to go in amongst his pigs with.

"Them two men stood outside our door for a long time. Then I heard 'em moving our horses from the corral. When I heard 'em leave, I crawled over to Ed. I figured him knocked cold. But he wasn't. I fetched him a couple of dippers of water, and he told me then he reckoned that rough bunch meant to starve us to death. I asked him what made him think a thing like that. He said he didn't know.

"Ed didn't come close to catching my pale joke. Then, after a time, as I sat there in that accursed, dark little room, I saw that our mean situation wasn't a joke.

Ed had caught on to that fact sooner than me. So I learned my sour joke was all on me."

7

Darnell Gage carried on with his strange, often mystifying tale.

Jack Mahan sat up now and then, wondering whether Gage was a hell of a good liar or if he might really be telling the truth. By and by, he admitted if Gage was a liar; he was no average liar. Darnell Gage firmly believed every word he related to him.

After many days passed inside the prison, Gage fell into complete despair, as Ketch had done earlier. He became mentally exhausted, ready for death, and even looked forward to it as an end to his misery.

But he wouldn't get off half so lucky.

Later, some men led the pair inside the house when they fell so weak from starvation they could barely walk. They propped them up and forced them to watch a fancy group of people at a sumptuous feast in a large dining room in the house, with lamps ablaze all along the walls. Hundreds of tiny mirrors hung by strings from the rafter beams. The mirrors slowly rotated and presented an impression the entire room was ablaze.

"Was the big man there?"

Jack dimly recalled the tight, squinted eyes of the man Ben Short had called Axel Twelvetrees.

"Not at first. Later on, he made his appearance, after the servants of his had set the food on that big table in the middle of that god-awful flashing room.

Lord, what a feast for them servants.

"I saw a shoat baked whole at one end of the table. There were chicken wholes by the dozen, baked fish, slabs of beef that knocked my eyes out. I was starved down, and it became a close race to see which would bring me down first, thirst or hunger."

"Where was my friend when all this took place?"

"Right there with them others." Darnell Gage swiped a hand across his face and conceded his debt to her. "She helped me out of that hellhole, Mahan. In repayment, she asked if I'd look you up, to let you know where she's at. "I've done that now, so I 'spect her and me are on the square."

Gage walked away, sprawled upon his cot, hands behind his head, and stared with blank eyes at the wall.

Jack got to his feet and left. He went straight to Emmit's store, bought several sacks of tobacco and an enormous book of cigarette papers, then went to his eatery and had Mrs. McWorthy make up a large plate of food, which he carried back to the jailhouse.

Darnell Gage gorged himself on Mrs. McWorthy's biscuits, gravy, mashed potatoes, and fried chicken. He licked the empty plate, and Jack saw that the man still had a deep hole in his gut.

"Thanks, Mahan," said Gage. He fired a cigarette. "I'll likely never get all the wrinkles out of my belly. its pure hell, nearly starving to death."

His clothes were worn, filthy and tattered. Both boot heels were gone, with holes in the uppers where the foot makes its natural bend at the toes.

He had truly suffered some hellish event.

Still, Jack wasn't entirely convinced of Gage's honesty.

Then Darnell told him more of the tale.

"There in that enormous room," he continued, while cigarette smoke bloomed above his head like a large, gray rose, and smelled to Mahan like hell's own foul breath, "Twelvetrees showed his ugly mug.

"An uglier sonsabitch ain't never been born.

"He took his seat at the head of the table. Already sitting and waiting was the ten others. Not to count Lenore, the person you called Carla. She sat at the far end of the table like the queen of that jolly feast. It soon became plain she wasn't, though. That old woman I first took for a Mexican was in charge, even though she let Twelvetrees act the part. "That entire bunch wore fine clothes, as if mealtime was equal to going to church."

Gage stubbed out his cigarette and built another one right away.

"When the meal got going full-bore, oily sweat popped out on the foreheads of all of 'em. The rattle of silverware on crockery erupted like artillery fire. Arms flew, elbows bent, jaws crunched, and slather escaped their mouths like calves at the tit.

Then I saw Twelvetrees catch the sleeve on one servant, heard him tell him to fetch a chair.

"Well sir, the servant went off and returned with a chair. Just one.

He set it down between us and left. I figured he was headed back for another one, but after he'd been gone long enough to've gone to the barnyard and back, I decided one was all we'd get. "I was in better shape than Ed. So I told him to go on and take the chair. He looked at me with gratitude in his eyes, and with both of us expecting any minute to be asked to eat with them.

"Ed sat down, but that big Twelvetrees, damn his evil soul, yelled out so loud it scared me so bad that if I'd had anything in my shriveled gut to lose, I 'spect I'd have lost it right then ... in the seat of my thin-assed jeans.

"'Who said you could sit down?' he demanded. 'Stand up alongside that chair.
If you get tired, you can put a hand on it, though, to steady yourself.
Both of you.
But there will be no resting on the job. You asked for one, didn't you?'

"Ed sprang straight up like he'd just sit down on a red-hot stove, scared nearly blind.

"I'd known Ed a long time. Saw him get on rank horse-creatures most sane men wouldn't even go near. He wasn't no coward. That big sonsabitch scared Ed, though. Hell's afire, I jumped too, when Ed did, and I wasn't even fixing to sit down.

"I thought of it a lot while I stumbled out of that pesthole, and I decided that what caused us to give in and cower so, was because of the simple fact we was rundown so bad. Hell, we wasn't far from death."

"How long did they make you stand up like that, Gage?" The tale had transfixed Mahan.

"Who knows? But it was throughout that meal. You can call me a damned liar, Mahan, but that meal went on for at least two hours. Everyone there was chomping like a fattening hog the whole time."

"Tom Easy, as well?"

"No, sir. He stood by the door. Which I took as damned strange, since there wasn't no way me or Ed could've escaped. Later on, I found out it wasn't just me and Ketch he was guarding that door again'."

As wild and outlandish as the tale had been, Jack soon found it even stranger.

"There was this one fellow, Blake, they called him. He sat on the right side of the lady called Lenore, and I saw him shove back in his chair, and just stare at his plate for a long time, like he'd just took sick.

"Then, without so much as a pause from his meal, Twelvetrees smiles at Blake, and says, 'What's the matter, man? I thought you were hungry.'

'No more, I aint,' he says.

"Twelvetrees says, 'You were damned hungry six months ago, as I recall.'

'I suspect I'm about full now, Mr. Twelvetrees,' came the man's answer.

"Then without another word, Blake leaps up, and makes a charge towards the door like he wanted to run right through Tom Easy and it as well. But the old boy didn't quite make it.

"That "big-talker" allows Blake to get within three or four feet of him and then shoots him right between the eyes."

Jack Mahan stirred on his seat at this. "He shot Twelvetrees's guest?"
"If that man was a guest, he wasn't no voluntary one that was plain.
Because after a couple of servants hauled off the body, Twelvetrees points to a man named Williams—a tall, ga'nt feller with crossed eyes.
'Looks like you got yourself a promotion, Williams,' he says.
"Williams then goes and sits in Blake's chair, and starts eating … and he put ever' nerve and fiber in his body into the act. Then, when Twelvetrees sees what a fine job, the man was doing as replacement for Blake, he smiles like a proud papa, and falls again on his food like the famine was at the front door.
"Don't you see, Mahan? Everyone at the table was there again' his will.
Then, when one of 'em got killed off, Twelvetrees just recruited another one of his servants. The servants themselves was just one rung above where me and Ed Ketch was."
Jack shoved back in his chair and sat fully erect. He studied Gage intently, trying to decide if he'd told him the truth, while Gage sat and rolled another smoke.
"You tell all this to the sheriff?"
"No, sir."
"Why?"
"Didn't figure it none of his business. Besides, it's well out of his jurisdiction.
He wouldn't believe me anyway. I doubt if you do, Mahan."
Jack figured Gage had noticed the indecision in his eyes.
"I'll get you out of here, Gage."
"No, sir." He raised a hand to ward off the offer, smoke streamed from the cigarette he held slack between his lips, eyes pinched to fend off the invasive smoke.
"They feed me in here, plus I got the sheriff's protection. Don't do me no kindly favors."
"I don't think you belong in here. I could use your help."
"You got horses to be gentled?"
"Of course not, I run a saloon."
"Well, I don't know nothing about saloon work."
"I'd pay as well as I can."
"Swamping floors?" Gage rolled his eyes. "Don't count me in on them plans."

Jack Mahan had seen other men drift into Sweet Home, down on their luck, starved out, bony knees poking through their pitiful jeans, filthy with dust and the high reek of sweat. Dry-land sailors, he called them. He always felt amazement at how quickly they regained their feet when they'd found a job, sat down to regular meals, cleaned up, and donned new clothes.

Darnell Gage, he felt, would be the same. All he needed was the chance.

Bridget McReynolds had the rhythm of the saloon down by now, but she couldn't run it all by herself. Possibly, in a week or two, Gage would leave the safety and comforts of the jail. Jack hoped that when he offered him the job a second time, he'd accept it.

He felt sure he finally had a firm direction to go in his search for Carla Daws and knew he'd have to be gone for quite some time. Bridget would need help.

A few days before he intended to leave on his search, he returned to the jailhouse, and once again drew up a chair in front of Gage's cell.

He said, "You ready to come out of that cage, Darnell?"

Gage sat up on the edge of his cot and rubbed sleep from his eyes.

He stood up, stretched and crossed over to the bars. Jack had purchased the man a new pair of jeans and a new shirt. He wore them now and new boots Will Twist had built for the drifter at the widow Blanchard's leather shop.

Twist was now running the shop for the widow. Darnell had cleaned up right slick and had shaved. As a result, he looked like a human once more, especially since he'd gained weight on Mrs. McWorthy's good food.

He hunkered on his heels, to face Jack eyeball to eyeball, and talked as he rolled a smoke.

"Thanks for the outfit," he said, and lit up. "I didn't ask for 'em.

But I'll repay you, soon's I'm able."

"That's a deal," said Jack.

Gage revealed the rest of his tale then. He informed him that after Tom Easy tossed him back in the bunkhouse, he nearly gave up. They took Ed Ketch in that night, with him on his last legs, figuring to feed him up some, then put him to work. Since Blake had been disposed of, they were shorthanded. Ed would have to take up the slack in the house.

Just when Gage had given up, he heard the latch to his prison lift. Carla Daws stood there in the darkness. She handed him a sack of food, a canteen of water, and told him to run for his life.

Darnell felt reluctant to leave without Ketch, but when she told him Twelvetrees had choked Ed to death, he caught up the supplies she handed him, took out at a trot, and didn't dare take time to hunt up his horse. He couldn't go into Scarlet, a shorter walk, for fear one of Twelvetrees's men would spot him, and drag him back to the ranch. It took him two weeks to reach Wilborn, where he hopped a freight train to Sweet Home.

When he finished his tale, Gage sighed, as if he'd suddenly found a great sense of relief.

"You've heard it all, Mahan. I reckon me and Lenore's square now."

"Yessir," Jack agreed. "I suppose you are, for sure. Thank you for the kindness you've shown to me and to Carla Daws."

Again, Jack Mahan offered Gage the job in his saloon, and this time Darnell took him up on it.

A week later, Jack felt ready to strike out on his search.

8

Jack Mahan saw by the way Bridget's pale skin turned ruddy, that she bore him animosity. Just why, he didn't know. She usually showed up for work as happy as a mockingbird.

In a blunt voice, she said, "Have you hired someone else for barkeep, Mahan?"

"Yeah," he answered. "He'll be in later. I want you to break him in.

Show him everything. He's never worked behind a bar before."

Bridget shrugged like a little girl in a way that showed her hurt feelings.

"What's wrong with my work?"

Bridget McReynolds had the palest blue eyes Jack had ever seen, and they now revealed the pain in her heart. He smiled. He finally understood what had set her off. She thought he was firing her.

He said, "You do a fine job, Bridget. But, I've got to make a trip, and I wanted you to have good help in the saloon while I'm gone."

He sat back and watched her face brighten. She realized now he was not turning her out. Her eyes flashed hot against her pale, freckled skin, surrounded by her splendid red hair.

"Surely you didn't think I would fire you, did you?" Bridget dropped her head in embarrassment, but then raised her face to him. A mist of tears dimmed her eyes.

"Yes. That's exactly what I thought."

"Well, you can forget that. As long as you continue to do your job properly, I won't fire you … not in a million years."

Darnell Gage looked like a newborn man. He'd gained weight on the hook of McDonald County. Jack had advanced him some money, and he stood before him dressed in a dark broadcloth suit he'd bought with the advance. His black eyes danced with humor when he spoke, despite the ordeal he'd been through. This, Jack reckoned, revealed the man's true character.

"I don't know how long I'll stay at this, Mahan," he said, as Jack showed him around the storage room, "but I promise you when I do go, I'll give you plenty of notice."

"Sounds fair enough."

"If someone comes in and offers me a job busting horses, I'm just apt to take him up on it."

Jack felt good about Gage. He felt he could trust him with the saloon right there and then, and walk out the door without a worry about the man's conduct. His natural cautious nature warned him against overconfidence, though. So he stayed on for a week longer to help Bridget break him in.

"You'll work a split shift," he told him.

Gage nodded in agreement.

"You'll open mornings," Jack continued. "I have a regular group of old-timers, who come in to play cards, swap lies, and order a beer once in a while. They set their clocks by when I open my doors. I open promptly at eight o'clock. They frown like hell if I'm even a minute late."

"Understood."

"Bridget comes on at two o'clock. You'll return around seven and stay until closing time. If you're a late sleeper, you might have to make some adjustments."

"I see no problem so far," said Gage. "I'm an early riser."

"Good. Now on Saturdays, if you have chores in town to do, just let Bridget know. She'll open for you. But be sure to return by two o'clock. You know how busy a saloon gets. Saturday is payday for the cowhands."

Gage said, "Yep. I know. These small towns are all the same, I reckon."

"You must keep your room at the Holloway House until I leave. Then, I'd appreciate it if you'd bunk in my room with the safe. You'll have to guard the daily take.

"Since you don't have a gun, I'll loan you one, or you can buy one.

"The bank opens at nine o'clock. I must trust that you to make the daily deposits. It wouldn't do for Bridget to go parading around town with a sack full of money."

Darnell Gage's eyes opened a shade wider. "You mean you'd trust me with your daily bank work?"

"It goes with the job, Darnell. It'd be better if you did it, than Bridget … wouldn't want to chance having her hurt. And I do trust you completely."

Jack shoved him a beer, which he accepted with a frown of mild trepidation at this unconditional trust that Jack had just thrust upon him.

"I'm an excellent judge of character, Gage. I figure I can trust you. The way I look at it, the only thing a man has in life worth a fiddler's dram is the ability to know who and when to trust … and be willing to meet a man's expectations of you when you've won a fellow's trust."

Gage sipped his beer, placed the mug on the bar with a satisfied thump, cracked a smile and said, "I believe you're all right, Mahan. I certainly do."

"Besides that, I'd hunt you down, Darnell." Darnell Gage chuckled at this, took another sip of beer. "I believe you would. I appreciate your faith. I mean to do my best not to let you down."

"One other thing," Jack told him. "That girl, Bridget, I'd appreciate it if you'd monitor her. She's plenty popular with the cowhands. I don't want to come back and find that someone has taken advantage of her."

"I'll see to it, Mahan. Nobody mistreats a decent woman in my presence."

By now, the entire town knew of Jack Mahan's intention to leave on his search for Carla Daws, and to track down the men who carried her off. Several people came to him to tell him he'd need help and warn him not to go off alone. But he knew none of them could afford to quit his job to go off on a chase through the northern counties on what might prove to be a fruitless pursuit.

Pete South, his good and truest friend, tried his best to talk him out of going, but Jack had firmly set his mind. He had to discover Carla Daw's true intentions for the satisfaction and peace of his soul. There was honest concern in Pete's eyes, and Jack felt in some strange way he was about to let the man down.

On the evening before he was to leave town, he rode out to the stock pens at the railroad siding north of town, to say so long to Sheriff Jordan, and his other friends from the Double O. Arnold ranch. He wanted to say so long, true, but he wanted also to secure a job at the Arnold ranch for Darnell Gage. He asked them for a job for Gage, and since everyone on the ranch had grown sick of gentling horses, they were pleased to give it to a man who made this work his lifelong occupation.

With this chore done, he got up from his animal in a trot, and headed back to town. He'd not gone far when Will Twist approached on a stately roan gelding.

When Twist drew alongside Jack, the boot maker slowed his roan to match the pace of Jack's horse.

"I'll ride along with you, Jack," Twist said. "I want you to be the first to know."

"Know what, Will?"

"Me and Irene are getting married. I want to invite you to the wedding."

Jack congratulated Twist and informed him he'd soon take off on his quest to find Carla Daws.

"If you can wait until we, or I return," he said, "I'd like to attend."

"For all I owe you, Jack, I'll see to it. You be careful, hear?" Twist said. He rattled his bridle jewelry then, and his animal leaped ahead, full out.

Jack watched as Will tore on up the street, bearing down on Blanchard's leather shop, pulling a long trail of dust behind him.

At closing time, Jack stepped inside the saloon to check on Bridget. Business had been scanty in the past couple of hours, so she'd turned Darnell Gage loose early.

She'd just finished stacking the chairs atop their tables, had brushed down the tops of the green felt-topped pool tables, racked the cue balls, and returned the cue sticks to their wall cases. All looked properly tucked in for the night.

"Hi, Mahan," chirruped Bridget. He entered the saloon from the storage room. "I figured you'd be asleep by now, getting up early in the morning and all."

"Came in for a little chat," he said. He poured himself whiskey and then sat down at a table with Bridget in the faint light of the lamp that glowed softly behind the bar.

Bridget gave him a bright smile, and suddenly a painful stab of hurt fired up in the center of Jack's heart. He and Carla Daws had often sat at this same table. He recalled that the lamplight had always chipped diamonds rays from her rich black hair. He recalled, too, the sense of peace he always felt as they shared such moments of intimacy, he with his whiskey glass at rest on his belt buckle, while she talked away the day's adventures, miscues and triumphs. He remembered the glow of warm, true quietude at those times and of a sense of intimacy that comes from being with someone a man truly enjoys being with.

After a time of deep silence, Bridget said, "What is it you want to say, Mahan?" She continued to count the day's receipts, as was her custom every night at closing time.

"You realize that part of Darnell's duties while I'm gone is to stash away the day's take in my safe, don't you?"

"Sure," she said, as she stacked the coins she'd already counted on the tabletop. "I wouldn't want to guard all this money. That's a man's job, Mahan."

He smiled and sipped his whiskey. He realized then he didn't need to worry about her. Bridget knew the ways of the world, even for her youth.

He said, "I want you safe while I'm gone. If someone attempts to rob you, you hand him the money with no hesitation. I'd rather have you safe than all the money in the world."

She laughed brightly. "Thanks. That makes me feel good." He watched as a long line of freckles scooted up her forehead with the contraction of her facial muscles in fierce concentration.

"There's a thing that plagues me, Mahan," she said. "If you bring back Carla Daws … will that leave me out in the cold?"

"No, it won't." "I really need this job. I like the work and feel I do a fair job. I'd hate to be let out … but I'd understand if when Carla returns you have to turn me or Darnell out. Me being a woman, I figure it'll be me goes."

"Darnell's working here as a favor to me," he answered. "When I return, he's going to work at the Arnold ranch. It's already settled.
Now rest your mind, Bridget McReynolds."

Later, he stood in the doorway and watched Bridget cross the street, and turned away only when she was safely inside the Holloway House.

9

Jack Mahan stepped into the saddle at the break of day, caught up the reins, and the mule's lead rope. He left town at a lope, while the mule stretched the lead rope straight out behind. The no-good creature must've been stricken by a lowdown mood to shirk its duties.

At the railroad tracks on the north edge of town, just before he reached the loading pens, where the Arnold ranch was camped out, still asleep all in a row in their bedrolls, the only tent being the cook's tall tipi, he saw old Tom Post, the Arnold cook, stretching lazily.

Tom Post waved with a lazy hand and lit his pipe before he turned to the business of cooking breakfast.

Jack hated to leave Sweet Home. The town was the equivalent of family for him … but it was not the same town without Carla Daws. He'd bring her home, if he was man enough, unless she told him she didn't want to return.

Fifteen minutes outside of town, he reined back to a more moderate pace.

The mule decided to co-operate, at least for the time being.

Three days later, just after noon, the town of Military Springs sprang into view. Jack stopped for the night. He figured it'd be great to have a bath and to sleep in a bed. He figured the mule wouldn't mind to spend a night in a stall either and eat a bag of oats. So he headed straight for the livery stable. Afterward, he took a room in the hotel, one in terrible disrepair. Mice had sacked it. Following a bath in tepid water, he made his way into the dining room. He ate a noonday meal of roast beef, potatoes, gravy, and grainy cornbread, with bitter coffee to drink.

After dinner, he ventured into the bar next to the eatery, and found the room heavily occupied. This suited him just fine, since he'd grown tired of being alone for three days, and had missed human companionship.

The barman must've been in his fifties, Jack guessed. He wore a white shirt with a black tie. Jack admired the man's green brocaded vest, just visible at the point where the apron he wore halted just below shirt pocket level. His shirtsleeves were puffed out at the cuffs and held off the wrists by dandy yellow sleeve garters at each elbow. The barkeep's face was bloated and red. Jack presumed by this he was well acquainted with the product he sold. His nose, with prominently enlarged pores, stood out huge on his face. The man's eyes were watery blue and nearly hidden beneath the overhang of a heavily boned structure of brows that were bushy as the tail of a squirrel.

The stub of a cigar perched unlit at the edge of his fat lips. Jack ordered whiskey.

The man poured. "Hunting work?"

"No sir," said Jack, then dropped coins on the bar to pay for his drink.

The bartender lit his cigar.

"No," he said, "I can see now by them hands, you ain't one to work.

Old man McCracken over on Sankey Creek's on the lookout for some extra hands.

I told him I'd turn him some if I could ... just to help him out. Shipping season, and all."

Jack nodded and sampled his whiskey. He found it fit enough to drink, but it was bar whiskey. It was a trifle too harsh, bit his tongue brutally, and burned his palate and throat like a kerosene-cure going down. A group of cowhands stood around a pool table, on which they were shooting a noisy, excited game of craps.

He watched them gamble for a while to pass the time.

One of the crap shooters—a slender fellow wearing new jeans and a crimson shirt with mother-of-pearl buttons that gleamed eyelike down the shirtfront, the sleeves, and at the pockets as well—was having a run of good luck as long as an eastbound cattle train. He made ten straight passes and increased his winnings, which were considerable already. He stacked his winnings out in front of him like fallen leaves a kid had gathered for a frolic. By and by, a few of the other players grumbled in the way men often do when they are in too deep to walk away from the table with any kind of dignity. The man who grumbled the loudest was a fellow with a sunburned nose, short and blocky of build, and wearing a derby hat, which had several dents in it, one of them quite severe.

After a time, the man in the crimson shirt's winnings grew to where they looked as if they might fill a bushel basket. The man beneath the derby hat stood up.

He eyed the winner and did so without humor.

"I'm wiped out," he announced. One player looked at him with sympathy on his face, as if he too would soon have to admit the same thing. But they all seemed compelled to continue their quest as if driven by a demon.

"Goddamn it, boys" the derby-topped man yelled. "I said I'm wiped out."

When he still didn't receive sufficient sympathy, he turned his spite on the shooter.

"Where'n hell did you get them loaded dice, Willis?"

Willis ignored him. He ignored everything, but his long string of good luck, without a care to whose money he was winning. For, very likely, if he became aware of himself, those around him, his incredible run might come to a sudden halt.

Who knew when, or if, it would ever return?

Now, completely disgusted, the man in the derby hat grew even louder, apparently invisible to those around him. Finally, unable to bear his loss and humiliation any longer, he pounced like a cat after a breeze, tattered feather, and snatched up the dice.

Willis plunged over the table after him and grabbed the transgressor in a death grip around the neck. His long, supple fingers, all muscle, thin bones and sinew, turned from sun-brown to a deathly shade of gray in his outrage.

They fell back against the wall, bounced off, and rolled onto the sawdust, going at it like Killkenny cats. The rest of the players suddenly found themselves spectators at what appeared to be a life or death struggle.

Sawdust swirled about the room with each attempt Derby Hat made to fling off the man that held him by the throat. The room filled up with the roar of the loud voices of spectators, and from Willis as well. He not only wanted to throttle his prey to death, it seemed, but wanted him to know why he was about to die as well.

"You took my run of luck, you sonsabitch. I've been looking for a run like this all my life, and you took it from me."

Tears streamed down Willis's face as if he were graveside at his mother's funeral. Eventually, the man in the derby faltered and fade. Twice, as Jack stood there, the unlucky man's hands dropped from Willis's wrists. Somehow, Derby Hat found the strength to continue the struggle for his life. The other man was nearly a goner.

Jack stared at the barkeep to see if he meant to do anything about it, and if so, when. By and by, the barkeep walked to the end of the bar to a small table upon which stood a water pail. He hefted the pail, and crossed the room toward the combatants, going slowly so as not to splash any on his pants legs, or so it appeared. He elbowed his way into the inner circle where the fight raged away.

Then one man who'd been in the game stepped lively to the table where the winnings were on display. He scooped up a double handful of greenbacks and stuffed them in his pockets. Something about this man appeared familiar to Jack.

The man scanned the crowd to see if anyone had witnessed his actions. Missing Jack, and emboldened by his success so far, he removed his hat in a sweep then stuffed the paper money inside. He packed and tamped away until he'd hidden every greenback dollar on the table into his pockets and hat. Quickly, he swept up the coins as well, and stuffed them inside his shirt.

With his hat filled his hat with greenbacks, it lost all resemblance to its original shape. The bartender raised the bucket of water high and dumped it down upon the two scrappers writhing wildly about on the floor like mating snakes. This sudden, cold dash of water broke them apart.

As they fell away from each other, the sneak thief slipped out the door and hustled off up the boardwalk. As he strode quickly away, he was jingling like harness chain from all the coins stuffed inside his shirt.

"Now," declared the barkeep, "get to hell up off the floor." He let the bucket fall to the end of an arm and clutched it firmly by its bail.

"If you boys can't gamble, win, lose or draw, like men," he added, "then get the hell on out of my saloon. Go to the alley if you want to, but you'll not carry on like dumb brutes in my place of business."

Willis was first to get to his feet. His crimson shirt was completely soaked with water. The other man rose up as well, chastened numb. First, because he'd probably just lost his entire month's wages, and, second, from the fine drubbing Willis had just laid on him.

"Sorry, Willis," said the throttled man. He cast about until he found his derby and stuffed it back on his head. "Don't know what came over me. Reckon I couldn't bear to lose my entire month's pay. I'm damned sorry for taking your luck."

Willis still had a dark, relentless scowl on his face. In the end, though, he thrust out his hand, and the two men made their peace.

"Thanks, Dutch," Willis told the barman. "I sure's hell ain't no murderer, but if not for you, I damned well might've become one."

"Well," said Dutch, "if you men want to continue to gamble in my joint, you must stop that kind of roughhouse play."

Willis smiled suddenly, flushed with a good cheer. "I'm buying," he announced. "Drinks for everybody."

This bold pronouncement caused a good-natured cry to strike up—one heard in bars everywhere when a man boasted of buying a round for all. They then charged the bar.

Willis stepped to the table for his money, stopped short, and stood as still as a stone monument. His eyes bugged wide in disbelief. The man's lower lip quivered like the frantic wings of a hummingbird.

He found his voice at last and howled as loud as a homeless dog baying at the sad passage of a midnight freight train.

"Who took it!" he demanded. "Who stole my money? It was right here on this table." He stabbed a finger toward the center of the pool table.

Strained despair and disbelief soon drained him of all color until even snow looked darker than did his stricken face.

Two men went to the table. They looked in every pocket, got down on all fours, and gazed into each other's eyes from opposite sides beneath the table.

"It's gone," one of them said. He got to his feet and brushed sawdust from the knees of his jeans.

"Damned right, it's gone," Willis cried out. He swept his eyes about the room, in an attempt of will to force the perpetrator to give himself up.

The saloon fell as silent as a snowfall.

All eyes stared at Willis, to project their innocence.

Willis walked up to everyone there. He stared into every sun-browned face and stopped when he reached Jack. His eyes lit up then, as if he'd just spotted a lady crossing the street with her bare posterior on display.

He cried out, "Where are you from, mister? Who in hell are you?

What's your business in Military Springs, anyway?"

Jack returned Willis's hard stare. "Jack Mahan. I'm just traveling."

"Just a traveler, eh?"

"Yeah. Passing through town."

Willis reached out and placed a hand upon Mahan's chest. Jack thrust it away angrily. Willis shoved him up against the bar.

Jack grabbed Willis by the front of his fancy shirt, tossed him away, and sawdust boiled up around him as he landed on the seat of his brand-new Saturday jeans.

Jack was far too strong for him to tussle with. But because of his loss and hurt pride, and because of the men standing about watching it all, he couldn't stand to be shown up.

He grabbed for his pistol and whipped it up toward Jack.

Jack eyed Willis cautiously as he got to his feet. Just as he did so, the barkeep thrust a pistol over the bar top aimed straight at the unlucky cowhand's face, whose bad luck continued to beat him over the head.

"Put it back in your pocket, Willis," Dutch said. "And see that it stays there."

Willis ground his teeth in near agony. "If he's got my money, I'll blow his guts out."

"Do it," Dutch told him, "and I'll shoot off your kneecaps. See then if you ever get to work again, poking cattle. That is, if the law don't hang you for murder in the meantime."

Willis finally realized. He put his gun away. The knot of men around Jack grew tighter. One of them pushed his burly face in so close that Jack detected the rare odor of the liver and onions he'd had for lunch.

The man said, "You take Willis's money, mister?"

"No. But I know who did."

"Why didn't you say so?" the barman snorted through his nose.

"Hell, you could've got shot."

"I don't recall that anyone asked. Willis had his mind made up when he first set eyes on me."

"Who was it?" Willis demanded. "I'll run him down, so help me."

Jack gave Willis a description of the man with smallpox scars, who wore a high hat creased in a forward slope.

"Withers?" one man cried out. "Was it Withers?"

"The man's gone, ain't he?" Jack said, as every eye in the room turned toward the door. He explained how, as everyone else there stood and watched the fight, the man they called Withers had stepped to the pool table, stuffed his hat and pockets full of money, and then fled, unaware that Jack had observed his every move.

The talk grew louder and more frenzied. Jack learned that Withers worked for a rancher up around Scarlet in Nebo County. None, however, could say exactly where the ranch was located.

Nebo County, Jack knew, was quite some ways off. Few cowhands traveled that far, unless they were out of work and forced to go off in search of another job.

Or maybe this man's boss had sent him out on some errand.

This rancher owned a large ranch somewhere to the northwest of Scarlet. According to the men in the saloon, he raised more hell on his ranch than cattle.

Some who worked for him were damned peculiar acting as well, or so the story went.

One man said he figured the whole damned lot of them were crazy as bats, and those who weren't crazy to begin with, soon caught up with the rest after they'd worked there for a while.

"What's the fellow's name?" Jack said. "This gent a large man?"

A short man with a wide bushy beard stepped forward. He spoke up, with his hands spread wide in demonstration. "I 'spect he's probably over four hundred pounds. Take a hell of an enormous horse to haul that man around."

"Bullshit, Sam," said an onlooker. "They ain't nobody that big, and you know damned well they ain't."

"Well, maybe not," Sam conceded, "but this gent's damn big just the same."

"Ever see him, Sam?"

Sam conceded even more. "Well, no. But, Ned Tull did. Said he worked on that ranch for a time. But when he divined the entire gang was slack bolted, he made his exit. Left in the dark of night. Didn't even bother to wait around for his wages."

"Was this man's name, Twelvetrees, Sam?" Mahan prompted.

Sam's eyes grew wider. "That's it, mister. How'd'you know?"

"I'm going after Withers," Willis said. "Anybody want to come along, I'd appreciate it. But if not ... I'll not hold it again' you."

It was Saturday. Most of the men declined to go off on a chase like that.

But two men did volunteer, and they followed Willis outside to their horses, got them up in the wind, and left town at a full gallop.

Later that evening, just before the big Saturday invasion of cowhands, Dutch, the barman, and Jack Mahan had a chat. "Have you heard the news about the legislature trying to pass a liquor prohibition law here in Kansas?" Dutch said.

"Yessir. I read some on it."

"If that goes through, it'll put me out of business," Dutch continued.

Finally, after they spent several minutes discussing the subject, Jack decided it was time he hit the hay.

"I'm leaving early in the morning," he told Dutch, and turned to leave.

Making his way across the room toward the stairs that led up to his mouse-eaten room, a large slug of Saturday night revelers burst into the saloon, loud and energetic as they swaggered toward the bar. He looked back at Dutch.

The barman lit a fresh cigar. Jack knew from experience this would be Dutch's last chance for a peaceful smoke for the next several hours.

"Good luck, Dutch." Dutch gestured with the match he'd just fired his cigar with, then shook out the flame. Jack left him as the crowd of rowdy, thirsty young cowhands rushed the bar.

He tried to sleep, but couldn't. Not because of the downstairs racket caused by the drunks, or from the irksome rustling of the mice that shared his bed, but because of a thing in his mind that was dealing him fits.

He felt sure he knew the man Withers, the sneak thief, but the act of attempting to force just where he knew him from caused him to roll from one side of the bed to the other in sleepless agitation.

At length, he decided to let the thought go, and just as he rolled over onto his side and clutched his pillow tight, he nearly leapt straight out of bed from the sudden flash of recognition that lit up his tired brain.

Withers, he recalled, was one of the hard cases who carried off Carla Daws on the night Bobby Sikh crushed his skull. Jack Mahan woke up before the birds, threw back the thin coverlet, watched in amazement as a dozen mice fell away with its short flight. When it struck the floor, the mice, in a mad rush, scampered for the safety of their snug holes.

Two evenings later, he was sitting on his bedroll holding a can of peaches, nibbling a slice of cornbread he'd brought with him from the eatery in Military Springs.

He turned to the sound of labored thumping of horses' hooves striking the ground in a slow trot. Someone had seen his fire and had come to investigate, or so he thought. He placed his pistol between his legs. He figured the visitors were probably cowhands from a nearby ranch sent out by the boss to give him the old eyeball, and caution him to be careful with his campfire, but he wasn't about to take any chances. It took only one crushed skull to turn a man wary, and he had good cause to think so. The insects ceased their racket when the two men rode up.

They reined in and sat their mounts just at the outer limit of the light cast by Jack's campfire. Behind the men, the sky had fallen completely dark with only a few faint stars at rest upon the far horizon.

The two men appeared unnaturally large, sitting above him on their horses in the dark purple evening.

They stood with their weight upon a single leg in the stirrups, and Jack figured he'd been wrong. They were tired and were not from a nearby ranch after all.

"Saw your fire."

Jack remained silent, but kept an eagle eye on them all the while.

"Smelled your coffee."

"The hell you say."

"We ain't eat in quite some time, mister."

Jack Mahan recognized this man's voice. It belonged to the burly faced man, raspy of voice, with the liver and onions on his breath. The man he'd encountered in the saloon back in Military Springs.

"You boys catch that sneak thief?"

"No sir," said the burly faced man.

"Didn't get nothing but empty bellies and sore asses for our efforts," the first man said. "Where'd you hear about it, mister?"

"I was there. Saw it happen."

Jack decided they were harmless. He invited them to step down for coffee and peaches—cornbread too, if they further proved their innocence.

He pitched them each a can of peaches and a slab of cornbread, and watched as they devoured the food like starved-down hounds. He passed coffee to them, leaned back on his bedroll, and slid his gun up alongside his right thigh, out of sight.

He trusted them, but he figured he'd be damned for a tramp if anyone ever caught him off guard again.

"Where's your friend?"

"Willis? He wouldn't give up the chase," said the burly faced man.

"That was a lot of money he lost. We warned him. Said he was crazy to go off alone like that.

Hell, he won't never catch that foul bastard."

"Wouldn't listen, though," the other man said. He sipped his coffee.

"Hot damn, mister, if this here ain't right fine coffee. I 'spect you're a lifesaver.

We was damn nigh starved." "I reckon Willis'll lose his job over this here," said the burly face. "Old man McCracken will probably run his ass off for laying out this away. Hell, he might even can us too."

Jack said, "I doubt it—shipping season and all."

"Might be right," the first man said. "But if I had to do it over again, I wouln't have taken off on that chase for Withers."

"It was the whiskey," said burly face.

His partner said, "Never again."

Jack smiled at the man's sick, sober refrain.

"Never again!" repeated the man, shaking his head. Jack figured this conviction would live until next payday, then they'd forget they'd ever said it. He'd uttered that same phrase himself, more than once.

The next morning, after coffee and tomatoes, sweetened with lumpy sugar, he outfitted the two men with cans of beans and peaches, and sent them on their way. After they departed, he tidied up his mess, rolled his bed, and struck out on the high road to Scarlet. His plan was to hit town late in the afternoon in time for supper. He'd grown tired of canned food.

But the nameless mule, for which Jack was sure the term, "stubborn as a mule," had been coined, delayed Jack with his humping and jumping. Full dark overtook him by the time he drew rein in front of the Scarlet livery stable.

His right arm and shoulder were sore from the mule's stubbornness. Jack felt like he'd towed the sorry creature half the way from Sweet Home to Nebo County. By the time he put up the animals, and located a room at the inn, the ten o'clock bell was striking. The doors of the eatery were shut up tighter than Uncle Tim's tomb. So he went back to the hotel, intending to bed down for the night. The night clerk, a man with sleepy eyes, told him to ask at the saloon if they had any stew left over from the free bar meal at suppertime. They sometimes did, or so said the clerk.

Jack Mahan changed his mind about going to bed hungry.

10

Jack Mahan entered the saloon, owned, as stated by a sign nailed above the door, by Bob Wilfong. He ordered beer, and to his great good luck, discovered there was still stew left over from the free supper, offered as an enticement to draw in customers. He ordered a bowl, and made a meal of beef stew, crusty bread and beer to drink. He'd been on the road long enough, dirty and tanned as he was, the barmaid took him for a cowhand. She asked him if he wanted work.

"Who's hiring?"

"You name it, mister," she said, and smiled to reveal two large upper teeth, capped with gold. The rest of her teeth were capped as well, but with nicotine from her habit of smoking a pipe which she held in the bosom of thumb and forefinger.

"All the ranchers are looking for help," she added. "Them cowhands ain't hardly even got time to come in for a beer. Be glad when shipping season's over. Circus is coming to town tomorrow, though, or so they say. Things should liven up, I reckon.

That'll keep me plenty busy." Jack finished his stew, and marveled at how quickly her tune would probably change, once she became busy.

"Twelvetrees hiring?"

The barmaid perked up at the mention of the name. "What do you know about Twelvetrees, mister?"

"Heard he's a good man to work for," he said. "That's about it."

The barmaid's head flew back. Her hair swished like the tail of a mare.

She roared with laughter, and then when she regained control she said,

"You got to be new to the area, for sure. Hell, mister, as far's I know Twelvetrees ain't never shipped a head of beef since he moved in out there. Whoever told you that one doesn't know what he's talking about."

She swung about toward two customers who stood down at the far end of the bar, the only men there besides Jack. Still in testy good humor she said, "Hey there, Bobby Sikh, this man wants to know is Twelvetrees hiring."

Jack's cast his eyes down the bar and there stood the man who fractured his skull. His toes turned cold in his boots.

Bobby Sikh pushed his empty mug back, stood erect, shoved away from the bar, and headed up the bar toward Jack. At first, Jack figured Sikh recognized him, but then he recalled his beard. The beard, and the fact that a lot of time had passed, brought him a bit of relief. So he relaxed.

Sikh stopped in front of him. His eyes were dark chocolate colored, darting about in their sockets like green broke horses. When he spoke, the tuft of hair beneath his lower lip moved up and down. The tip of the spade, keen and neat, pointed arrow-like toward his chin. "Where'd you hear about Twelvetrees, mister?"

Just listening to Sikh's voice fired barbs of pain straight into Jack's brain, as if he'd just bumped his crazy bone. He felt a strong desire to knock the man down and stomp on him for at least ten minutes. But he knew if he did so, he might as well forget about squaring his debt with Twelvetrees. He'd never get in touch with Carla Daws then, for sure.

In as calm a voice as possible, he said, "A man in Military Springs. Said he treated his help decent, fed good, paid well."

The crusty barmaid cackled again. This time she sounded like a hen on a full nest.

"He hires occasionally," Bobby Sikh said. "What've you got to offer, mister?

He doesn't just hire any old trail bum comes down the pike. You got to have a specialty. You good with that gun you're packing?"

"I'm cool under fire, and usually hit what I aim at," he said. "If that's what you're looking for."

Sikh studied him for a time, and then said, "I ought to know you … but I 'spect I don't." He continued to study Jack, as if close-scrutiny might make up for what his memory lacked.

Behind him, with the patience of a well-trained dog, Sikh's friend stood and watched.

Bobby Sikh stared too long at Jack. Jack shifted his weight just so, in case he needed to knock him down, but then Sikh swiveled his head to the barmaid.

"Nope," he said, "I reckon Twelvetrees ain't hiring." With that, he swung on his heels, moved back down the bar, and took up his former spot. He raised a finger for another mug of suds and continued to study Jack. "Still look sort of familiar, mister," he said. "I ought to know you."

"Ain't going to say you don't, Sikh."

"You know my name … what's yours?"

"Waverly," Jack replied. "Been on the road a good long time. Money's about gone. Thought I'd go to work for a while."

"So you can travel on?"

"Yeah. So I can travel on."

"Nope." Bobby Sikh tipped his beer mug back and forth nervously, then removed the mug from his lips. "I reckon Twelvetrees can't use your kind. He needs men who tend to stick around."

"Count me out, then."

"I've already counted you out, Waverly."

Jack ordered a fresh beer. Before he finished it, Bobby Sikh and his bar chum shoved off and strode on out the door. He listened to the heavy fall of their feet, the thump of boot heels as they shuffled up the boardwalk. A keen sense of clairvoyance, born of being in tight spots in the past, alerted him to danger. He felt he'd see those two again, and soon.

He turned back to the barmaid.

"Haven't seen a fellow named Willis, have you? Wears a bright red shirt."

Her crafty old eyes lit up. She said, "Yeah. I saw that man. Wearing that smart shirt. Couldn't very well miss him. Ain't seen many shirts that loud. Didn't know his name, though."

She puckered her mouth around the stem of her pipe, and puffed away as she reflected, brow wrinkled in concentration. By and by, she added, "I don't recall exactly which day. A couple days ago, for sure. Man said he was looking for his cousin. Fellow named Withers, wearing one of them high-crowned hats, creased to the front.

"Didn't bother to tell him I knew Withers. I don't spill my guts on any man I know. Unless I see a good reason. I didn't bother to tell him that Johnson's across the street held a sale on that kind of hat either. Them hats are pretty common around here."

Jack left the saloon. On his way to the hotel, he expected at every alley for Sikh and his pard to waylay him. To his surprise, he made it to the hotel without incident, mounted the steps of the wide porch, then pushed on inside.

The hotel parlor appeared muted with a faint glow of lamplight. Shadows lay upon the floor, behind every stuffed chair, every footstool, even behind the thin hat rack. The night clerk, the fellow who'd checked him in earlier, lay sprawled out on one of the stuffed chairs with his shoes off, belt loosened for comfort, eyeglasses at rest upon his ample gut, gone to the world. But to his good credit, the man slept lightly as a cat. He jumped awake and settled his spectacles upon his enormous nose.

"What time is the kitchen open for breakfast?" Jack said.

The clerk reeled toward him with an expression of guilt on his face.
Probably because Jack had caught him on the nod.
"The cook gets in about four o'clock. But you just try to enter her kitchen before five and see what it gets you. You'll play hell getting any breakfast till she deems it time, and not a minute earlier, mister."
Jack headed for the stairway to go up to his room on the second floor.
"Catch a nap," he said over his shoulder.
The clerk cracked a wide smile and raised a finger to his lips as if they'd just made an alliance of great secrecy.
The hotel looked new as Jack moved down the upper hallway toward his room.
He smelled fresh paint, heavy in the hallway. This hotel was much nicer than the bag he'd slept in at Military Springs. The wallpaper trim that bordered the wainscoting—what he could see of it in the dim light of the hallway—looked as fresh as the paint on the walls above the paper. None of the seams of the paper had yet separated and curl up. But what he liked best about it was, so far, he hadn't seen a solitary mouse or mouse hole.
The doorways to the rooms along the hall were recessed at least a foot, and he couldn't help but note how easy it'd be for a man bent on skullduggery to hide within one of those clefts and spring out on a man in the gloomy hallway. When he arrived at his door unmolested, Jack smiled at how good he'd become at trying to dredge up dire afflictions from mere shadows. He dug out his room key, opened the door and stepped inside.
An acute burn and tingle rushed down from the part of his skull Sikh had crushed all the way to his left foot as he stepped inside.
He sprang deeper into the room.
An object, solid and probably metallic, stuck him high in the back, just below the shoulder that hurt like a live coal. Jack glimpsed someone poised in a low crouch in the unlit room.
He lashed out and slugged the shadow man full in the face with a quick, fleshy left hand, followed by a hard right, and slammed the man up against the partially open door. The door struck the inner wall hard. The door grated in loud protest, slamming back against the wall, sprung out of shape on its hinges.
"Help me, goddam it.
Help me," the low shadow squalled out his distress.

Jack spun just in time to catch an arm loaded down with a candlestick as it started its downward flight toward his head. He crunched the fellow's wrist, and the candlestick clattered onto the floor.

He spun with the man at the end of his arms.

The man he'd busted in the chops scrambled out of the room.

He continued to spin with the intruder on the end of his arm like the deep man in the old schoolyard game called "crack-the-whip." Then he released him.

The luckless fellow twirled off in a knock-kneed half-run, half-flight.

Jack had meant to knock him senseless against the far wall.

But he'd had no experience at flinging hard cases about hotel rooms, and as a result, his aim failed him.

Instead of bouncing off the wall as he was supposed to do, the man crashed out through the window, and took window frame and all outside with him in his long plunge to the ground. He rushed to the window, in hopes to be in time to drop to the ground, and run him down. But when he saw the bushwhacker sprawled out in the alley, head twisted on his shoulder at an unhealthy angle, he realized the man's career as a head-crusher was over for good.

He turned from the window, rushed into the hallway, down the stairs, barely avoided a collision with the night clerk on his way upward to discover the source of the commotion that had no doubt disturbed his sleep, and then continued his downward plunge.

When he burst through the front door onto the street, he saw he was too late to catch the man he'd popped twice in the mug. The man sat low in the saddle, and Jack watched helplessly as the cutthroat spurred his mount as if a demon had drawn a bead on him. Jack then grew hot that he'd been waylaid.

He watched the fellow's departure, and decided he was watching the departure of Bobby Sikh, although he didn't get a good look at him.

His fist-marks were on the gent's face, though. This would reveal him if their paths ever crossed again. The horse, with white mane and four white stockings glowing bright like lamplight in the dark, would tell on him as well.

He bent to a knee and squeezed off a round. The roar of the discharge in the street boomed unnaturally loud.

He missed. He'd taken the shot as an expression of his anger and frustration with little expectations that he'd hit the man, and sure enough, he missed.

At length, he came to his better senses, exhaled a long held, hot breath, and stood up. The horse and rider were quickly swallowed up by the dark night.

He holstered his pistol, turned and hurried back into the alley.

He knelt then alongside the man he'd tossed out the window. He placed a finger upon the man's carotid artery. He felt no pulse. He was dead, as Jack feared.

He started to stand up, but felt a sudden cold sensation upon his left jawbone.

No one had to send him a letter. He held still.

"Get up, mister. Get up slow."

Jack didn't argue, but did what the man told him to do, turned and faced a man with a shotgun in hand. The shotgun man removed Jack's revolver from its holster, stuck it behind his own belt buckle. "Just what'n the hell're you up to, mister?

Get on out in the street. Let's see if I know you. I'd like to know just exactly what you're doing bent over a man who looks plenty dead, alongside old man Pride's hotel."

Lights blinked on inside many of the business places on the street. The pale yellow glow they cast lay in wide slashes upon the street.

"Let me have a peek at you."

Jack stood facing a short, stocky man, wide at the shoulders, thick at the chest, but slim of waist.

"You the one fired off that pistol?"

"Yessir."

"You kill that man in the alley?"

"Yessir … but I didn't shoot him."

"You expect he cares now just how you killed him?"

"No sir," Jack said, but the man with the shotgun cut him off before he could tell his side of the incident.

"What was you shooting at, if you didn't shoot him?"

Jack Mahan tried again to explain, "Look, when I entered my hotel room, I was jumped…"

Once more, he was interrupted. This time by the loud slam of the front door of the hotel.

He turned as a tall man, bare of foot, clad only in trousers, the wide galluses of which hung down his sides, hurried toward them. The sleepy night clerk followed him.

The tall shoeless man bore a scattergun across his body like an infantryman.

Jack figured him for the owner of the hotel.

"What's all the shooting about, anyway, Sheriff Hyde?" he said in a high, squeaky voice. Even though there had been only one shot fired, the man added, "Hell's fire, sounded like a regular artillery exchange out here."

"That there's him, Mr. Pride," said the clerk. He stood with a finger cocked and pointed at Jack. "He's the one I told you about."

"It's all right, Henry," said the shotgun man to the fellow Jack guessed to be the owner of the hotel. "Now take that gun and lay it on the porch there before you shoot somebody, or maybe your own self."

Henry turned to the night clerk and thrust the shotgun into his hands.

"Do as the sheriff says, Alfred."

He turned back to Jack for an explanation of the racket raised by the furious scuffle that had occurred upstairs.

By the time Jack Mahan finished his explanation, he was tired, clear to the bone from all the backtracking, the filling and grading he'd made.

"You must pay for that window you broke, mister." Henry stood close, and shook his finger in Jack's face.

Jack said, "Charge it to the old boy that flew through it. He's the one who damaged your window." Henry saw no humor in this and continued to rack up charges against Jack's bill. "And for the door, too. Alfred says it's sprung all out-of-round."

Jack protested. He realised it wasn't his fault a couple of hard noses attempted to rob him just as he was about to bed down.

This sent the hotelkeeper off again. He raised such a fuss it was enough to wake up the rest of the downtown.

It seemed at least half the merchants were already standing in the street.

They ventured into the street in small knots of three and four to better hear and see who or what had caused the disturbance.

The shotgun-man—Hyde, the sheriff of Nebo County—aimed the barrel of his shotgun toward the jailhouse across the street.

"Get along, mister," he said. "We'll sort this out in the morning. Meantime, you'll spend the night in jail, courtesy of Nebo County." "I already have a room for the night, Sheriff."

Hyde ignored Jack's sorry stab at humor. "When it's time to pay up, Mr. Pride will probably deduct the cost of the room from all the other damages he's fixing to stick you with."

"Like hell, too," said Henry Pride. "It ain't my fault if he don't use the room as intended. I provided it for him all in good faith."

"Go on back to bed, Henry," said Sheriff Hyde, and his tone of voice allowed no further debate.

"And the rest of you as well." He swept his free arm toward the men crowding the street.

Hyde escorted Jack toward the jailhouse, and Henry was still roaring loudly, protesting his hurt in an offended voice to call there.

Hyde opened the door to one of the jail cells. Jack decided further argument would be just more lost air, so he slinked on inside, noticing that all the other cells were empty. This was because of market season, he figured. Sheriff Hyde, if he wanted to be re-elected, knew better than to arrest any cowhand right now, short of a murder charge.

His bunk, he discovered soon enough, was a solid sheet of iron attached to the wall. It lacked even a tick of cobs on which to nap, or a brick to rest his head on.

He saw right off that he'd get precious little sleep this night.

"What're you doing in Nebo County, mister?" Hyde said.

"Passing through. Looking for work." "Bullshit," snapped the sheriff.

He stepped closer to the bars.

Jack stood, gripping the iron bars tightly with both hands.

"Don't pull sly stunts on me. You'll find I'm too big a turd to shit. You don't come into my county passing as a man looking for a job. Asking questions, like the funny man hisself.

"Any common dummy can see by them hands of yours you ain't no working man. You ain't no lawman, either, else you'd have come to me first thing.

"Now, whoever you're looking for, or whatever you're up to, you'd be wise to let me in on it. I might lend a hand. I'm acquainted with every man in the entire county.

If I can't find who you're after, they ain't no need for anyone else even giving it a shot.

"Now spill you guts and stop pussyfooting around. Judge Lodge is apt to hang your sorry ass for killing that no-'count Art Shell … unless I speak in your favor. So you better wise up, and give me the lowdown."

11

Jack Mahan saw no other way but to go along with the sheriff. He had to trust Hyde. So he told him his tale. "My name's Jack Mahan. But I registered at the hotel as Jack Waverly." He revealed to Hyde all that'd occurred between Twelvetrees and himself in Sweet Home.

Hyde studied him from critical eyes, and after listening to it all, he said, "Twelvetrees is surrounded by a virtual army, Mahan. I've been trying to bring the man down myself. But have had little success.

"The man thumbs his nose at the law and does whatever he wants to do."

"Can't you call in outside help, Sheriff Hyde? There has to be some way to bring him to justice."

Hyde's face fell. "He's got money and a lot. You got money you can buy good legal help" This might all be true, but all Jack wanted was a good shot at Twelvetrees, and to talk to Carla Daws to learn just exactly what her side of the arrangement with the big man happened to be.

Hyde continued, "Twelvetrees takes the law with him wherever he goes. He is the law, as far as that goes.

"Recently, he strangled a young local man to death because he couldn't get to the boy's father, and so far I haven't been able to do a thing about it. Neither has the boy's father. This feller is a merchant in town, by name of Tillman Dead. Tillman's an Indian, married to a white woman. Twelvetrees can't intimidate Till, and that's another reason he hates him so."

"All I want to do, Sheriff," Jack said, "is get out of jail, settle my debt with Twelvetrees, and get on back home.

"I prefer to take Carla Daws with me, but if she says she doesn't want to return, then that'll be the end of that. I'll go back to Sweet Home and get out of your hair."

"You make it sound simple," said Hyde. "If it was that easy, I'd already have Axel in jail.

"On top of the other problems that face you is the little matter of the man you killed. Art Shell was a no-'count bastard … one of Twelvetrees's men. You never know what Judge Lodge will do in a case like this. He might just throw the book at you.

"He's trying hard to get on Twelvetrees's payroll, but ain't got no chance. The judge doesn't realize it, but Twelvetrees hates him nearly as much as he does Tillman Dead. Lodge ain't got sense enough to figure it out.

"By the way, the coroner will have to get out of bed, and pick up Shell's body. One thing the man can't stand is to get woken up in the middle of the night. I reckon you ain't making many friends around here."

"I killed that man in self-defense."

Hyde sighed. "Well, one thing's in your favor, the judge is in town. You won't have to wait in that cell for a couple of weeks until he finished his circuit. You'll go in front of him in the morning. You can explain it all then."

Jack slumped down onto his cot. A few minutes later, Hyde mumbled something about going over to the coroner's house to awaken him, then left the office.

Jack got up from the iron cot then and camped out on the floor where it proved to be a bit more comfortable.

12

The sun stabbed dagger-like rays in through the front window of the jailhouse and woke Jack Mahan up. At first, he couldn't say just where he was. But sadly he recalled all that'd transpired last night, rolled over reluctantly, and sat up. He ached all over. So much so, it was as if his balky mule had kicked him a good number of times in the small of the back.

He fought his way to his feet, then paced the floor as if he were breaking in a new pair of boots. Minutes later, he heard a bright whistle tune approaching the jailhouse. Suddenly, the front door burst inward, and bounced viciously off the inner wall as if a tornado had just ripped through the center of Scarlet and struck the jailhouse full blast. An old man then entered with both hands full. He held a tray of food in one hand, a pot of coffee in the other. The man was dressed in scuffed boots, faded jeans and worn plaid shirt. A brand-new black beaver hat set upon his head that contrasted with the rest of his faded attire. If not for the new hat, and because the man had recently come from the barbershop, leaving the lingering scent of lily of the valley powder in the air around him, Jack might have taken him for the town bum.

"If I kick the bottom of the door just right," the man explained, "it flies open. Do it wrong, I have to set down all this mess."

He stood before Jack, whistling again, while he waited for the surprised prisoner to accept the food. After a time, he wrinkled his face in a stormy cloud. "Damn it all, man, don't you want to eat?"

The bearer of the food tray looked like an Indian, but since he spoke English better than Jack did, he felt unsure of his guesswork. Eventually, he caught on, and drew the food through the bars one item at a time. The door was handmade and had no meal slot. With this done, he sat down on the iron cot and ate.

He found it good food, oatmeal, bacon and eggs, fried spuds with one enormous biscuit, and coffee to drink.

The man stood by all the while, waiting for Mahan to finish his meal.

Jack figured the old man was the swamper and houseman at a nearby diner.

"So, you're the old boy, eh?" the man said, rolling a smoke.

"Which old boy?"

"The old boy who's been going about town asking questions about Axel Twelvetrees. The words out on you already, feller."

"That bad?" he said, between bites.

"There are only two people in this entire county who ain't scared shitless of that fool. You're looking at one, and the other one is Sheriff Hyde."

Jack figured the old man liked to brag a bit. "Is that so?"

"Damned true."

The man stood there, puffed on his cigarette, and waited. With each drag, his cheeks drew inward as if a puckering-string tugged away at them from inside his mouth. After each drag, he removed the cigarette as he inhaled, and raked off the ash that had accumulated there from his last prodigious puff.

"There are people who have been known to go missing from Scarlet. Everybody in town knows it's Twelvetrees behind it all. But most of the folks around here are too chicken-shit to go out to his ranch, haul his lard ass outside, and string him up."

Jack stopped eating, interested now in the man's rant.

"They just lay it off on everything except Twelvetrees. They go on about how the missing person grew tired of Scarlet, his family, neighbors or whatever and just moved on. I reckon it makes 'em feel better to let things slide.

"Now how many men you know will do a thing like that? Going off without saying goodbye, kiss my ass, or any other kind of a damn thing?"

Jack shook his head, then fell again to eating. By and by, he said, "I'm searching for a friend."

He explained it all to the old man. How Twelvetrees journeyed to Sweet Home and carried off Carla Daws. Jack trusted his instincts, feeling safe revealing all this to the man.

"I know that place, Sweet Home. Used to kill buffalo where the city now sits. This was many years ago with my uncle. Uncle was a great one to kill buffalo. Killed 'em off by the numbers, he did. Then he'd give 'em all away.

"His old woman would tear up his ass right good when he came home empty-handed. Off he went again. By then, of course, the buffalo—being migratory creatures—would be way off on their northerly loop. Uncle would be gone sometimes for a month. He always had plenty of game, though when he finally returned.

"Uncle took me along a few times. Taught me a lot of stuff that soon fell out of favor after the railroad hunters killed off all the buffalo. That left me with a lot of useless knowledge. I suppose you could say I was over-educated for the times I grew up in.

"Later on, a good Christian white man took me in."

How The old man ground out his cigarette, reached inside his leather vest to an inner pocket, drew forth a pint of whiskey, and took a long pull.

When he removed the bottle from his lips, he shoved it in Jack's direction.

Jack said, "No thanks. I'm not really all that keen on whiskey before breakfast."

The old fellow took another pull and put away the bottle. "I offered, son. It ain't my fault you're a man to eat late in the day."

Tillman Dead wiped his lips with a backhanded swipe and rolled another cigarette. "Anyway, go ahead with what you were fixing to tell me."

"Twelvetrees and a few of his men sliced up my face with a razor."

"I've seen that razor. He wears it around his neck on a silver chain. That the reason for all the facial hair?"

"Yessir. I didn't want to go scaring off every child I met."

The old man laughed at that, then said, "Being ugly won't kill a man. If so, I'd have died at birth. Course, scaring children—well, I reckon I've scared my share."

Jack carried on with his tale, "They cracked my skull. My friend, the one Twelvetrees kidnapped, is Carla Daws." "Don't know the name."

"Twelvetrees called her Lenore. She was my barmaid."

"I do know that name. She's been with him a good long time. She was gone for a couple of years. Then suddenly, returned. She must've run off on him, and he took her back when he found her tending bar in your saloon. That'd be my guess, anyway. I allowed all that time he'd killed her."

Jack finished his meal and handed out the dishes. "I mean to find her," he said. "And I wouldn't mind too much if I paid Twelvetrees back for all the grief he put me through."

The old man's tight black eyes burned hot and glinted bright, deep within their sockets.

"Tell you what, mister," said the old fellow, "you flush that brainless bastard for me, and I'll take him … on the wing, or shoot him aground. Doesn't matter a whit to me. "This community will be a far better place when it's done. Call on me, son. I'll be glad to lend you a hand."

Jack still figured the old man was a harmless braggart. He told him this, but then decided he didn't want to hurt his feelings.

"I won't keep you from your job, sir," he said. "I wouldn't want to see you get in trouble with the owner of the dining room."

"Don't let that worry you, sonny," replied the old-timer. "its mighty kind of you, but I am the owner of the dining room. My swamper, Luke, is out with a bad case of the snakes. I'm filling in for him.

"Luke's a fair enough feller. Just can't hold his liquor's all. I own a saloon here in town too, although I got a white feller who runs it for me since Twelvetrees killed my son. My name's Tillman Dead."

This took Jack Mahan aback, and his shock stood out plainly on his face when he recalled that this man was the one Sheriff Hyde had spoken of last night.

"It ain't good for business for an Indian to be serving whiskey to white folks," he went on. "I own the millinery and half-interest in the hardware store with Abner Johnson. Lots of money in picks and shovels, nails and all like that. I would have learned the trade of undertaking too, but I felt folks would draw the line at that."

Tillman Dead seemed to be quite a successful man, even without the buffalo to follow. The old white man who'd raised him had made an enterprising entrepreneur of Tillman Dead.

"You're going in front of Judge Lodge directly. Lodge is a foolish bastard if ever you wanted to see one, but he exercises fair to good judgment at times. I figure the signs are all in your favor today. Lodge has made some harsh rulings here of late. Time he changed. I predict he'll rule pretty much in your favor. Art Shell was a well-known bum, and even though he worked for Twelvetrees, I figure you'll get off. At least, I don't see you swinging."

Tillman Dead departed, whistling away like a mockingbird as he strolled back down the street.

At a quarter till ten, Sheriff Hyde showed up in a rush. He opened and slammed desk drawers, searching through stacks of paper.

Jack watched from his cell. Finally, having found what he was looking for, Jack figured, he took down his ten-gauge from its seat in the wall rack, approached the cell, unlocked it, and motioned with the barrel of the gun for him to step out.

Hyde said, "Let's move, mister. We got to be in front of the judge by ten. It'll not do to be tardy for Lodge's court."

Jack caught up his hat, knocked out a few wrinkles from the front of his vest, and stepped out of the cell.

Hyde dodged his head toward the front door, and they stepped outside together in the bright sunshine, and crossed the street to the courthouse.

Judge Lodge turned out to be a dandy. He was an extremely thin man, perhaps fifty years old. What hair he possessed stood upright in cottony islands of disrepair, as fine as the mane of a racehorse, and between broad oceans of shiny, taut skin that covered his bony skull. His face looked drawn up at the mouth in a loose crumple, and his eyes were blue flints that danced in their sockets like water droplets atop a red-hot stove.

He kept his upper lip clean-shaven, but a thin ribbon of short gray whiskers ran from just below his ears around both sides of his lower jawbone and on to the peak of his pointed chin. His chin whiskers stood out long, in a wispy beard that hung all the way to his small potbelly.

Judge Lodge and Sheriff Hyde deliberated in soft whispers at the bench. By and by, Hyde gestured for Jack to step forward at the conclusion of their confab, which he did. He stood at attention awaiting the verdict.

In a sudden loud, arrogant voice Judge Lodge said, "You, Mr. Waverly, owe the city of Scarlet three dollars for firing a weapon in city limits after eleven o'clock p. m., and an additional two dollars paid to the county for the same infraction. Our citizens need their rest, sir, and you disturbed it."

This stunned Jack, not merely at the size of the fine, but because of the added penalty awarded to the county. He fixed his mouth to protest, but the judge cut him off before he widened his trap.

"As to the death of the vagabond and rank ruffian, Mr. Art Shell—the man who attempted to burglarize your room, but was foiled in this when you flung him through the window, whereupon he broke his neck when he struck the ground—I dismiss all charges."

Judge Lodge banged his gavel and pronounced court adjourned for the day.

A short time later, inside the jailhouse, Hyde passed Jack's personal possessions over to him. The silver money he placed in his pocket, the paper he stuffed in his folding wallet. He strapped on his holster with a pistol, and reattached his watch and chain, looped the fob, and secured it in a buttonhole of the vest.

"Leaving Scarlet, mister?" said the sheriff.

"Yes, after I've located Carla Daws."

"Better watch out Twelvetrees don't tan your hide and use it as a liner for a steamer trunk. The man's dangerous."

"Thanks for the tip, but I already have first-hand knowledge of just how dangerous the man is."

He heard the distant strains of music and cocked his head toward the sound.

Hyde got to his feet, went and stood in the doorway, and stared off up the street.
Presently he said, "Here comes the devil now." He returned to his desk and packed his pipe.
"What's the music all about, Sheriff Hyde?"
"Oh, that's just Axel. He wants to show his gratitude to the citizens of Nebo County. He's hired a circus to entertain us.
"I heard he had, but figured even he wasn't that brash as to make the same bribe twice." Hyde fired his pipe and set about filling the room with tobacco smoke.
"A circus?" said Jack. He then recalled the gold-toothed barmaid's pronouncement from last night.
"Yeah," Hyde said, "but I don't think there are many animal's though.
Just a few tired bears. Mostly a bunch of performers. Acrobats, magicians and the like.
"Axel had 'em in a few years ago. Guess they're back for a return engagement."
Sheriff Hyde exhaled tobacco smoke, turned to the hat rack, donned his hat, and strode toward the door. He spoke to Jack over a shoulder. "Nothing to do now but go out and remind Twelvetrees he can't take over the entire town.
We made an agreement last time he was in, when his rough lot damned nigh tore down the entire town. "City council still hasn't ruled on the agreement yet.
Supposed to do that today, or so the mayor tells me. We're trying to bar him from town except for twice a month."
Jack Mahan followed Hyde outside where the sheriff stood on the sidewalk, one hand on the butt of his revolver, and with the other one he tugged the brim of his hat down to cover his forehead against the bright sun.
Jack studied the slow approach of the long line of circus wagons.
By now, the news of the circus caravan's arrival must've spread across town.
A mob of young boys charged out to meet it, yelling at the top of their lungs in their youthful enthusiasm.
Soon the lead wagon bearing the band, an octet, arrived. The musicians stood on the flatbed of a wide wagon and played away at an inspired march tune to draw a crowd.
A grand pair of mules, their manes neatly clipped and as erect as the stiff bristles of brushes, drew the wagon.
Behind the bandwagon, a group of jugglers gave a hot display of their skills as they proceeded up the street. The tumblers strutted along next, throwing their feet high, cutting nifty shines and elaborate didoes, raising enormous clouds of dust.

A good number of clowns followed the tumblers, marked bright of face, decked out in outlandish, garish costumes. They pulled faces and played exaggerated pranks on their fellows. All the performers were herded along by a black coach, trimmed in gold paint, drawn by four magnificent white horses, driven by a stiff-backed fellow seated upon a high seat.

The driver of the coach waved a shiny top hat above his head occasionally and wore a somber black suit with white gloves. The occupants of the coach had the shades of the elegant vehicle drawn to reduce the dust, or so Jack assumed. Out in front of all, rode four heavily armed horsemen. They were riding two abreast. The entire company drew along in its current, a group of hard-looking men and women of the circus.

At last, the coach came to a shuddering halt, rocking fore and aft upon heavy carriage springs. Sheriff Hyde tugged again at the brim of his hat and said, "Come on. You might as well have a look at the man you plan to bring down all by yourself."

Frank Hyde stepped down onto the street. The two men walked side-by-side up close to where the coach stood upon the dusty street. Axel Twelvetrees, himself, emerged first from the coach, helped down by a man dressed in similar black funereal garb worn by the driver. Twelvetrees stood there, tricked out in a white silk suit that contrasted boldly to all the black.

Atop his head set a high hat as if it were the crown of some great royal nabob. An old woman, also dressed in black, which included a veil, filigreed with thin silver thread that partially hid her face, followed Twelvetrees.

A younger woman stepped next from the coach, in a bright red velvet ball gown. She paused just outside the coach door for a second, as if waiting for someone, but then hurried after the old woman, who was now ascending the steps up to the shaded porch of the hotel.

13

Jack's heart lurched like an eager horse against the bit. "Carla," he muttered.

The sheriff crossed over to face Twelvetrees, who stood upon the boardwalk, out of the sun, beneath the porch roof of Tillman Dead's saloon.

Jack first felt he should follow Carla, but there appeared to be a barrier between them now, one, possibly, she wouldn't allow him to breach. So he stood by and watched.

"Twelvetrees," Sheriff Hyde called out, "you realize you're violating our agreement, don't you?"

Twelvetrees stood straight as a ramrod, unconcerned as if he hadn't even heard Hyde. He stood and gazed out over the crowd, made up mainly of young boys, who'd come to see the show. Slowly, he extended his hand toward his valet, and said, "Give me the sack, Marv."

The valet passed Twelvetrees a large leather sack and stepped aside to wait for any following orders. Twelvetrees opened the sack, removed a handful of coins, many of them coppers, and tossed them out into the crowd. Two sick-eyed alcoholics joined the boys, battling furiously for the coins.

Tom Easy, the gunman, stood in a relaxed slant against one of the rough, unpainted posts that held up the roof of Dead's saloon. He watched every move made there. Mainly he kept his eyes on Sheriff Hyde. Jack felt an increase in tension—felt it grow steadily with the passing of every moment. "Axel," said Hyde. "You and your bunch of lowlifes ain't welcome in Scarlet today. If you recall, we had an agreement."

Twelvetrees continued to ignore Hyde. He tossed more coppers down into the crowd, as if he were feeding a flock of chickens.

Twelvetrees's lack of concern caused Hyde to blow up in anger. The blood veins in his neck bulged. They grew thick and pulsated with the blood of his anger.

"We made an agreement that you weren't allowed in town but twice a month," he said. "What happened to that agreement?"

Twelvetrees broke his silence. "You know what they say about agreements, Sheriff."

He turned his eyes on Hyde for the first time. "They're made to be broken."

He continued to toss coins out onto the street where the youngsters and the two alcoholics continued to battle for them, raising a thick boil of dust. "I'm sure you've heard of that, haven't you, Sheriff?"

Hyde thrust a hand out in anger. He snatched the bag of coins from Twelvetrees and said, "Now, I figure its time you listened to what I have to say."

Like a swift shadow in front of a full moon, Tom Easy stepped up. He swiftly lifted his gun and placed the barrel against Frank Hyde's head.

Twelvetrees reclaimed his sack of coins and handed it to Marv. "All right, Hyde. You've had your say. Now go on back to your office before you get someone hurt."

He grabbed Hyde up with a huge hand, drew him close to his face, stared at him like a practitioner of Mesmer, and then flung him away. Hyde fell down the steps and landed on his rump in the street.

"And," continued Twelvetrees, hands on his hips, "I suggest when you get back to the safety of your office, you stay put until we leave town. Everything will work much smoother that way."

Just then, four men came lugging a large iron box out into the middle of the street. The box had one small window, covered by bars. Someone was inside the box, but it was hard to see into the interior. It appeared as though the man had drawn as far back in the box as he could.

With closer inspection, Jack made out the man's face, and learned it was Withers, from Military Springs. He must've fallen into disfavor with Twelvetrees.

Twelvetrees turned his attention to the box, ignoring Hyde for the moment.

"That man in the box there will soon learn what it means to cross Axel Twelvetrees," he said. He did not elaborate, but whirled to enter Dead's saloon. He didn't get far.

"Just take one more step toward this door," said Tillman Dead in a dry crow-like voice, "and I'll blow your guts out and feed 'em to the hogs."

He shoved the barrel of his ten-gauge into Twelvetrees's gut.

Slowly, a smile widened the big man's large, round face.

"Why feed them to the hogs, old man? Being the great businessman, you would profit more if you listed them on the menu of your dining room. Hell, make them the special of the day."

"Not likely," Tillman said, not missing a lick. "I figure even a hog would turn up its nose at your stench." Axel Twelvetrees attempted to step forward. Tillman Dead stepped gracefully backward and fired off a round. The low blast tore the fine top hat from Twelvetrees's cannonball head.

The white silk hat burst apart instantly. The fabric that composed it swarmed high above the street like flies off a gut wagon.

The blast sounded much like a landslide in such close quarters there upon the porch. A sudden, sharp rise of fear flashed briefly in the eyes of Twelvetrees before he regained his swagger.

"You mean to kill me, old man?"

"I plan to do the job all right, but not yet. Unless you back me up where I can't back no more. I'm in no rush. But don't put me in a bind."

"You have only one round left, Dead," warned Twelvetrees.

It was clear though he'd have to do more to frighten Tillman Dead than throw puny words at him.

"Hell, Axel, I can count. Old Silas Dead, who reared me, taught me that much and more."

"If you were somehow able to kill me, Tillman," Twelvetrees said, "my man would cut you down before you could fumble more loads into the beech of that shotgun."

"I've had my grip packed a good long while, Axel. Probably before your mam dropped you from between her befouled legs. It's a shame she made the mistake of keeping you and tossing out the baby instead."

"You're not funny, Dead," Twelvetrees countered. Dead had gotten to the big man at last. "Not a damned bit and leave my mother out of this."

"Why is that, Axel? That woman's into every other means of filth known on earth.

"I'm an old man. I've lived my life, not as rich as you have, and I don't have as much to keep me yearning to hang around ... not the way you do. "Are you ready to give up all you have?" Dead continued. "I'm betting not. Either way, I figure you'll hit hell long before me."

Tom Easy had his .44 trained now on Dead, and his hand looked as solid as stone.

Forgotten in the rumpus, Sheriff Hyde raced back up the steps with his revolver in hand, aimed at Tom Easy. "Better change your tune, Twelvetrees, and damned fast.

"You tore Till's saloon all to hell last time you were in town. So while you got that sack of coins handy, you can settle your tab with him.

That is, if it has more than coppers in it."

Twelvetrees grinned widely and added a low chuckle. He tossed the sack at Tillman Dead's feet, where it jingled flatly. A few of the coins rolled free of the mouth of the sack and traveled on edge in short circles before lying down on the floorboards.

One gold coin, though, stood up on edge and rolled across the surface of the porch to the boardwalk, crossed it, and dropped a step at a time down to the street, with the eyes of the youngsters and the alcoholics glued onto it.

When the coin struck the street and fell on its side, the boys fought like men with the drunks for possession of the valuable coin. Sheriff Hyde regained his authority and pressed on. "Turn your caravan around, Axel. Get on back to your ranch. Stay there till it's time to return ... as per our agreement."

Twelvetrees spun away from Tillman Dead, and when he did so, Tillman took this opportunity to fetch forth a fresh load from a pocket, kick out the spent hull, and insert a fresh one.

Just then, Judge Lodge showed up, and stood next to the sheriff. "What's the ruckus all about, Sheriff Hyde?"

"It's Twelvetrees again, Judge Lodge," he said. "As you know, we made an agreement the last time he was in town. He was supposed to stay out of Scarlet for a couple weeks yet before he came back. His men have a knack for damaging other folks' property."

"I always make amends, Judge Lodge. Everyone knows that.
Why, only just now, I settled with the noble red man here, and I paid dearly too. Also, I doubt my people caused all the damage. We're not the only crew that comes into Scarlet."

"That true, Tillman?" said the judge. "Did Axel reimburse you for the damages to your property?"

Dead dipped his head in a reluctant nod.

"I spend big when I come to town," Twelvetrees added. "All the merchants know it. I don't think it would be so good for them to bar me from a town in an agreement like the sheriff's proposing."

"Proposing, hell," said Hyde. "We had an agreement." Judge Lodge held up a hand for silence. He stroked his long billy-goat beard in contemplation. Presently, he raised his head to the sheriff.

"Regarding this agreement, Sheriff Hyde, the city council just now, this morning, determined that your agreement is void."

The sheriff's face fell in disappointment. The judge turned to Twelvetrees.
"As far as you're concerned, Axel, I must caution you to rein in your men—and yourself, as well. You must exercise restraint. "But since it's clear you pay for everything your people destroy—not that I condone any such behavior—I see no reason to ban you from Scarlet, especially since the city council agreed you should be allowed to come to town whenever the need arises, negating whatever agreement you might have made. Nonbinding agreement, I might add."

Twelvetrees stepped up to Sheriff Hyde, and said, "You hear that, Hyde? You've just been overruled."

Frank Hyde held Twelvetrees's gaze for a considerable time. His face turned red. Finally, he whirled, descended to the street, shoved his way through the crowd, and strode back toward his office in a slow burn.

As Hyde strode off through the crowd, Twelvetrees flung back his head and roared with laughter.

Then in a loud voice, he called out, "Come one, come all. Let's step inside the old man's saloon. I'll spring … drinks for everyone for the entire day." Twelvetre surged forward, pushed along by the crowd toward the door of Dead's saloon.

The old man pushed the lengthy barrel of his ten-gauge into the big man's stomach again and stopped the forward surge right away.

"I told you, Axel. You ain't welcome. A man has the right to defend his own property. Now I'll thank you damned kindly to step down off my porch. I'll not tell you again."

Twelvetrees turned an expectant, defiant eye toward Judge Lodge. "Judge?"

"Now, be rational, Till," Lodge said. "Step aside, please."

"This man killed my son, Judge, and everyone knows it. I'll be damned if I allow him into my place of business, serve him drinks, and listen to him crow."

"Now you know full well there is no proof of who killed your son. So be reasonable. Life is harsh, sir, and we all need a break from its drabness from time to time."

"If it's a break you need," Dead told him, defying the judge and the world as well, it seemed, "then take it across the street to Bob Wilfong's joint. I figure he'll be more than pleased to serve such an illustrious bunch of turd-hounds."

Lodge turned to Twelvetrees with a resigned look on his face.

Twelvetrees glared at the old man for a time, then without further argument, whirled, walked down the steps to the street, and crossed over to the other side with the wind driving whirlwinds up against the large crowd that followed the big man.

All in the crowd were eager to accept Twlevetrees's largess and cared none about which side of the street they celebrated on. They reached the porch of Wilfong's saloon, and Twelvetrees turned and stared back across the street, through the film of dust in the air to where Tillman Dead stood with his shotgun held across his chest. At length, Twelvetrees strode on inside and dragged with him the noisy mass of carefree men. On the street, the entertainers, who'd stopped to watch when the blast of Dead's shotgun roared alive, took up their acts precisely where they'd left off, and didn't miss a single beat or a step.

Jack Mahan stepped up and stood on the porch alongside Tillman Dead.

"Judge Lodge is messing with dynamite, boy," Tillman said. "And it's just apt to go off in his face, and he won't even know what killed him."

"How's that, Tillman?"

"The man made some rulings that went again' Axel."

Dead took his bottle of whiskey from beneath his vest, popped the cork, and took a long pull. When he put the bottle away, he wiped his mouth absently with the back of a hand.

"Judge Lodge's forgot all about that, seems to me. But one thing's for sure, Axel ain't. He don't forget a damned thing."

14

Jack Mahan tromped down the boardwalk, back to the jailhouse, and left Tillman Dead on guard at the door of his saloon, watching with the concentrated look on his face of a hawk on the hunt.

The street was crowded with the circus troupe that included mimes, jugglers and acrobats that required ample room to perform their specialty acts, and so the street became their stage.

The white-faced mimes were at work in their tight-fitting costumes. Acrobats carried out their acts to perfection. Two bears performed tricks between pulls from bottles of honey, which was the incentive they needed to coerce them to perform.

One sad-looking clown, face painted gaudily, beat slowly and steadily upon a huge bass drum, as if counting time to the end of some great event.

The boardwalks teemed with spectators. These were citizens of Nebo County, who were not interested in wallowing in the beer and whiskey served in Wilfong's saloon. Instead, they seemed content to watch the performers, who, to them, were bigger than life in the ease and grace with which they carried out their acts—a notable diversion from the boredom of their daily routines.

Jack stood and studied Withers, encaged in his iron prison. The man's hair fell down in his eyes. He had terrific purple contusions and deep cuts on his face that showed the evidence of a fierce beating. Jack figured Withers was probably dying of thirst.

When the sad-faced clown came up behind him, whaling away on his noisy drum, Jack moved on. Jack stepped inside the jailhouse. Sheriff Hyde sat stiffly erect behind his desk. A man with a long, square jaw, dressed in a suit of light broadcloth, sporting a pair of low-heeled shoes, the toecaps of which outshone the sun from the good, vigorous work of a shoe brush, sat across from him.

The man swiveled in his chair to see who'd just entered.

Hyde clenched his pipe between his teeth. The pipe had gone out, and now it seemed as if he'd forgotten where he'd put his matches and lacked the humility to borrow one.

"Well, Waverly, did you enjoy your visit so much you came back for another night?"

Jack raised his hand in defense. "I don't think so, Sheriff."

Hyde introduced Jack to the man with the shiny-toed shoes, the mayor of Scarlet, Jeff Sloan.

"Waverly spent the night in one of my cells, Mayor," said Hyde. "You the man who tossed Art Shell through Pride's hotel window?"

Hyde answered in Jack's place. "Yep. That's him, and an act long overdue, if you don't mind my opinion."

"How often does this sort of thing go on?" Jack said, referring to the commotion the circus created.

Frank Hyde dropped his pipe onto the desk and relaxed. He fell back in his chair, and clasped his hands across his flat, lean stomach. "We put up with similar behavior from Twelvetrees constantly. Except now, instead of twice a month, as we'd agreed to some time ago, he's jumped it up to every week."

"Won't be long till it's every day," the mayor said.

"No doubt," agreed Hyde.

"Twelvetrees aims to take over the entire town," said Mayor Sloan. "He'll bring his gang of cutthroats into Scarlet one day, and all those with good sense will leave."

"It ain't just everybody can own a town," Hyde said. "But you might be wrong about everybody with good sense leaving town, Jeff. Axel might not let them leave. Just run the town through fear ... same as he runs that so-called ranch of his."

"How did all this get started, Sheriff Hyde?" Jack said, wondering aloud.

"The man uses oppression," said the mayor. "Like all tyrants."

Sheriff Hyde picked up his pipe and packed it full, graded it smoothly and evenly with a thumb, then lit up. As the smoke wafted in a gentle cloud toward the rafters, he explained the difficult position that faced the town of Scarlet. It turned out that when Twelvetrees first moved to the area; he was a great one to perform acts of charity. He rebuilt the schoolhouse and built a home for the aged. All three of the churches in the area went to him next for help with pet projects. Twelvetrees met their every need and even more. Helped them all, no questions asked.

"And the merchants all love him," the mayor added.

"The man spends enormous sums of money in town each week. This morning the city council decided, despite my protests, to allow him to come to town whenever he wants to. They wouldn't go along with the deal the sheriff had set up to ban him from town for all but twice a month."

"You didn't carry any water as mayor?"

"They overruled my veto."

He spread his hands in an appeal for understanding. No one spoke a dirty word against Twelvetrees, their benefactor. Axel had been the man behind the wherewithal that allowed Ted Maxwell's wife and children to survive after they found Ted with deeply indented finger marks and contusions upon his neck, likely strangled by Twelvetrees. He granted Bridey Morris, who'd fallen and broken her hip, a nurse, to tend her until she regained her feet.

s wife The list of Twelvetrees's generosity was indeed long. They set him up as a saint-like being.

Jack recalled seeing the depraved savagery on Axel's face that night in his saloon, when the big man had attempted to take one of his eyeballs. The saloonkeeper felt at a loss as to how anyone could ever mistake him for a saint.

"He must've changed since he was in my saloon," he said, scarcely above a whisper.

"Naw," said the sheriff. "Axel's a born bastard. He can't change. Not for the better."

"I'd have to say it's Axel's mother," Mayor Sloan said. "She's the one behind all the benevolence. She realized early on that in order to keep the law off their backs, they would need to win the trust of the citizens. She coached Axel.

Now it's nearly impossible to touch the man. The townsfolk, especially the merchants, treat him as if he truly is a saint. Hell, it would be downright disgraceful to speak against the man—to hear them talk." "No. He ain't changed," said the sheriff. "He does what he pleases. Gets away with it too. But, he's still a no-good sonsabitch."

"Why did he kill Tillman Dead's son?"

Hyde said, "Twelvetrees began frequenting Till's saloon, ragging Till, him being an Indian. He might've been put out that Till had done so well for himself in business, I don't know, but he damn sure belittled him.

"Then, one day while Till was out, his boy, Raymond, was behind the bar, and Twelvetrees started running Till down. Raymond got hot damned quick.

He ordered Axel and his gang outside, and pushed Axel out the door with that same ten-gauge you saw Till with just now. He just walked up to him, stuck it in his gut, and continued walking, with Axel forced to step backward all the way outside."

"Where was Tom Easy?"

"Tom wasn't along that day. Bobby Sikh was though, and when he opened his mouth to protest, Raymond took Bobby's gun, just like snapping his fingers. He shoved him outside too.

"Afterward, Axel being showed up, and all had it in for Raymond. Wasn't long before a man found Raymond strangled to death, out on the prairie. Near to where they found Ted Maxwell earlier … dead, in the same fashion." "You think it was Twelvetrees, Sheriff?"

"Yes. Of course, it was. Had to be. Twelvetrees killed 'em both."

Sloan said, "We figure the reason he had it in for Ted Maxwell was because of Ted's young daughter. Axel took a shine to her, and tried to lure her out to his ranch, the way he had done other girls in the past. Ted thwarted his plans. Later, Axel strangled him to death."

"Caught Ted alone, I'd say," Hyde joined in. "Rode him out on the prairie where they wouldn't be no audience … and just strangled him to death, while his gang held his arms."

The tale flipped Jack for a quick loop. "And everyone still thinks he's a great man?"

"Money …" said the sheriff and fired his pipe.

"Now," said the mayor, "he's got the young Peavey girl, Nancy, out at his ranch. He came to town one day and as he rode up Main Street, he saw Lillian Peavey and Nancy. Nancy is fourteen, but nearly grown-up, physically, at least.

"She has a lot of long, springy blonde hair that hangs down her back, springy as coiled wire. Blue eyes nearly the color of ice. She is—or was—a frolicsome, spirited girl.

"Then, when Axel laid eyes on her, he stopped and struck up a conversation with Mrs. Peavey, eyeing the girl all the while. He said that a girl like Nancy belonged back east in a fancy boarding school.

"Mrs. Peavey said there was no way they could afford to send her to one of those fancy schools. Axel offered to send her to school on his own hook with no hesitation. Mrs. Peavey said it was nice of him to make the offer, but she would have to talk it over with Mr. Peavey.

"But Mr. Peavey blew up when he heard the offer. He forbade it, which should've. put an end to the matter.

"Several months later Nancy disappeared."

"Everyone got upset over the girl's disappearance. We searched all over this town for her," Hyde said. "I wore out a couple of good horses, my damned self, looking for her. Poked my head into every cubbyhole and small cave, up and down all the draws, in every deep coulee … everywhere. But no Nancy.

"We put up notices in newspapers as far off as Lewisburg. Still nothing. It seemed the girl got whisked off into the sky."

"Such a pretty girl, too," said the mayor, then shook his head.

Outside on the street, the crowd that watched the performers grew even more clamorous. Jack peered out of the jail's one window, bespattered by generations of flies, and stared awhile at the prison box in which the sneak-thief.

Withers sat dehydrating, a little more with every minute.

A group of bothersome boys jabbed at him with long sticks through the gaps between the bars. Withers had given up bothering to defend himself. He sat slumped, resisting the sharp jabs of the sticks in silence.

"Yeah," Sheriff Hyde said, "damned pretty girl. And I hope she still is, although I've got my doubts."

"Twelvetrees has her," said the mayor. "There's no question."

When the sheriff and Mayor Sloan had spoken all they meant to on the subject, Jack turned his thoughts to Withers. He said, "That man out there in the box. I saw him in Military Springs. Watched him steal a man's gambling winnings, and skip town. He was one of the men with Twelvetrees that night in my saloon."

Mayor Sloan pushed himself up on the arms of his chair for a better look, and the sheriff craned his head toward the dingy window as well. The clown's drumbeats were still loud and obnoxious, even though he stood farther off down the street.

Hyde turned to Jack. "So?"

"So, why is he trapped up in a box with bars on the windows, in the hottest part of the day … right outside your door?"

"Withers works for Twelvetrees," said Frank Hyde. "Looks like his luck run out."

"He must've done something Twelvetrees didn't approve of," the mayor said, and settled deeper into his chair. Jack recalled hearing Twelvetrees declare that the man in the box had brought disgrace and danger down on him, and that he meant to deal with him. Withers surely wouldn't last much longer in such heat without water. Someone needed to do something for the man, and soon.

"What will Twelvetrees do to him—considering he survives the heat in the box?" Jack said.

"Who knows?" said the mayor. "Usually he makes the men he considers foul-ups suffer some public humiliation. Maybe he'll make Withers's sit outside in the sun all day long as punishment."

"He won't last all day. Someone needs to free him and soon."

Hyde made to remove his badge in a big dramatic display. "Here," he said, "take my badge. Go on out there. Straighten things out for me. Lord knows someone should."

Jack raised a hand to appease him, and Hyde dropped his fingers from his badge, took up his pipe by the bowl, and rolled it between his busy, nervous fingers. He said, "I have to deal not only with Twelvetrees, or try to, but when Judge Lodge is in town, this doubles my work. You saw how he took Axel's side back there at the old man's saloon. Hell, they're two of a kind."

"We spend most of our working hours attempting to find a solution … a way to handle things properly and legally," said Mayor Sloan. "So far, as you can see, we haven't done so."

"I was surprised this morning Lodge let you off so easy," Hyde said.

"Art Shell was no good," said the mayor. "No one liked him. Not even Axel. He used him for the dirtier jobs no one else wanted."

"Like lying up in my room to waylay me?" Jack said.

"They were there to ransack your outfit," said Sloan. "See what you had worth stealing. Shell did that a lot … pick up a few extra bucks. He must've talked Sikh in to going along with him."

"That fellow, Sikh, broke my skull with a gun butt," Jack said. "Addled my brain. Laid me up a long spell. The doctor was amazed I survived."

"And you came back for more?" said the mayor.

"Yes." Jack told his tale to the mayor, even down to Carla Daws, which was the main reason he'd chased all the way up to Scarlet in the first place.

"You know all this, Frank?" said Sloan when Jack Mahan finished his tale.

"Yes. He claims he knows when he can trust a man."

Sloan said, "I don't think I would have had the guts to have let that out. Not in this town."

"He's going by the name, Waverly," Hyde told the mayor. "So, for his safety, don't let the cat out of the bag." Mayor Sloan agreed with a nod of the head.

"What's next, Sheriff? Just allow them to run wild in town till they're too tired to carry on any more?" Jack said.

Frank Hyde filled his pipe, lit up, and inhaled with a look of appreciation on his face for the tobacco.

"Yes. That's about all I can do. Wait till he steps too far over the line. Then, I must deal with it … whatever it is."

"You saw how Axel's bodyguard is always at his shoulder," said Sloan. "Tom Easy's a cold killer, and Bobby Sikh is nobody to sneer at. How can the sheriff fight alone against the likes of those murderers? Bobby or Tom Easy is with the big man always."

Jeff Sloan shook his head as if he were amazed at the sad predicament in which his town found itself.

Jack took his leave and walked back out through the crowd. The sad clown's drum banged away loud enough to rattle windows.

15

Jack Mahan fought his way through the heavy crowd of spectators to Wilfong's saloon, relying on his beard to hide behind. If someone learned his true-identity—well, he figured, there'd be hell among the yearlings then, for he wasn't about to go down easy.

The walls of Wilfong's saloon bulged outward with men. A heavy cloud of tobacco smoke hung above the noisy mob of patrons, all of them smokers, and the saloon looked to Jack as if it were on fire. He stood for ten minutes before he found elbow-room at the bar. At last, the short, portly barmaid stopped before him. She was the same old pipe-smoking, gold-toothed woman who'd served him last night.

"What'll it be, mister? Don't make it nothing fancy, neither. 'Cause we ain't got it."

She had forgotten about Jack. At least, he saw no flash of recognition on her face.

At the far end of the bar to Jack's left stood a large, red-faced man engaged in rapt conversation with Twelvetrees and Judge Lodge. He figured him for the saloon owner, Wilfong. His heart lit out like a jackrabbit when he saw Carla Daws elbow to elbow with Twelvetrees.

"Drinking, mister, or did you just come in to gawk? I ain't got all day.
So shake a leg if you want a drink. Axel's buying."

He ordered beer. She turned to draw it as he studied the group around Twelvetrees. His eyes remained glued onto Carla Daws. He was scarcely able to stifle the urge to rush up to her and drag her off with him. This would be a terrible mistake, he knew, but felt inclined to do just that. This was the wrong town in which to pull a dumb stunt like that. He had to wait, as much as this disturbed him. The chubby barmaid fetched him his beer. In her haste, she splashed most of the foam onto the bar top.

"Thanks," he said, and jingled a few coins before him, refusing the free beer offer from Twelvetrees. "Busy today, I see."

"Ain't got time for chitchat, mister. Can't seem to get the old man to turn a damned tap today."

She nodded down the bar at the man he figured was Bob Wilfong. Evidently, he was her husband, or the old man, as she'd just termed it.

"He's busy jawing with Mr. Bigshot hisself, and his fancy woman, not to mention snuggling up to Judge Lodge." Jack sipped his beer, and watched her move off down the bar, while men hefted their empty beer mugs high, and yelled out for refills.

After a time, he felt a sharp jab in the ribs. He turned to face a short man with a pasty face. He wore the rough clothing of a cowhand, but looked too sick or too lazy to be of any help poking cattle up the loading chutes out at the stockyards.

The cowhand, in a high whine, said, "How's about giving somebody else a chance, mister. I'm about dead of thirst, as it is. And I ain't one to miss a free beer."

Jack took his own beer and went and stood against the wall near the door. Sooner or later, Carla would pass through this door. He meant to be there for the occasion.

His beer tasted flat and was bitter as raw coffee beans. By the time he finished it, Carla Daws had turned her back to the bar, and stood with her eyes on Jack Mahan.

She looked like a red rose in her bright dress. She spent considerable time scrutinizing Jack, turned to Twelvetrees then, and touched his forearm. He turned to her. She spoke into the big man's ear. He nodded in assent, then turned back to his conversation with the judge and the bar owner.

She pushed away from the bar then and flowed through the crowd like a silken red wave. As she approached, he could see she recognized him.

She stopped two feet from him, facing the open door, staring at the crowd outside. By and by, she whispered, but with her eyes set upon the antics of the performers on the street, "You were crazy for coming here, Jack." "I came to take you home," he said, barely able to keep his hands off her, not in the least worried because she had recognized him through his beard. In fact, he felt blessed she had.

"Axel will skin you alive, if he catches you here."

"You don't belong here. Come and go home with me."

"If you're in contact with Axel too long, Jack, he'll recognize you, even behind the beard. It will be too late then. I won't be able to stop him. You must listen to me. Now, please go."

"I can't. Not till you go with me. Or until you say you don't care for me."

Her eyes found his, then darted away like two minnows in search of shelter on the bottom of a pebble-strewn stream.

"That's easy enough to do. I don't want you. I won't return with you. Now leave, before Axel recognizes you."

Her words cut him, even though he thought he knew the reason she'd spoken them, or at least, hoped he did. "You don't mean that."

"I do. I hated it in Sweet Home. I hated working in your saloon. I hated your every touch."

"Carla…" She turned again to the door. Her face grew stony cold. She had locked up the muscles that controlled her facial expressions to hide her true emotions, or perhaps to reveal them. Which one, Jack couldn't truthfully say.

He shifted on his feet, and fought a powerful urge to reach out to touch her, just to see if she was as cold as she appeared to be. The tiny muscles of her eyelids twitched slightly. Her expression turned cold again. She stood as still as a blank of granite in a mason's yard, set aside for use as a tombstone.

She whispered, "Don't you touch me." He felt he was indeed speaking to a rank stranger. "Tom Easy watches my every move. I'll scream if you dare touch me. Tom will shoot you like a dog. Do you want that?"

Jack couldn't have felt worse if she'd just stabbed him through the heart.

He thought of all the good times they'd shared.

He prayed she was doing this to protect him.

But as he continued to study her, it seemed she'd just nailed shut the door to her heart.

As he stood there searching her face for the truth. His soul shriveled up like a dead insect baked in the sun. It was true. He saw no way to deny it.

"I'm going outside for a stroll," she said. "Don't follow. If you do, Tom will kill you."

She floated out the door, light on her feet. Her scent lingered behind to torment him.

Soon, Tom Easy brushed past him, and strode on outside, following Carla silently like a shadowy actor from a nightmare. Jack stalked to the window, bound to his torment like a man indentured. He continued to watch her as she strolled up the boardwalk. By now, she'd raised her parasol against the sun, going slowly, and became a dream character from that same nightmare that included Easy, following ten feet behind her with dust rising from his feet, and heat waves wavering like a far off pool of water. When Carla Daws had entered his life, Jack felt an intimacy as brilliant as the brightest glow of the most powerful star in the night sky. Although he was no longer a young man, she'd made him feel young, and wanted.

More than that, he wasn't yet totally convinced of her sincerity, or if she might've invented her actions just now for his protection, and for her own.

This hurtful uncertainty grew until it became an enormous pain, most difficult to bear.

His beer stein slipped absently from his grasp and clattered noisily to the floor.

He rushed up to the bar, kicking men out of his path as he went. Because of his large size, and probably from the terrible look of pain upon his face, the despair in his eyes, they gave him a wide berth, for he was emitting discharges of defeat and crushed hopes like the slow smoky tendrils of a fire built of waterlogged wood.

He stood there with such a heavy, hurting heart he felt it surely must burst.

These doubts weren't unfounded, he knew. For Carla had turned down his proposals of marriage, after all. He'd grown so spellbound by her he'd simply brushed away her refusals, figuring she loved him too, and that soon she would give in. All he needed to do was continue to pursue her. Perhaps he should've given up, forgotten all about Carla Daws. Her betrayal just now flared up in his guts, and ate away at his vitals like the abrasive action of pumice stone.

She'd been the one who'd helped him ward off the wolves of pain, the pain he'd experienced by his abandonment as a child. Standing there now, he sensed those same wolves, as they lie in wait, on the edge of the feeble ring of fire he'd built as protection for his soul. Their bright eyes reflected the light of his fire in brilliant rays.

Their teeth were bared, saliva escaped from the hinges of their powerful jaws as they sat patiently, just waiting for the fire to die.

Carla had entered his life, and that feeble fire of protection he'd managed to build burst into full flame. She'd made him feel whole and needed, had banished his sense of mistrust and misuse. She'd put him at ease in the world, and as a result, he grew more open and had learned to trust her completely.

He downed another drink. Then in a sudden lucid perception, like a bright beam of light on the darkest of nights, he rediscovered his place. Then, along with this, his self-worth returned.

Presently, he glanced down into the face of the barmaid. "Mister, Bob says you must either share the bar, or get to hell out of here. You've done hogged up all the damn space."

He glanced in the direction she was nodding her head. The men who earlier were involved in such an intense discussion had stopped their conversation, staring at him now from cold, narrowed, distrustful eyes.

"Sure," he said, "I'll share."

Promptly then, men crowded in on both sides of him. But they stared warily into his face to judge his temper, or maybe wonder about his sanity.

He noticed a man who stood with one foot behind him in order to get a step up, in case the need for a hasty retreat arose. A man with a severely sunburned face struck up a conversation with him. And just that quick, the crisis passed. His bar mate turned out to be the engineer on a surveying gang out of St. Joe, plotting out a new road, seeking a quicker route between Scarlet, Black Horse, Linden and on, all the way back to Topeka.

The man led him on a fine chase, uphill and down, across streams and over plains, and Jack attempted not to be so rude as to nod in all the wrong places.

The man paused and yelled out for a refill, and Jack felt other eyeballs fall upon him.

He turned and stared down on the scarred baldpate of Axel Twelvetrees.

The man wore a small parody he probably thought of as a smile. Jack saw that it'd become trapped instead, somewhere in a grimace. He studied the man's eyes, found them dead as a dried up streambed. Twelvetrees thrust forth a pale, corpulent hand.

"The name is Twelvetrees," he said, as if he were the Czar of Russia.

Jack couldn't force himself to shake hands with this walking perversion.

Instead, the best he managed was to say, "Good for you, mister." With this said, he left the proffered hand stranded in no-man's-land.

"Perhaps you have heard of me," Twelvetress continued. He dropped his hand, and did so as if he hadn't offered it in the first place, then wiped the charade of a smile from his face.

"I hear I owe you the burden of a thank-you," he added.

"If it's a burden, don't offer it."

Bobby Sikh stepped up and stood just off Twelvetrees's shoulder. One finger worked nervously at the small patch of hair beneath his lower lip.

Sikh, Jack noted, wore a sizable shiner. He felt the urge to repay him in full for the dazed state he'd lived through back in Sweet Home. Instead, he banished his need to the deepest reaches of his mind. The shiner he'd given Sikh was but the first installment in his overall payback. But he needed to be patient.

"I hear you killed one of my men," continued Twelvetrees.

Jack heard a voice of caution inside his mind, warning him to step with care.

He ended the sharp aleck answers.

"The man's name was Shell, before you ended his unfortunate life."

"I caught him in my room," Jack said. "He and another fellow were trying to waylay me."

"I felt sorry for Art Shell," Twelvetrees explained. "Gave him a job—barn work mainly. Then, after he got his gut full—likely for the first time in his miserable life—he took up skullduggery on the side. Art caused me more trouble than all my money, which is considerable." He paused, exhaled as if in despair, and continued, "I hate to lose one of my people, Mr. Waverly, but Art was what they call an incorrigible.

I gave him more chances than any ten men deserve. But he and that damned Withers have a certain roguish charm, and well I was unable to kill Shell, even though I knew I would be better off if I did so.

"Now, well, I've learned my lesson. I won't make the same mistake with Withers, you can bet on that. He'll soon learn he can't continue to misplace my trust, even though he does have that same crafty charm that Shell possessed.

" Thank you, Mr. Waverly, for performing a deed for me, one I felt was damned distasteful. Now that you have shown me how it's done, I won't have any qualms when I kill Withers, which is what I mean to do shortly, in plain sight of the entire town. That should serve as a fair warning to other men not to cross me."

Twelvetrees's scarred face rendered the man incapable of revealing emotion. As he spoke in terms of death and killing, his features remained as neutral, as unfathomable as those of a corpse in its casket.

His eyes were now a different matter. They lit up like sparks thrown from the wheels of a locomotive under an application of the brakes on the blackest night. A certain glee burst from them like a violent kid who'd just tortured to death a defenseless animal. Axel Twelvetrees placed his hands upon the counter, palms down. Massive veins throbbed and tunneled blood vigorously throughout his body. Those hands were white from the death of pigmentation caused by the same fire that'd, without doubt, scarred his face and head.

He turned one hand upright and revealed the pink in the creases and lines of his palm. The man's fingers were incredibly large. He made a fist that showed its full bulk. The knuckles were tall and ridged, not the blunted fists of a fighter, but made instead to grapple, to exert tremendous pressure.

He said, and it didn't sound like a boast, "When I was younger, I could straighten horseshoes. Believe that?" Jack shrugged.

"But, no longer. Time has its way with all, rich and poor, mighty, all."

He croaked in sudden laughter, slammed both hands down flat on the top of the bar. The echo of hard flesh upon wood rounded the room like a shotgun blast. Everyone stopped and stood still, as if to wonder who'd just gotten shot.

Twelvetrees raised his hands, studied them for a time, flexed them, and said, "They're not what they once were, Mr. Waverly, but they will do."

He paused, and then added, "Judge Lodge told me your name, in case you wondered."

Jack nodded. "Yes, I was wondering." Again, Twelvetrees attempted his outlandish smile, and talked on, "These hands aren't what they once were, but they can still exert tremendous pressure. Enough to strangle the life from any man." He stared at Jack from a sharp angle, as if squinting against the sun, then went on, "I mean to use these hands today to right things, not once, but twice."

Finished, he strutted back down the bar and stood again with Bob Wilfong and Judge Lodge. His laughter rang out shrilly, and he demanded, in an unruly, but welcomed voice, "Drinks! Drinks for the house!"

With that, Jack Mahan nodded to his bar mate, the engineer, and departed, while all at the bar sang the big man's praises.

When he hit the boardwalk, he blinked to ward off the sunlight. But that same sun falling gently on his skin felt good and pure to him, and reminded him again of which side he was on.

Confidence surged upwards from the pit of his stomach to the peak of his skull, and when it struck his brain, it caused a slight giddy elation to fire up within his inner being.

He had no choice now. He'd take Carla Daws back to Sweet Home, or die in the effort, even if he had to tie her face down across a horse to get the job done.

The sad-faced clown still hammered away on his drum.

The performers were still going through their paces, even though the heat of mid-day had driven the spectators to the shade beneath the porch roofs of business places along the street.

Jack Mahan strode to the city well pump on the courthouse lawn and reveled in the sight of the living grass at the base of the pump. He pumped water until it gushed cold and tasted sweet. When he'd had his fill, he felt himself a better man.

So he hefted a dipperful and moved to the center of the street to where the box that held the sneak thief stood. He didn't know, nor care just then who watched him or what reaction this might bring. Withers was sitting with his head between his up-thrust knees. He sensed Jack's presence and lifted his eyes.

The suffering man's eyeballs were red, and as alien as those of a cicada's.

"Loan me your gun, mister," he croaked through cracked and bloody lips.

His breath was foul from the abuse heaped upon him. "Your gun and one shell."

"Cup your hands," Jack told him.

Withers complied. Jack poured Withers's hands full of water. The water-starved man downed it all in one long swill and gulped a lungful of precious air. Jack poured again He swilled until his palms were dry. Jack stepped back to the well and drew another dipper of water and returned to the box. As he watched Withers drink, he wondered if perhaps it might be more humane to hand him over his gun, as he'd requested. No telling what torture Twelvetrees would put him through before he killed him.

Withers downed another dipperful of water, and said, "Been in this box for three days already. Won't make it much longer.

"I ain't no great one at religion, mister. Ain't been to church but once or twice, and them times as a child. So at the risk of being a hypocrite, and for your kindness, I want to say, God bless you, sir."

"To you as well," Jack returned.

It was plain to Jack that Withers would soon die inside that iron box under the full bore of the sun. He needed to fetch the man more water. He turned to go back to the well, but Withers fell then into a long, entangled commentary on the failure of his entire life, and how much he'd do differently if he but had the opportunity.

Jack found his chance and asked him just who Twelvetrees had in captivity in the bunkhouse at the ranch.

Withers told him it was a young girl. So far, Twelvetrees's tactics hadn't subdued her spirit enough to force her to submit to his depravity.

"How old is the girl?"

"I'd say she's shy of sixteen. But she looks much older than that now.
She'd be better off dead than living the life Axel has planned for her.
Damned shame too. She was such a pretty thing when I first laid eyes on her."
He shook his head sadly in contemplation. "But, she ain't so pretty now."

Withers talked on. He told Jack how he'd ended up in the box.
After he'd stolen Willis's money in Military Springs, he'd gone straight back to Twelvetrees's ranch, and then a few days later, Willis rode up to the big house.

"He raised three kinds of hell," said Withers. "So I'm told, for I wasn't there.
He told Twelvetrees he wanted to go inside for a look around to see if I was there.
Said he didn't trust their word.

"Axel asked him how he found out where I worked at, and he told it all. Told how I stole his money a few days earlier in Military Springs.

"By the way, I hid that money at the base of a cottonwood tree over on Shippen Creek.
It ain't hard to find. It's the only tree growing out there for better than a mile.
I 'spect I won't never get the chance to go out there now and dig it up. "Anyway, Twelvetrees and Tom Easy and Bobby Sikh took Willis's gun from him, and offered him a job. They often do that to men who come in on 'em uninvited. "He refused, then cursed them all out pretty damned savage. Tom Easy and Bobby Sikh beat the boy damned near to death.

They took him and sit him on his horse, and rode him out to that big gate where you enter Twelvetrees's property. They tied a rope around his neck. Tossed the other end over the archway above the gate. Them boys let him come to, then hung him.

"He's still out there, swinging away. Vultures and crows eating him.

'Bout all's left of him now's his boots, jeans and that red shirt he was so proud of.

"I done thought things over, mister, and I've decided if there was one thing I could do to redeem myself in this sorry world, it'd be not to have stolen that boy's gambling poke."

He paused for a time before he continued, "It ain't been nothing but the downfall of us both. He's dead and hung by his neck. Right shortly now Twelvetrees'll come in a full strut out of that saloon, yank my pitiful ass out of this box and strangle me to death with them hellish big hands of his.

"That's his favorite way to kill a man. I've seen him squeeze a man till his eyeballs pop out of his head, and then release his grip long enough for the man to revive, then commence squeezing again. Then, when the old boy is finally lucky enough to die, Twelvetrees goes into a rage, and kicks the body for dying on him too soon.

"That there's the reason I asked for the gun. Be easier for me that aways."

"You'd be better off killing Twelvetrees."

"Mister, the slug that kills him ain't been dropped from the shot tower yet."

Jack set his mouth to ask about Carla Daws, Lenore to him, but a voice rang out from the shaded porch of the mercantile store, and this stopped him.

"Better get on to hell away from there, mister, unless you want to share that box with Withers."

Jack peered into the gloom of the shaded porch. The man was short and heavy-set, wearing greasy trouser held up by a grimy-looking set of canvas braces.

He stood there shirtless, and as hairy as a rough collie.

He pointed his shotgun at Jack Mahan, the butt plate at rest against his hip.

Jack casually lifted a hand to him and strode off. He left Withers there, dehydrating more and more by the minute, still dry as a feather duster.

As Jack started off, Withers said, "Wish you'd ride out to Shippen Creek, mister, recover that money, and take it on back to Willis's mam.

She lives over close to Military Springs. Don't look like I'll get the chance to do it myself now."

'Jack clenched his jaws, crossed the street, and entered the sheriff's office.

That's Nancy Peavey," Sheriff Hyde said. Jack had informed him that Twelvetrees had a young girl in captivity out at his stronghold.

"Where'd you come by this information, Mahan?"

"Withers, in the hot box, told me."

"They let you get close enough to speak to him?"

"I think the guard must've been asleep. By the time he realized I was there, I had already given Withers some water, and had a friendly chat with him.

"But you'd already told me you figured Twelvetrees had the girl. Wasn't such a great surprise, I guess."

"No. I just hoped I was wrong's all." Jack told Hyde of Twelvetrees's plan to make a public spectacle soon, when he strangled Withers in view of everyone.

Hyde jumped to his feet, and stormed around the room, face clouded with frustration.

Jack said, "We need a plan, Sheriff. Let's figure a way to take Withers away from that hairy guard."

"Man's name is Murphy," said the sheriff. "He ain't a bad sort. Needed a job, though, and took the first thing to come his way.

"I need your help, Mahan. To take a stand against Twelvetrees. Will you help me?"

"Yes. As long as it doesn't interfere with what I came here to do, and that's take Carla Daws back to Sweet Home."

Hyde paced the floor and planned his moves. "There's the old man, too. Tillman Dead, he'll help."

"You really think that old man will be of any great use to us, Sheriff Hyde?"

Hyde stopped pacing. He stared at Jack in an attempt, or so it seemed, to judge Jack's sanity.

"Tillman Dead, you'll learn, if you hang around long enough, is one of the toughest men ever born. He could sit you and me both in the shade without a sweat.
Don't worry none about Till."

"How about the mayor?"

Hyde shook his head. "Naw. You saw him. He's a good man, but he ain't no kind of a fighter."

"What about Judge Lodge? Can't you go to him, and have him send outside for help, after you explain what's going on?"

"I've tried to do just that for years, Mahan. Lodge's tried to get on Twelvetrees's payroll for all those same years.

"He's been over there at Wilfong's, sucking up to Axel all morning.
The less he knows about this, the less he has to blab, and the better off we'll be."

The door suddenly burst inward. Judge Lodge, the devil Hyde had just spoken of, sprang up before them. He stormed into the room in a flurry of noisy, energetic activity. He nodded in a brief jerk of his head to Jack.

"Hyde," he shouted in his theatrical voice that rattled the timbers.

"What is it, Judge?"

"I have a chore for you to handle."

"That so, Judge?" Frank Hyde sat there poised now, peering closely from suspicious eyes.

"You recall that scamp, Thompson, the fellow in jail over in Staley?
The fellow charged with stealing old man Henley's chickens?"

"Yessir, I do. So?"

"So, I want you to ride over there and fetch him back here. I plan to deal with him while I'm in town this time, instead of waiting until next month as I'd first planned."

"Sure, Judge. I'll do it first thing Monday morning." "No, sir. You will do so now, Sheriff."

The judge's long, wispy beard stood out from his birdcage chest as he thrust forth his head. He'd grown exceptionally pushy now, with self-importance. "Naw, Judge.
Can't do it. I got other, more important matters to tend to right now."

Jack watched as Sheriff Hyde labored to hold his temper.

"Today, Sheriff Hyde! Right now. I mean to try that man tomorrow morning."

"I ain't going to wear out my ass today on a ride clear over to Staley to bring in a chicken thief, Judge Lodge. It must wait until Monday. I tell you, I got more important matters to tend to."

"Oh, but I must insist, Sheriff," said Lodge. "You'll take your wagon and go right now to Staley, and bring back that man. But if you insist on belligerence and insubordination, you will find yourself answering some lengthy and nasty letters, sir."

Hyde lifted himself part of the way out of his chair, broad hands gripping the chair arms tightly, knuckles turning white. At last, however, he relaxed and eased back down onto the cushions.

"I shouldn't leave town while Twelvetrees is running wild like this.
You know that well as I do, Judge Lodge."

The judge sensed he'd won the war of wills. He fluffed up even more with pride and looked to Jack like a turkey gobbler with its tail feathers spread to their fullest.

He said, "I just spoke to Axel about that very thing. He's promised me he won't let anything destructive happen in your absence."

He spun on his heels, and over his shoulder, added, "I hope I've made myself clear in this matter, Sheriff Hyde."

Hyde nodded in acceptance and watched Lodge leave.

The judge banged the door shut on his way out.

16

Frank Hyde sat in a brooding silence for a time, then reached for his pipe. Slowly he packed the bowl with tobacco.

"Damn near gave it all up just then. Axel wants me out of town."

"Looks that way," Jack agreed.

"He wants to assassinate Withers, just like you said, and wants me out of the way.

"He wants the law, but don't want it to interfere with him. He thinks the law should protect him, and to hinder those who don't agree with him."

"We have to have the law, Sheriff. Without it, we'd all be rolling around in an enormous pile to determine who came out on top. The powerful would take it all and leave the rest of us to slave for them."

Hyde struck a match, placed the blue flame over the bowl of his pipe, then lit up. The air, as it passed through the pipe stem, created loud screeches.

When the lengthy stem filled with smoke, the sound backed off.

Hyde said, "Sort of like what's now going on in Nebo County?

The way Axel runs everything, using the law when it works in his favor, ignoring it when it doesn't." He continued to puff his pipe in thought for a time.

At last, he removed it, and looked Jack in the eye. "That was what you were talking about, wasn't it?" Jack, forced to, nodded in agreement.

"Well, Lodge and Twelvetrees have got another think coming. I'll be damned if I'll run off to Staley right now to haul in a chicken thief.

"I've got bigger birds to pluck right here under my nose. I'm staying here in Scarlet. To hell with all nasty letters."

He caught up his hat and pounded loudly and swiftly to the door. "I'm going to call Murphy over," he said. "First thing to do is take his scattergun from him.

I don't believe he'd use it on me, but I ain't big on unnecessary chances."

"I can take his gun without too much fuss. He's not that big. Just hairy is all," Jack said.

Hyde stared a minute at him, as if he were facing a rank braggart. By and by, he said, "Good. Together we should be able to pull it off."

"Just lure him in through the door, Sheriff, and make sure you enter right behind him. Just in case. Leave the rest to me."

This gave Hyde another cause for a pause. "You must've got your snoot full while you were over at Wilfong's saloon, Mahan."

"Just bring him through the door. I've worked in saloons all my life. I can handle the man."

"Just make damned sure you take his gun without him setting off an alarm. Don't want him running wild through town screaming his head off for Twelvetrees. We need to keep things quiet as long as possible."

The sheriff stepped outside. Jack heard his booted feet striking the boardwalk, followed by silence, save for the distant and persistent beat of the clown's drum.

After a few moments, Hyde called out to Murphy, and then the sound of their footsteps upon the boardwalk was loud as they returned to the jailhouse.

He held himself as still as possible behind the door to make good on his claim to the sheriff.

Then Murphy stepped inside. Jack moved quickly forward and struck the hairy man with a good right hand squarely on the right temple.

The big guard exhaled as if in complete joy, and crumpled, knees having lost all strength. Murphy hit the floor hard, with the sound of a tree striking the ground. Jack didn't need to look twice to know the man was out cold.

Frank Hyde scooped up the fallen shotgun, broke it down, ejected both shells, placed them in a pocket of his trousers, and set the gun on the floor behind the desk.

"Why, hell, Mahan. If you ain't just a regular knockout artist now."

"I fought for prize money for a time, back in St. Louis. That was years ago, but working in a saloon keeps me on my toes." He latched onto Murphy's heels, dragged him inside one cell, and left him there on the floor. He knew from experience the unconscious guard would be much more comfortable there than on the cot.

Jack stepped out of the cell. Behind him, Murphy was mumbling gibberish, and attempting to sit up.

"Let's go get Withers," Hyde said, and took along a crowbar from the closet.

The sun struck Mahan with its powerful heat, and he wondered if they were perhaps setting out on a useless quest. He figured Withers had probably already succumbed to the heat.

The man surprised him. Withers's shirt still ruffled faintly with each slow breath. He lifted his head. His lips bled from ugly cracks created by the fists of Bobby Sikh, or so Jack figured. His face was white as the corpse of a drowned man, for there was little air inside the tiny iron box. He rested his chin upon the narrow ledge of the barred window and panted for air in painful-sounding gasps.

"We're taking you out of there, Withers," Jack explained. He studied the street then to see if anyone watched their rescue attempt. All eyes, it appeared, were on the circus performers.

Hyde wrenched the lock off the box with the crowbar, dropped it and the bar both in the dust, then swung the door open.

"Come out of there, man," he said.

Withers was drastically weak and rigid from the cramped space inside the box, and was unable to climb out by himself. Jack and Hyde hauled him out of the cage.

He fell to his knees when he tried to stand. Jack picked him up.

"Watch our back trail, Sheriff."

He lugged the man inside the jailhouse.

"What the hell's going on?" muttered Murphy. Jack entered the cell next to the guard's, and placed Withers down on the floor. The sheriff followed with a large dipper of water, then began feeding it to the dying man.

"Is it time?" Withers said.

"Drink up," Hyde told him. "Nobody'll harm you in here."

Withers fell upon the water with a strong devotion.

"Why've you got me locked up, Sheriff?" Murphy said.

He stood at the bars, watching all that took place, unable, it seemed, to make sense of it.

"Lay back down, Murphy," Hyde told him. "Catch a nap. I'll keep my eye on Withers for you. You just rest easy." Trusting the matter was in hand, Murphy settled back down on the floor. Soon he was snoring away.

When Withers grew more alert, and sloshing with water, he declared his hunger.

"You want to go down to Dead's eatery to fetch him a plate of food?" Hyde said.

Jack headed for the door.

"And tell Tillman I want to talk to him," Hyde said, as Jack stepped outside.

Halfway across the street, Mahan stopped short at the sight of Carla Daws.

She came toward him from the opposite side, followed by Tom Easy.

Fearful of drawing the gunman's attention by stopping to await their approach, he went straight at them.

Carla looked fresh and cool beneath her frilled parasol, a feat that came naturally to her, despite the heat. She nearly stunned Jack in her red gown. Her radiant black curls bounced nimbly off her shoulders with every step. They passed, and Jack saw her lips part just slightly, as if to speak. She caught herself, though, and walked on.

The familiar scent of her perfume hovered just above Jack Mahan's head.

Easy came next. They passed without incident.

Jack looked back after reaching the opposite side of the street, unable to refrain from stealing another look at Carla. He wondered briefly what he'd done by becoming more and more wrapped up in this tightly woven web of no-good. All he really wanted to do was go straight at Tom Easy, rap him right good and proper, grab up Carla, and get out of Nebo County. He'd promised his help to Frank Hyde, though.

He wouldn't go back on that. He wondered then if his aunt Anne had taught him too well that virtue makes the man. He figured he was stuck with her guiding hand for the rest of his life, whether he liked it or not.

"By god," Tillman Dead said, marveling as Withers attacked his plate of food.

"This man eats more than a pus-gut preacher at a Sunday afternoon feed."

For his age, Tillman Dead was a lithe, lean and capable man yet, filled with the enthusiasm of one much younger.

After the meal disappeared down Withers's gut, Dead strode with a grace that bordered on arrogance to the desk where the sheriff and Jack sat. He drew out a chair, sat down, brought forth a bottle of whiskey, caught up a good long pull, and offered it around. He roused no-takers, though, so he put it up and rolled a smoke.

"What is it you want to jaw about, Frank?" He stuck the cigarette between his lips, fired it, and dropped the dead matchstick on the floor.

Hyde wised him to his plan to run Twelvetrees off.

Dead listened to it all, eyes squinted tightly against the smoke.

"Sounds like an ambitious chore, and a long time in arrears."

"Then, you'll help?" "Bet your skinny ass."

After a lengthy discussion, they decided Hyde should remain in town with his prisoners. Dead, with Jack, would go out to the Twelvetrees ranch to see if they could locate the Peavey girl, and create what mayhem they could.

Jack voted to give Withers his horse, a bag of grub, and send him on out of the county. But the other two men overruled him. He supposed they were probably wiser in these matters. Finally, he conceded that if Hyde cut Withers loose, he'd probably head straight for that lone cottonwood where he'd stashed Willis's gambling winnings, then hang around until Twelvetrees recaptured him while he attempted to spend it all in a saloon.

Dead and Jack left Hyde there with his prisoners. At his dining room where Dead headquartered for most of his working day, he caught up his horse's reins, and walked with Jack to the livery stable to pick up Jack's horse.

Jack saddled quickly and watched the no-good mule retreat deeper into the stall when it saw Jack headed its way. It humped its back and rolled its eyes.

Jack said, "Don't worry, you sorry knobhead, I wouldn't dare think of disturbing you."

17

Within sight of the elaborate gate leading up to Axel's ranch house, Jack witnessed a large tribe of vultures at feast upon the small portion that remained of the unfortunate gambler, Willis. One of the feathered creatures shifted positions for a better point of attack, and Jack caught a glimpse of Willis's bright red shirt. This shot his gut full of pain.

When the two riders approached the gate, the scavengers took air with a loud whirr of wings. A few of the detached feathers drifted on the slight wind until they fluttered to the ground beneath the gate.

Jack and Dead stopped beneath Willis's remains, which looked like nothing more than a small length of rags a group of women had ripped apart to create a quilt.

A stench hung strong in the air. The fetid odor threatened to turn Jack's stomach wrong side out. He watched the old man's nose wrinkle in disgust too and felt relieved that no one but Dead could see his own look of disgust.

Nimbly, he stood up on his saddle to cut Willis down. He snapped open the blade of his pocketknife, and Tillman said, "Just what are you doing there, boy?"

"I'll cut him down, Till. Ain't right to leave him up here."

"You got a shovel?"

"No, sir."

"Leave him be then."

"It's not Christian, Till."

"If you don't have a shovel with you to bury him, you better leave him up there."

"But the vultures," Jack protested.

The old-timer pointed to where the vultures strode upon the ground nearby, agitated and angered because of the interference of the two men.

"They'll get him, anyway. Up there or on the ground. You don't intend to haul him around behind your saddle till we get back to Scarlet, do you? I certainly hope not."

The old man was right, Jack figured, but he had bad feelings about it all the same.

"No. I guess not."

Tillman said, "We come out here to fetch home the little Peavey girl. As for me, I've just about had my fill of this old boy." He gestured toward Willis's woeful, ragged remains. "We'll have the coroner come out with his wagon and haul him in.

We pay him to do such chores as this." A few minutes later, Twelvetrees's large, three-story house popped up off the floor of the prairie like magic.

They halted to reconnoiter. Dead pointed out the church Twelvetrees had built when he'd passed through some absurd religious phase.

He pointed to the barns, and all the other buildings, which included the prison, where they hoped to find Nancy Peavey.

"They say that twisted sonsabitch held some right fine services in that church," Tillman said. "Course, I don't know that firsthand, thank God."

This struck Jack speechless. He wondered what might make a man go so far astray. He rode alongside Dead at a trot. They rode through heat waves standing out boldly upon the dry earth before them looking like shallow pools of water shimmering bright as sunshine off water.

Jack kept his eyes in constant movement in search of any sudden flash of color that might suddenly become a man with a gun.

Dead appeared to have eyes only for the windowless cabin used as a prison that held the Peavey girl. The old man rode along in an exaggerated slouch.

"I just won't think of what that little girl's been through all these past months," Dead muttered. "Her such a young thing, too. We'll go there first … fetch her out of that hell house. Axel ain't a man to go off and leave the joint unguarded like it was open house, though. Bill Bolt's around here somewhere, I believe."

They drew rein two hundred yards from the bunkhouse. In front of the bunkhouse, a man sat all kicked back in a chair propped against the side of the rough structure, apparently asleep, rifle across his lap.

Old man Dead raised a supple hand the color of coffee. He pointed to the east end of the structure. He muttered, "Go on off to the side there. I'll come at him straight on. We'll catch the bully ruffian from two sides. See then how he likes it.
We'll not give the bugger any room to squirm."

Jack got up from his horse, riding at a fast trot toward the small, brushy gully he needed to cross in order to circle the bunkhouse.

Rocks and small stones rolled noisily from beneath the feet of his mount, and what with the swish and loud talk of the brush he disturbed, Jack figured for sure the door guard would hear his approach. But as he climbed clear of the gully, the guard was still seated there, hard at his rest.

Tillman Dead had already advanced on the sleeping man. Jack walked his horse up before the guard, then halted. Tillman raised a hand for him to stand tight.

He then reached inside his vest, drew out a partially filled pint bottle of whiskey, and placed it behind his back, wedged tight between his backbone and gun belt, out of his way.

He then stepped with minimum effort from his horse, tossed the reins over a rail of the corral, and trod up silently until he stood before the guard who snored loudly away in his peace. Dead made sure his shadow didn't fall across the neglectful guard's face. He glanced at Jack with a half-smile on his eggplant-colored face, drew his revolver, and slapped the side of the unlucky man's head with the barrel.

The collision of metal upon hard bone created a loud smack in the silence of the lazy day. The guard fell into a deeper slumber, lost all rigidity, and slid sideways off the chair, leaning upright against the bunkhouse, chin at rest on his chest. Tillman squatted next to the man, took his Winchester, stood back up, and pitched it atop the bunkhouse, out of reach.

The old man motioned for Jack to dismount and approach.

"Sleeps peaceful, doesn't he?"

"Damned if he don't."

Dead turned toward the main house and cut out at a brisk walk. Sunlight winked at Jack off the pint bottle as Tillman strode toward the massive ranch house.

Over a shoulder, Tillman said, "I might as well check out the house while we're at it. No telling what I'll find. Go on inside the bunkhouse. See if Nancy's there. If she is, get her on behind you, and get to hell out of here, posthaste."

"What about you, Till?"

"Don't fret about me. Now, get on, boy. Do what I told you." Dead walked off as unconcerned as if he were crossing the main street in Scarlet. He reached the steps of the house, uncorked his bottle, took a large hooker, and then put it up, and mounted the steps.

He stopped at the stage of the wraparound porch, turned, and saw Jack still rooted before the bunkhouse. The old Indian fanned the air angrily with a hand for Jack to get on with his chore.

Jack turned and lifted the heavy wooden bar from the door. He propped it against the outer wall and tugged at the door. It didn't give an inch. He tugged even harder and soon felt a slow give of pressure. Presently, he heard a female voice frantically sobbing on the other side of the door.

"I'm a friend," he called out. "I've come to take you home."

"Stay away," she replied, still holding to the door with all her strength.

"Nancy, I'm with Tillman Dead. We've come for you."

Evidently, she didn't believe him, and the two continued their tug of war.

The struggle created more of a ruckus than Jack thought. He sensed someone behind him, released the door, spun and grabbed for his revolver.

He was far too late on the grab and stood face-to-face with two men. Their guns were in hand, trained on his brisket.

"Go ahead on," said the nearer man through tobacco grimy teeth, "and reach for it. Might as well die now ... like a man, in place of waiting around for Twelvetrees to have a go at you. You'll wish then you had."

Jack relaxed his grip on his pistol, aware it would be suicide to try to have at them while they had the drop on him.

The second man, a tall, skinny fellow with teeth even grimier than the first old boy's, stepped forward, and disarmed him, then passed the gun to his superior, who immediately slipped it behind his belt buckle.

"What're we going to do now, Bill?"

Bill ignored the question, and said to Jack, "I see two horse mister, but only one rider. Where's the other feller?" "I needed two horses."

"Bullshit," Bill said. "What for?"

"I planned to take the Peavey girl home," he admitted.

The guard Dead had knocked unconscious, by now was up on his hands and knees. He muttered and mumbled—all craziness.

Jack figured he didn't even know what county he voted in, if he voted, and this reminded him of his failure in the plan he and Dead had concocted. He should already have Nancy Peavey up behind him on his horse by now, headed back toward Scarlet.

If Bill had been alone, Jack was confident he could've taken his gun from him. He'd pulled off the stunt before on meaner-looking customers than Bill. A slight show of misdirection, a quick left hand to latch onto the gun, a pivot of the toes, a right-hook to the jaw, the gun would be his, and Bill would be out cold.

But with two of them—well, the odds were wrong. He let the thought die. This man, Bill, he now figured, was Bolt.

Jack Mahan waited for whatever lay in store for him, resolved that if Bill Bolt even looked as if he were going to rap him with his pistol, he was going to do his best to tear off the man's face. By and by, Bill turned to his sidekick. "Hunt up some rope. Might be some up at the big house. We'll tie him up for the time being."

The skinny man left for the ranch house, almost on tiptoes, looking as if he were sore afoot.

Jack watched Bill grow lax with his revolver. The man said, "I can't figure you, mister." He stepped closer. Jack longed for him to step even closer. Just one more step, he figured, and he'd drive his fist right on out the back of his skull.

He planted his feet, and gathered his soul for the assault, but just then, the fellow Bill had sent on the errand stopped in his tracks.

"Bill," he cried out. "Somebody's in the house besides Lana and Jeff."

"What makes you think so?"

"Why, hell, the door's wide open. They always keep it shut."

Just then, two quick shots erupted from inside the house.

Tillman Dead had run into trouble.

Bolt took two quick steps toward his pal, who by now, frightened by the unexpected gunfire, started in a lope back toward his partner.

Bill made a bad mistake and caught on too late.

He tried to whirl back on Jack to rectify his error.

The saloon owner this time was faster. Jack hit the man hard behind the left ear. Bolt didn't even quiver, but went down hard. A thick cloud of dust rose above him.

Jack Mahan snatched the revolver out of the air, bent to the fallen man, recovered his own revolver, and stood confident, cocky, with two guns in his fists to show his power.

The door guard, awake now, scurried in his fright, slipping and sliding, trying to gain his feet. At last, he managed to put his feet under him, and lit out for the deep, brushy gully Jack had ridden through earlier. Jack raised Bill's pistol to shoot him, then pulled back. The man was no threat now without a weapon. He probably wouldn't have been much of one if he'd had a half-dozen. Not with how he'd cut and run. Jack swung back around.

Slugs were ripping up the soil at his feet by now. Small clods of dirt pelted his trousers legs like hail. He looked up from this spectacle. Bill's pal was firing at him from over his shoulder as he made tracks for the barn. Jack snapped off three shots, and this stopped the jets of dirt from leaping up around his feet.

Even though Jack didn't hit him, he'd had enough. He threw in the fight and turned all his efforts to reaching the safety of the barn.

The ranch house, by now, sprang alive with a heavy barrage of gunfire.

After ten explosions, Jack stopped counting.

He turned again to the bunkhouse door and yanked it hard. He'd expected Nancy Peavey still to be holding him out. Instead, the door rushed back at him. He quickly regained his balance, then plunged on inside.

"Nancy," he called out.

He stopped just inside the door to regain his proper vision. It was unnaturally dark inside, in contrast to the full blast of the sunshine outside. He scanned the room patiently, waiting for his vision to clear, and when it did, he found the room very much as Darnell Gage had described it. Low cots, stove, water bucket on a shelf, but not much more. He saw no place for her to hide out.

"Nancy, where are you?"

He was wasting valuable time that later might become crucial if things got any hotter than they were already. He fixed his mouth to call out again, but before he could do so, he felt a sudden presence behind him, like the flush of wind a ghost might've stirred up.

He whirled on his toes, and the girl rushed him. Her only weapons, her two bare hands, fingers extended like claws.

Jack grabbed her wrists, and the fear, pain, and hatred he saw on her face distressed him for a moment. Desperation had compelled her to charge a man of his size empty-handed.

He tried once more to reason with her, "Nancy, please. I'm a friend. Listen to me."

They wrestled about the room while he attempted to get through to her. "Please, I'll take you home to your mam."

Then, as soon as he spoke the word, "Mam," the girl fell limp, and would've fallen had he not held her erect.

She mumbled, "My mam?"

"Yes. I'm here to take you home."

He explained as swiftly as possible the tight fix they were in, and of how important it was for her to trust him.

She nodded. Then, for the first time, he had a close look at the girl. It was true, just as Withers had told him. She in no way resembled a girl of fourteen. She truly must have gone through a hellish experience, locked up with scarcely enough food and water to exist. He got hot. As hot as he had been in his life. He vowed not to leave Nebo County until Axel Twelvetrees was in jail or dead.

"Let's go. Can you ride double with me?" "Yes," she muttered.

He guided her to the door. They stepped out into the outdoor brilliance. Nancy caught at her breath in noisy gasps and covered her eyes against the severe glare of the sun.

The undersides of her forearms were overlaid in thick pads of sores that had healed, and others that were fresh and livid.

Her face, too, was a field of rank sores in varied stages, some old, some fresh. Her hair was thickly matted and filthy. The bunkhouse likely was swarming with rats, bedbugs, and other vermin.

Just then, fresh gunfire erupted from inside the ranch house, and he feared for the old man's safety. He doubted if Tillman would emerge from such a gun battle all in one piece, and maybe not even alive.

A man dove headfirst from the house just then. He landed in the center of the porch, gathered his feet beneath him, and fled down the steps.

This was not Tillman Dead, Jack realized. He breathed a sigh of relief.

The old man had held his own, at the very least.

The fleeing man caught a slug from behind just as he gained the yard, then slumped forward, cold, dead, Jack assumed.

A large woman followed the unfortunate gunman. She stood sky high, privy wide, and backed slowly down the steps with a gun in each hand, firing them off in alternate blasts. Gun smoke lifted above her head like the nimbus of some angel fallen in disfavor from paradise.

Jack couldn't see who she was shooting at, but had no doubts who it was.

The woman was no shabby slouch in the guts department, but instead a hellion trueborn. When she stepped from the porch to the yard, she whirled on a heel, caught air, and pulled foot for the barn.

Tillman Dead emerged from the house at a causal pace. He snapped off two quick shots at the woman, whose long black hair was now streaming out behind her like the tail of a racing-mare. Dead missed with each shot. Finally, the gutsy woman gained the safety of the barn. Tillman Dead reloaded his weapon, steadily studying the barn all the while, as if he thought he might just go ahead and storm it.

Jack reckoned the barn would likely hold a good number of defenders, and now loud rattling gunfire issued steadily from the safety of the heavily timbered barn-fortress. Dead finished his reload, took up his bottle, tipped it high and downed a drink. Afterward, he sauntered back inside the ranch house as if he had all the time in the world.

Jack stood on hot coals of tension, wondering how much longer it'd be until Dead finished his mischief. He was eager to get off the property.

The old man returned later, bent over. He walked backward and awkwardly across the porch, and on down the steps, pouring a steady stream of some sort of liquid out of a five-gallon demijohn from which he'd knocked off the neck to allow a smoother, faster flow.

"Kerosene," Jack mumbled.

Dead poured the kerosene from the demijohn in a long trail.

The container ran dry at last. He tossed it aside, drew out the whiskey bottle again, and took another pull, then tucked it back behind his belt. He scratched a match, dropped it upon the long combustible trail of kerosene, and strode back toward the bunkhouse with full contempt for his safety.

Clouds of dust leapt from the ground all around the old man's feet.

The rattle of gunfire from the barn bounced off the ranch house in a steady echo, with two voices.

Dead continued his carefree stroll toward the bunkhouse, as if he were out for his evening constitutional. Behind Tillman, the fire trail he'd ignited flashed up the steps, crossed the wide porch and penetrated the house. Flames licked up the outside walls, crackling industriously, sizzling fiercely, spitting and hissing with a loud nervous energy.

Jack lifted Nancy up into the saddle, ready now to mount up behind her.

He thought to fetch Dead's horse to him as the old man seemed to be in no great rush. But his own animal threw high its head and rolled its eyes in fear.

He swung about in time to see Bolt rush him; the bar used to lock the bunkhouse clutched in his hands, raised overhead as a club.

Jack threw up a forearm and deflected the blow. The bar caromed off his arm, fetching him a right smart lick, setting up a severe burning and tingling in his arm all the way to the shoulder. He hit the man hard, three times with his fist, watched him fall in a heap, and then leapt up on his horse behind the girl. He grabbed for the reins of Tillman Dead's mount in the same motion, but found, instead, the old man already seated in his saddle.

Dead dug in his spurs, and Jack struck out behind him, none too soon, to suit the barman. His animal sprang ahead in a great lunging leap, and they abandoned that hellish den of no-good. He cast eyes back over a shoulder. Tremendous flames sprang forth in ragged tongues through the windows and doors of the big house, and the brave army which had defended the barn so honorably, made its slow appearance. The men stood idly about, as the fire consumed the house, too smart at least, to fight the conflagration, for, by now, it'd broken free of the interior of the building from every opening. It sucked hard at the air, and roared as loud as a beast that'd just suffered some horrible, killing injury.

Nothing now, short of a miraculous downpour, could extinguish those flames. Jack Mahan figured Twelvetrees had never performed a solitary deed to qualify him for the granting of a miracle. So the house was surely doomed.

Dead's horse tore huge divots from the earth, and this kept Jack and the girl plenty busy dodging them. They thundered beneath the tragic remains of the swaying ex-gambler, cowhand, in a windy blast.

Jack hoped the girl hadn't had time to figure out what hung there by its neck like a scarecrow someone had forgotten and left out to turn to tatters.

Then, passing from sight of the arched-over gate, the twice-disturbed vultures, and the grisly remains of their meal, the swift riders slowed to a walk to give their horses a good blow in case they needed to make a hasty side-trip through the brush.

If Twelvetrees and his royal court rode up on them, it'd then be prudent to have rested animals.

"What kept you?" said the old man.

Dead stopped his animal and stood up, one foot at rest in a stirrup.

He tugged out papers and tobacco and rolled a smoke.

"You should be back in town by now, mister." He lit his smoke, and cut Jack down with a withering stare from his stern, raptor's eyes.

Suddenly Jack's headache fired up again. "I ran into a few problems."

Dead eased back down into the saddle. "I gave you the easiest chore, Mahan. Damned if you didn't go off first thing and screw it up."

"Some days are just worse than others, Till," said the saloonkeeper.

Dead scowled at Jack's answer, reached and produced his bottle, but found it empty. After he studied it forlornly for a time, he gave it a good, healthy fling into the brush.

"Let's get," he said in an urgent command. "I'm so dry I can't even whistle."

By the time they reached Scarlet, Jack's horse was spitting thick foam that looked like calf slobbers, and foam boiled up from beneath each piece of leather that touched its hide.

When they reached sight of her home, Jack Mahan said, "You see Nancy, I told you we'd take you home."

18

Tillman Dead dismounted, took Nancy Peavey down off Jack's horse, and assisted her to the front door of a modest white house with a broad front porch. Dead and Nancy entered the house, and seconds later, loud screeches of joy burst forth from inside. Jack guessed the mother of the girl had been the one who had set up the loud wails of thanksgiving. Directly, a short, baldheaded man hurried from the house, down the steps, and toward Jack, who, by now, stood in the shade of a tall pine tree to await Dead's return. The man approached him. His hand outstretched in welcome.

"Thank you, mister," he said.

Jack saw from the joyful reddening of his eyes he'd been weeping.

Nancy Peavey's father attempted to persuade him to go inside with him to continue the festival of joy in the Peavey home. It was a private affair, Jack figured, and cordially declined the invitation. When Dead rejoined him, they left the Peavey's to themselves to enjoy their glad reunion. Jack mumbled to himself, "Now, if I can rescue Carla Daws and strike out for MacDonald County, my satisfaction will be complete."

The circus was still in progress on Main Street as he followed Dead toward the jailhouse. Much of the earlier enthusiasm and vigor had fled the performances by now, and many of the spectators had gone home, which didn't surprise Jack since it was close to suppertime.

Frank Hyde had a deck of cards spread out on the desktop in a game of solitaire, studying them intently as Jack and Dead entered the office. "What'd you find out about the Peavey girl, Till?"

"We fetched her. She's home right now … with her mam and pap."

Hyde had been about to toss the ace of diamonds to the upper row, but dropped the deck on the table, and rose halfway out of his chair. "You found her?"

The sheriff sounded as if he didn't believe Dead. "Damned true. That's why we went out there for, wasn't it? Me and this feller here," he said.

He touched Jack briefly on the shoulder, and then continued, "We worked up a right fine mischief out at the great man's stronghold. I flushed out the ranch house and torched it. I 'spect it's burning yet. There's a damned sight of timber in that building."

This, too, was nearly too incredible for Hyde to swallow.

"You burned Axel out?"

"Yessir, I did. I knew you wouldn't or couldn't since you're the law. But somebody had to do it. So I just went in there and did the deed myself. Try to arrest me, and I'll deny it all. And this old big boy here'll back me all the way."

Hyde turned to Jack, as if he might confirm Tillman Dead's claim. Jack's confirmation sent him into another brief spell of headshaking.

"Arrest you? Hell, I ought to kiss you."

"Don't even think about it, Hyde."

While they had been off on their mission to the ranch, no one had yet missed Withers or Murphy. So they still had that little fracas staring them in the face.

Jack worked at a plan to rescue Carla Daws. He often heard it said in his aunt's house that there was a solution to every problem. He already had the problem, now all he had to do was discover the answer.

Hyde told him he'd seen Carla pass by his office recently, followed by the wicked man Easy. He'd watched her enter the hotel. Easy had gone inside, following closely behind Carla. After a few minutes, he'd returned, and was standing there now in the porch's shade.

Jack informed the two men he needed to check on his outfit in his hotel room. He slapped his pants legs free of dust, then left the sheriff and Tillman Dead.

"We're counting on you," Hyde said as Jack passed through the door.

"I'll be back, Sheriff Hyde."

He crossed the street, tromped up the steps, and onto the hotel's porch.

He walked past Easy studying the street from cautious eyes. The clerk, Alfred, got to his feet as Jack entered.

Jack signed the register for another night's stay. Alfred slid him the bill for the repair of the damaged window and door.

Jack paid up with a grudge, but at last decided that he'd come out the lucky one. Lenore Twelvetrees's room, he noted from the register, stood three doors down from his own. He climbed the stairs, went straight down the hall and tapped softly on Carla's door. She opened it cautiously.

Her eyes widened in surprise at first when she saw him, but she opened the door wider and looked fearfully up and down the hallway, reached out and tugged him into the room.

He didn't need to ask a single question. He read what he wanted to know in her eyes. He took her in his arms, and wrapped her up tightly, afraid she might turn to smoke and disappear. Her arms wrapped around him, clutching his back. A powerful urge swept over him to carry her home that was almost too strong to override.

He reckoned he should scoop her up, fine dress and all, haul her out of the room, mount his horse, and get on back to McDonald County.

They sat on the edge of the bed, and she related to him the long, sorry story of her ill-abused life.

"When I was fourteen, Axel saw me on the porch of my father's house.

He kidnapped me. I tried many times to escape in the years he held me captive.

"Finally, one night when I'd taken all I absolutely could stand, I picked up a lighted lamp, and threw it in his face. The lamp broke and set his clothes on fire. I ran as fast as I could with a song in my heart, so great was my passion for freedom. I didn't care what might become of Axel. I actually prayed he would die.

"I caught up a saddled horse and fled."

Jack recalled, back in his saloon that horrible late fall night, how Twelvetrees had made the remark that Carla Lenore, as he'd called her, loved to play with fire.

Carla had made good her escape while all hands were busy battling the blaze created by the burst lamp. This same fire had accounted for the degenerate's horrific, scarred face.

"Was this in Nebo County, Carla?"

"Yes. Right after we left Missouri where I was born, and where he stole me from my family."

"The same way he stole the little Peavey girl?" "Yes. There were girls before Nancy, too. Those who bent to Axel's will survived. He kept them until he grew tired of them and then set them to work in whatever house he lived in. He often moves, and owns several hideaways, like the one he has here. I escaped before, but he always hunted me down.

"The girl's who could not bend, had the hardest time of it. Axel kept them locked up, starved them, deprived them of light and human companionship.

"I've tried many times to free the girls, even Nancy Peavey, but have never done so without leaving myself open.

"Axel claims Nancy is as pretty as I was when he abducted me. He feels he has plenty of time to break her. But it now looks like she isn't far from losing her mind.

I mentioned this to him, but he ignored me."

"Axel appears to be sane. In those times, he uses people. Judge Lodge has fallen into Axel's trap. He has plans for him. He hates the judge because of some verdicts that didn't go his way. Someone should warn that man before it's too late."

Carla told Jack essentially the same story Ben Short had related to him back in Sweet Home. She also told him how she arrived in his saloon as his barmaid. After she'd made good her most recent escape, she existed as a maid in houses in the larger towns she passed through. In other towns, she tended bar. Eventually she landed in Sweet Home and went to work in Jack's saloon. The rest of her story he knew.

Finished with her sad tale, Carla drew away from him on the bed, but held his face in her tiny hands. He caught the fully flowered scent of her sachet as her fingers explored his beard.

"I had to grow it. Axel cut up my face with a razor, and I couldn't bear to look at my reflection in the mirror."

She fell into his arms again. "You could never look ugly to me, Jack Mahan. Someday you'll shave it off."

Her words strengthened his soul, his determination to win.

He said, "We have to bring Axel down. If we don't, we'll spend the rest of our years hiding from him. We'll be looking for him behind every door, in every closet wherever we go."

"I'm afraid, Jack. He'll kill you if he discovers your true identity. He still speaks of the bartender who owes him an eye."

"I owe the man, all right, but it's not an eye I plan to give him."

Carla squeezed his hand. "Be careful. Axel is strong. Just to think of the evil acts I've seen him perform … is nearly too much. But, if he were to kill you, I don't know what I would do.

"Let's leave, Jack. Please take me away. Now!"

"I can't. Not yet. I told you … we would live in fear every day that he would show up. It's time the man gets locked up, or dies."

Carla pulled back from him, and her eyes filled with helplessness.

"The law will never jail him. Or if it does, he will just escape.
He would tear you apart. Shoot him down from a safe distance, Jack.
For me, please." Jack could do that easily enough, but then he saw in his mind his aunt Anne's stern look of disapproval, and realized he couldn't kill the man that way, even though no one except the law would see the harm in doing so. "It's the only sure way," she went on. "It would be no different than killing a mad dog. Believe me … it's the only way."

He felt of two minds over the matter. From the viewpoint of survival, she was right. He had to admit that deep inside, where the natural push for survival at all cost resides, her argument made perfect sense. But he just couldn't do it that way.

He didn't want to spend the rest of his life on the edge of his bed at night—when and where the restless mind roves most vindictively—with a heavy regret in his heart that he hadn't found a different way. It had a great appeal, though. There was no denying that.

"I just can't do it, Carla."

She rose from the bed, took his hands, pulled him to his feet, and smiled up at him in a bright beaming smile filled with a warm glow of pride and full love.

"I know. I knew it was impossible when I proposed it."

She exhaled sadly, and continued, "I knew you weren't capable of such cowardice, even though it would be justified ... and I'm glad. But I just had to try."

He drew her to him again. He realized then that no matter what might come his way, no matter the outcome in Scarlet, he had Carla's love, and this meant more to him than anything else in the entire world.

His heart pounded hard against his ribs. "I was afraid you didn't love me.
I had the craziest thoughts when you turned down my proposals."

Her tears soaked through his shirt. He felt them on his skin and cherished them.

"There was no way I could have married you, Jack. Axel had already forced me to marry him."

Jack had known she was married to Axel, but still it hurt to hear it from her lips.

They held each other for some time, and it became a preview of things to come, or a requiem for the death of them. He didn't exactly know which.

She stepped away from him, and said, "You need to monitor Tom Easy.
He has no qualms about shooting someone from ambush, or in any way he can."

He nodded. "My room is three doors down. When I leave here, go there. Stay there, no matter what happens. If they come for you, there's a rifle on my bed, loaded and ready. Defend yourself, Carla. Don't let him take you again."

Carla nodded in agreement. "Don't go, Jack," she whispered.

"I have to. The sheriff and Tillman Dead are counting on me. When this is all over, we'll go back to Sweet Home. Maybe we'll be in time for Will Twist and Irene Blanchard's wedding. That will be a happy day for the entire town. Someday they'll say the same of us ... when we get married."

"Don't say it now, Jack. Not if you can't make it come true. Save it for later."

He told her then that they'd rescued Nancy Peavey and had brought her back home to her parents. He also told her Tillman Dead had burned Twelvetrees out.

He saw a bright fire of hope light up her eyes, and a strengthening of her will to resist Twelvetrees.

He swung toward the door, but she stopped him. They embraced.

When they parted, she eased him away from the door, opened it, and looked up and down the hallway for Easy.

Satisfied the way stood clear, she said, "Sometimes Tom stands just outside the door, but it's safe to go now."

He slipped past her into the hallway, and couldn't help but notice her tears as they slid down her cheeks. He strode swiftly down the hallway to the stairs, descended, and pushed on outside in the late afternoon heat, trying to erase the memory of her tears.

19

Jack pressed through the crowd which was on its way back from supper in order to watch the last acts of the circus. He stepped up onto the boardwalk to go into Dead's eatery for a bite to eat and then cast his eyes back across the street.

Tom Easy continued to watch him from suspicious, hostile eyes.

After his meal, Jack walked back toward the jailhouse. Just as he reached the enormous crowd of men, women and children, he stopped as a half-dozen horsemen galloped up the street. Spectators and entertainers alike scattered for safety.

The riders slid their lathered animals to a halt in front of Wilfong's saloon.

Thick dust plumes from the feet of the horses rose in the air when the riders skidded to a halt.

He lingered there on the street as the men dismounted. The man in the lead was Bill Bolt, the fellow who got the drop on Jack out at the bunkhouse. Bill merely dropped the reins to the ground, and pounded on up the steps, with his boot heels as noisy as a hailstorm on a tin roof. The quaking horses tossed their heads, blew loudly, and shifted their hindquarters, wound up tight from the punishment of their lengthy run.

A noisy group of youngster ran toward Jack.

Bolt was in a hurry to inform Twelvetrees that Dead had burned him out, Jack reckoned. He elbowed his way through the oncoming crowd of youngsters who'd come running to discover what lay behind this latest commotion.

Sheriff Hyde sat at his desk. Smoke from his pipe curled skyward as Jack entered the office. Hyde had forgotten the card game he'd been engaged in earlier.

The deck lay scattered upon the desktop. He looked up at Jack through breaks in the clouds of tobacco smoke. "Where've you been?"

"Had a bite to eat." "That Axel's men just hit town?" Tillman said.

"Yeah. Same bunch we had the row with earlier. They just went inside Wilfong's saloon."

"Well," said the old man, his feet propped on the ledge of his side of the desk, "'bout what I figured."

He shoved back in his chair and tugged his hat down over his eyes. "I guess they're in the saloon now, crying to Sir Twelvetrees how we treated 'em dirty, and burned down his fine house.'

"Probably," Jack agreed.

Dead could not sit still. He pushed his hat off his broad nose, let his feet fall gracefully as a boy to the floor, then in one supple movement, stood upright. He dug out tobacco and a cigarette paper from a shirt pocket, all in one smooth motion.

His crafty fingers crimped a neat sleeve in the paper, and then he poured from his tobacco sack the proper amount into the sleeve. He then leveled the tobacco, rolled it between thumbs and fingers until it became a tight tube, and then lightly licked the edge of the paper to seal it, spitting a few flakes of tobacco from his tongue.

"My god, Sheriff," the man Murphy called out from his cell. "When're you going to set me loose? I'm supposed to be guarding this Withers feller."

"Just fall back on the cot, Murphy," Hyde told him. "It'll be awhile yet. Relax and enjoy your brief vacation."

Murphy grumbled about the uncomfortable cot, his detention, the biting flies, but eventually he sat down again, and shut up. Withers lay at his rest across from Murphy, snoring away, loud as a mill saw.

Later, a loud uproar erupted from out on the street. Jack glanced up, and saw Twelvetrees heading toward the jailhouse, his shadow immense on the ground.

His man, Bobby Sikh, Jack's fond friend, walked to his left and Bill Bolt to his right.

Judge Lodge was absent, though, which struck Mahan as odd.

"Here comes the grandee now, Sheriff."

Sheriff Hyde sat composed at his desk, at peace with the world, now that the big wrangle seemed about to start.

Tillman Dead lit up. He looked unperturbed too now.

Sweat stood out on Jack Mahan's forehead, though. Beginnings and uncertainty were always troublesome for him. He figured he'd calm down though, just as soon as the heavy-lifting started.

Twelvetrees filled up the space in the doorway. Other men of his ill-smelling breed—the taller ones—stared over the big man's scarred head.

"What's this I hear, Hyde," Axel said in a determined voice, "about Dead burning down my house?"

"That what you heard, Axel?" Hyde took up his pipe to pack it with tobacco.

"Yes, that's exactly what I heard. And why is it you have my man Murphy in a cell? And this reprobate, Withers? His time is up, Sheriff. I've come for him."

"Nope," said Hyde. He graded the tobacco in the bowl of his pipe with his thumb. "Can't let you do that. It's again' the law, Axel. Try it, and you'll find yourself waking up in one of my cells."

Twelvetrees shot Tillman a malicious look. "You burned my house, didn't you, old man?" He stepped deeper into the room until he stood within leaping distance of the wary old-timer.

"Damned true," replied Dead. "You killed my boy. You still owe me, Axel."

Dead paused for a second, stared down the big man, and then added, "I plan to send you a dun … and right soon."

Twelvetrees stepped one-step too many.

Dead's gun flashed into his pink padded palm faster than a card-cheat hiding a card.

"Come on, Axel," he said, "take one more step, and I'll free up the space your lousy hide occupies on this good earth. Your days are over around here. It's time you hunted up another sty to foul."

Axel's face reddened by slow degrees. His massive jaws ground loudly upon his teeth. His eyeballs flashed fire, hot from the depths of their sockets, all the way back into the foulest section of his brain.

At last, he said, "What do you have to say about all this, Sheriff Hyde?"

Hyde fired his pipe, and spoke from inside a large tobacco cloud like some old-time prophet, "Me? All I can truly say is, Amen."

"You call yourself the law, and that's all you have to say?"

"For now, Axel. I reckon that's plenty."

"Damned true," Dead agreed. "That's aplenty said."

Twelvetrees deflated slowly, smiled a crooked smile, lifted a fat finger, and pointed at the old man. "If the law won't do anything about your lawlessness, then I suppose I must find other measures."

"Do something stupid to carry out your threat," said the sheriff, "and I'll back Tillman in court. You'll answer to Judge Lodge then."

"Don't worry about the judge. He won't have anything to say in this matter," Axel said.

He stared from Hyde to Dead. Finally, his eyes settled on Jack Mahan.

"What's your concern in this matter, mister? What are you doing here in Scarlet?"

"I reckon you'll find out soon enough," Jack replied. He watched the murderer toss off the frayed remnants of whatever remained of his tiny portion of sanity. Axel dropped his hands to his sides and roared with outrageous, inappropriate laughter.

When the storm surge passed, he wiped his eyes and backed out of the doorway, swung around, knocked men onto the street, and then pounded off up the boardwalk. His laughter boomed like thunder as he strode away, and overrode even the obnoxious, slow measure of the clown's drumbeat.

A long silence then ensued. By and by, Dead spat his cigarette stub onto the floor, ground it slowly with the toe of his boot, and holstered his revolver. "Somehow or other, I 'spect I might be haunted by my clemency just now. I should have shot that sonsabitch, like I started to."

"You couldn't do that, Till," Hyde said.

"Yeah, I could've, Sheriff, and should've. I'm an Indian. I'm not tied to things the same way as you old white boys are."

"That'd make you a criminal, Till."

Dead answered, "A man who has to have his businesses recorded in his white wife's name, is already a criminal … or treated as one."

Jack crossed to the open door and stared out at the street. All stood as it had earlier in the day. The performers still played on, even though much of their audience had already gone home. He saw the door of the prison box, wide open now, and smiled at the simple irony of how even a thief such as Withers could appear a child of innocence compared to an honest-to-god hell bringer like Axel Twelvetrees.

On the street, a brisk breeze carried dust into the air in a dark whirl.

Through a thin screen of light tan dust, he saw Tom Easy on the porch of the hotel. The man looked as if he'd become the main pillar holding up the roof. Jack swung his gaze from Easy then and watched the approach of two men. One of them was a short fellow. His bare baldhead shone in the sun from the sweat that poured off onto his face. The other man carried a medical bag. A doctor.

As the pair neared, it became obvious their destination was the sheriff's office. Jack stepped out of the way and allowed them to enter the jailhouse.

The doctor was a heavyset man, past middle age, heavy of jowl, with a thick dark growth of whisker stubble. Dark splotches of sweat stood out on his light-colored suit.

As he approached the sheriff's desk, he said, "Sheriff, I've just come from Wilfong's saloon, where I attempted in vain to revive Judge Lodge..."

The sheriff sprang up straight in his chair.

"He had suffered a constriction of the trachea…"

"Of the what, Doc Katz?"

"His windpipe was crushed, Sheriff Hyde. As a result, he died of asphyxia—a lack of oxygen."

The bald man with the doctor shuffled on his feet. So great was his desire to add to his part. Unable to hold back, he blurted out, "Twelvetrees choked the judge to death, Sheriff."

Hyde stood up. His tanned face had grown white. "That so, Dr. Katz?"

"That, I don't know, since I was not present at the time of death. But I can say for sure that Judge Lodge's death was not a natural occurrence."

"Axel did it, Sheriff," the bald man pressed on. "I saw him do it.

I was the one that fetched Doc Katz."

Sheriff Hyde drew a deep breath, held it for a considerable time, and then released it in a slow, audible sigh.

"Will you swear to that, Wee Willie?" said Hyde. "In a court of law?"

Wee Willie looked from the sheriff back to the doctor.

At length, he said, "Why, sure, Sheriff. But hell's kaflootie, we ain't got no judge now. How can there be a trial?" "Just fix your mind to be in court to speak up, when the time comes," Hyde informed him. "I mean to see you back up your word."

Wee Willie shrank from his earlier firm commitment. Since he'd enjoyed his moment of notoriety, he now seemed satisfied to fade away.

Dr. Katz took up his handkerchief and mopped the sweat at the back of his thick neck. He exhaled a large blast of pent-up air.

"I haven't slept in over twenty-four hours," he said, visibly disturbed.

"I rode the seven miles out to the Exeter ranch, reached there just at midnight, and delivered a fine healthy boy. In the process, however, Lydia, Mr. Exeter's wife, died. There was just no way to staunch such a terrific flow of blood.

"Then as I left, I felt like the lowest creature on God's earth for my failure."

He drew another ragged, emotional breath.

"Wasn't your fault, Doc Katz," Hyde said. The man looked downright exhausted, physically and mentally.

"We couldn't get along without you, Doc," Dead said.

Dr. Katz waved them both away with a tired, shaky hand, and said, "Oh, I know. I'm just tired, is all. But it's bad when you meet with so many failures all on the same day.

"After I arrived home from the Exeter's, Jimmy Moody showed up, and I traveled with him to his ranch to deliver another child. Another boy. This time I saved the mother … but lost the child.

"And now this, the death of Judge Lodge. He was my friend. We spoke a common tongue. Often when he was home for court, I would have him over to my place for cigars, coffee, and conversation. We spent many fine evenings in discussion. I'll miss those evenings of relaxation and conversation with a close friend and peer … especially now, since Mrs. Katz has passed on.

"And if this was not bad enough, Mr. Exeter has no one at his ranch to tend his new-born son. I first thought perhaps Jimmy Moody would take the child in, but he turned the tyke down." Katz sighed, and it sounded much like a sob. He wiped the back of his neck with a sodden handkerchief once more.

"I'll tell you what gentlemen this surely has not been the best day of my life. However, it is one that I'll not soon forget … if ever."

Hyde and Dead consoled the distraught doctor as best they could. They reminded him he'd feel better once he had rested. By and by, Sheriff Hyde commanded Wee Willie to assist the doctor home, and to stay on guard to see that no one disturbed him until he recovered. Then off they went, Wee Willie with Dr. Katz's medical bag in one hand, and the doctor's arm in the other.

After their departure, Hyde turned to Tillman Dead. "I think Axel's stepped in over his head now, Till."

Jack accompanied Hyde to the saloon, while Dead stood guard on the prisoners.

They entered the saloon, finding only three customers standing at the bar. The rest of the patrons, and Bob, had gone off on some quest with Twelvetrees. The men who remained were too drunk to care what happened, unless it happened to them, or at least took place right before their faces.

The dead man lay upon the floor. An oilcloth covered his face and chest. Hyde and Jack paused before the body. Lodge's legs from the belt down and his feet were visible where the oilcloth fell short.

The barmaid, Wilfong's wife, stared at them from bored and tired eyes. She pinched out a measure of tobacco, placed it into the bowl of her pipe, dropped the sack on top of the bar, and leveled tobacco to the top of the bowl. "He's dead, Sheriff." Hyde ignored her sarcasm. "Anybody send for the coroner, Gladys?"

He dropped to one knee and lifted the oilcloth from Lodge's face. A cloud of flies took noisy flight.

"Yeah," Gladys Wilfong replied. "I did. Who else? I do everything around here."

Judge Lodge looked gruesome. The tip of his tongue was visible, clenched between his teeth, and his eyes bulged out in a gross display of death. The cloud of flies soon made a strong comeback, eager to get on with the job nature had set down for them, with a devotion more instinctive than was their fright.

"Uh-huh," Gladys declared lazily. She'd just lit her pipe. "Just had to do that, didn't you, Sheriff? I did tell you the man was dead."

She shook out the match that threatened to burn her fingers, inhaled deeply, pleasure flushing and relaxing the deep, age worn creases of her face. She exhaled in a long steady skyward stream of blue smoke, then dropped the match onto the floor behind the bar.

"What'd you mean to do, Sheriff—lay hands on the man and bring him back to life?"

Hyde spread the oilcloth back onto Lodge's face, stood up, and walked to the bar.

"What can I get for you, Sheriff?" said the harried barmaid.

"Who killed Judge Lodge?" "Damned if I know. I've been so busy today I haven't even had time to scratch my ... ear, let alone keep a-track of who's doing what to who. This here's only my third smoke of the day." She tipped her pipe stem in Hyde's direction, to dramatize her point.

Hyde turned from her to the men at the bar, benumbed by drink.

He said, "Anybody here see who killed the judge?"

No one had seen a thing.

Gladys laughed, and the deep wet gurgle in her chest announced the slow advancement of serious lung damage.

"Shoot, them boys is lucky to even know their names, Sheriff Hyde. They been here all day long drinking on Axel's hook." A tall man, attired in a lightweight suit, sensible for the heat of the season, entered the saloon followed by another man, bearing a folded canvas stretcher.

The coroner-mortician, Jack reckoned.

The coroner-mortician stopped at the body, and addressed the sheriff in a deep voice, "You through here, Frank?"

Hyde nodded, then said, "Been out to Axel's gate yet to cut down that hanged man?"

"Just got back," answered the coroner. "I'm catching 'em faster than I can string 'em today."

Hyde produced a pad of paper, a stub of a pencil from a vest pocket, and took down the names of the men at the bar. He told each of them to be ready for court, and to think long and hard on everything that had occurred here today.

Jack figured it unlikely Hyde could learn much from them.

They looked like a sorry lot, and were far off the main road.

Hyde put away his pencil and pad. "You boys try real hard to recall something of importance. You too, Gladys. You must go with them to testify in court, I 'spect."

Gladys Wilfong's liquid laughter followed Jack and Hyde to the front door.

She called out after them, "Well hurry to hell on up, Sheriff. I could damn sure do with a little time away from this here bar."

20

On the street, Hyde said to Jack Mahan, "I'm going out to visit the Peavey's. I'd consider it a favor if you'd stay with the old man. Help him monitor the prisoners.

"I think Withers will spill his guts in court, if we can assure him Twelvetrees can't get to him while he's under my care. And Tillman—well, he's as fine a man as you'll likely run across, but he's a bit of a hothead. The man has absolutely no concern for safety, his own or anyone else's. Monitor him, if you will. I'll not be gone long. I need to talk to the little Peavey girl and her folks."

Jack stood and watched the sheriff amble toward the livery stable for his horse. When Hyde entered the barn, the saloonkeeper from Sweet Home went back to the jailhouse. He paused before the open doorway, looked up and down the street, looked for a second time, surprised to see that Easy had now flown his perch.

This troubled him.

"He's with Axel. They went off down the street awhile back," Tillman said, from the doorway. "Figured, you were wondering."

He shoved on inside the jail with Tillman Dead, to await the sheriff's return.

"If I was the law here," Tillman said, as he sat down at the desk, tossing his heels upon its top. "I would've already made my move on Axel. Course, I'd have to handle Tom Easy first and perhaps Bobby as well, although he's not the hard sonsabitch Easy is. Bill Bolt, now, he ain't much."

"Is Easy bad with that gun, Till?" "Anyone with a gun in hand is bad enough to suit me. Easy's rank and is a no-'count bastard.

Tom's veins flow full with snake blood, and he'd rather shoot you in the back, but he can do it manlike as well.

"Tom and Axel are both the scum of perversion. This town's got a crick in its neck from kissing Axel's ass. He figures he can toss out a few coins from time to time and be allowed to get his own damned way. The sad part is he's 'bout right."

Dead stared out the door in contemplation. The wind kicked up a powerful blow that gave birth to whirlwinds. They twisted off in a mad reel, and lifted up dust and papers, then cast the debris over the tops of buildings. Jack watched as people scurried for cover. Some took refuge in the lee of business places to await the end of the vagrant blasts of wind.

Tillman peeled off a single paper from a book of cigarette papers and rolled a smoke. He fired up, shook out the match and added, "Folks will reach the end of their patience, I reckon, someday. Just how many will die before they reach their limit is a question nobody can answer."

The old man smoked then in silence and watched the wind drive the dust past the open door. Then when he'd smoked his cigarette down to the coal, he dropped the remnant on the floor, kicked back in his chair, and pulled down the brim of his hat.

"I'm taking me a little nap, boy." Jack Mahan sat there and watched as the falling sun behind the hotel across the way cast the tall dark image of the building onto the street, while other shadows grew larger inch-by-inch migrating eastward with the approach of night. Suddenly, as it often did in this land, the wind just upped and stopped.

Thirty minutes passed.

Tillman Dead jerked awake.

He stood erect, pushed back his hat, and leapt for the door. He'd heard, smelled or sensed something amiss, that Jack hadn't detected.

"Something's wrong. Something's wrong with May, my wife."

Jack hadn't heard or seen anything out of the ordinary and wondered if perhaps Dead might suffer from the remnants of a troublesome dream.

He called out after him, "Till."

The old man didn't respond to his query, but stepped with caution onto the boardwalk, and gazed down the street toward his eatery.

Jack stood up. He felt the eyes of the two prisoners follow his every move.

"Let me out of here, mister," said Withers, approaching the bars. "Give me a fighting chance. If Twelvetrees gets hold of me, he'll throttle me to death."

"Me, too," Murphy said. "He won't like it I couldn't keep my eyes on Withers. Let us both out of here, so we can make a run for it. That old man smells trouble, sure's hell."

Jack Mahan ignored them both and stepped outside alongside Dead.

He saw that the circus had moved down the street to perform in front of Dead's dining room, and Jack puzzled over what might take place down there.

The sad-faced clown passed in front of the jailhouse. He banged away on his bass drum, still in the same even beat he'd employed all day long, obviously headed down the street to rejoin the rest of the troupe.

"Shut that damned thing up," Dead shouted. "I can't hear a thing but that drum."

He sprang down onto the street, and in a running start, smashed a boot through the skin of the startled clown's drum.

The clown drew up fast, staring in awe at the old man, his sad, painted face animated at last.

"You've banged on that thing all day long. Take a break. Go get yourself a beer. Rest your ears … and mine too."

"But, Mr. Twelvetrees said…"

"Go!" Tillman growled and pointed toward Wilfong's saloon.

The clown didn't know whether to cry or laugh. He turned at length, and started off, with the drum cradled in his arms as if it were a good pet just run over by a drayage vehicle.

"Them scurvy bastards are in my dining room," Tillman Dead announced.

He stood fully erect, broad nose extended. His eyes leapt like popcorn in a hot pan. Seconds later, as if a short fuse in his mind had been touched off, he charged forward in a run toward his dining room.

"Wait up," Jack called after him. "I'll go along."

"Stay where you are," Dead yelled back over a shoulder. "This could be a ruse to get us away from the prisoners." Then he ran toward his eatery like a young man.

Dead stopped at the entrance of his eating establishment, drew his gun, and entered the old wooden building. Smoke curled skyward at the rear of the building.

A chill of great intensity passed through Jack Mahan, well aware that all these buildings were old, the wood brittle. They'd explode like bombs.

The entire downtown district would go up in flames.

"Fire!" he yelled.

He pounded down the boardwalk, pausing at every doorway to alert those inside that Dead's eatery had just burst into flames. He rushed onward, and a crowd gathered to his call.

Soon men ran with pails in hand, and old blankets to soak down at the well with which to fight the fire. Everyone in Scarlet knew that if one place went up in flames, the rest would be in danger as well.

The men set up a bucket brigade, and they seemed to work as hard at combating the conflagration as they had at any work they'd ever performed in their lives.

They battled the blaze feverishly, with no sense of time or fatigue.

But after some time, it became obvious the dining room was damned.

All hands turned then to wetting down the sides and roofs of the buildings next to the devastated eatery, in order to prevent the spread of the fire.

Jack wondered what had become of Tillman Dead. He fell out of the fire line to look for him and strode to the front of the eatery to offer his help in whatever chore he might've undertaken.

The fire had eaten through the roof at the rear of the building. Monstrous flames struck like snakes at the heavens. Jack figured the fire had started from spilled grease, ignited by a spark from the kitchen cookstove.

He reached for the front door, yanked it open, and just as he did, the old man plunged out of the smoke like some lost soul in flight from the depths of hell.

He carried a small woman in his arms. Blood stained her full-length apron.

She lay in his arms, with head aslant like a doll with a broken neck.

This was Tillman Dead's wife, May.

Jack stepped up to lend a hand, but Tillman looked into his face as if he were an enemy. "Don't you touch her."

Jack followed him across the street. On the far side, in front of Johnson's store, Tillman knelt, placed the small woman on the sidewalk, took up both her hands, and the paleness of her complexion highlighted his much darker hands.

The storekeeper in his long apron appeared then, followed shortly by a short, robust woman. Jack figured them to be Mr. and Mrs. Johnson, co-owners of the hardware store.

"Till," said the man in a soft, considerate voice and knelt alongside Dead. "Tillman," Mr. Johnson tried again, but Dead still ignored his business partner.

At length, the wife of the store-owner stepped up. She placed a hand on Tillman Dead's shoulder. "Bring her inside now, Tillman, please. I'll clean her up." But Dead continued to hold his wife's hands. After a few tense moments, he looked up into Mrs. Johnson's concerned face, and said with lips atremble, "She's dead, Dolly. May's dead."

"Yes," Dolly replied in her gentle voice, "I know. Now, bring her on inside.

She mustn't be allowed to lay out here on the sidewalk this away, please, sir."

Dolly Johnson's concern finally broke through to Tillman Dead. He lifted May and held her across his arms. May's head dangled down, and her gray hair fell in a cascade toward the boards of the walkway.

Jack Mahan saw where two pistol balls had pierced her heart. This had forced the blood flow—stopped now, at her death—which had drenched the front of her apron and dress. Mr. Johnson's face blanched white, and it seemed he could scarcely breathe, so compassionate was his nature. He said, "Who did this? Who did this to May, Tillman?"

Dead paused before he stepped through the doorway into the store.

"Twelvetrees's gunman," Dead answered. He clenched his teeth against his hatred so tight they ground so loud Jack could hear them easily. "Tom Easy. He's the proud kid done this."

Jack learned then that Axel Twelvetrees had just taken his revenge for the destruction of his ranch house—in spades.

The three old friends passed from the street into the store. Jack stood and watched as the fire consumed the rest of the dining room. Fortunately, the wind had lain, and the flames didn't spread to the other buildings—thanks also to the well-drilled fire brigade. The flames that had laid waste to the dining room were now contained. The firefighters stood back to take a break, but still alert for sparks and hot spots in the rubble of the ravaged eatery.

Crossing the street, Jack became entwined in a large knot of men that made up the circus, heading back up toward Wilfong's saloon to take up residence just outside the door to where he figured the great man had just returned.

Jack stepped up on the boardwalk in front of the jailhouse, and just as he did so, Murphy, inside the jailhouse, screamed for help.

He hotfooted inside, paused long enough to discover the source of Murphy's distress, which didn't take long. Axel Twelvetrees was standing in the cell—with Withers.

He must've given his own crowd the slip, gone to the jailhouse, taken the cell keys down from the peg on the wall behind the sheriff's desk, and barged into the cell with Withers, Jack guessed.

Axel stood with his huge fingers wrapped around the sneak thief's neck, throttling him to death.

The veins in the murderer's hands looked to be the size of spring-born snakes as he gripped Withers by the neck. The sneak thief's lank body fell slack. His legs offered no support at all for his body, held erect by the strength of Twelvetrees's powerful arms.

Jack glanced at Murphy for a quick assessment. The man's face was pale from fright, and he'd backed up in a corner, cowering at the rear of his cell.

His eyes were bulging out, and his mouth fell like the mouth of a puppet with a broken drawstring. Jack rushed across the room and plunged into the cell with Twelvetrees and Withers. He gathered his strength, felt it swarm like a hive of bees in his muscles, aware too of the same great rush of excitement he'd often felt in the boxing ring barging in for a knockout.

He lashed out with a powerful right, and caught the barrel shaped man just behind the left ear, a favorite target when going in for a knockout. His fist caromed off Axel's solid, heavily boned skull and burst alive with sudden pain, as if he'd just struck a concrete wall. Twelvetrees trembled from the blow, lashing his huge, scarred head crazily about, and by and by, fell to one knee.

Jack had knocked him down all right, but not out. Even worse, the rank criminal still had a death grip on Sheriff Hyde's star witness.

Since he'd fetched Twelvetrees his best punch, but didn't knock him out, and since he didn't want to injure his fist more than he felt he already had, Jack Mahan took his own best advice. He drew his revolver, flipped it over in the air, caught it by the barrel, and struck Axel a right handsome blow with the butt end of the weapon.

Twelvetrees crashed like a tripped-up horse, releasing Withers as he fell.

The heavy blow broke the skin behind Axel's ear. A slow trickle of blood meandered down the depraved man's skull and pooled up on the floor.

Jack disarmed him, then searched the pockets of his suit for anything Axel might use as a weapon, finding none he carried Withers out of the cell, and placed him upon the floor by the door so he could recover his wind. He then returned to the cell that now housed Twelvetrees.

"The razor," shouted Murphy. "Get his razor."

Jack recalled the small razor Twelvetrees wore on a chain around his neck—the very razor he'd used to cut up his face. He removed it and stuck it in a vest pocket.

"Damn it to hell, man," cried Murphy, "slam that cell door. Hurry. Then let me out of this cell."

Jack slammed the door shut, and it rang like a hammer blow off an anvil.

He twisted the key in the lock where Twelvetrees had left it, with no idea when he entered the cell he'd end up being the latest resident of the Nebo County jail.

He returned the cell keys to the wall peg, swung again to Withers, dropped to a knee alongside him, bent deeper, and placed an ear on his chest.

Wither's heart was still chugging faintly along, weak but there still.

He removed his beaver hat and started fanning it before Withers's face.

After a considerable time and much arm work, color returned to the face of the sneak thief, and his respiration grew stronger. The saloon owner left him by the door and stood up.

"Let me out of this cell, mister," Murphy pleaded.

Jack realized then the man had been begging for his release all this time, and he'd simply blocked out his wild panicked voice.

He stepped up before Murphy's cell.

"Get the keys, mister." "When Sheriff Hyde tossed you in there, I 'spect he had a good reason. If you mean to be turned loose, you must take that up with him."

"Aww, come on. I don't even want to be in the same county with Twelvetrees when he wakes up, let alone in the cell right next to him. Besides that, what'n hell have I done?"

"Take it up with Hyde." Jack turned back to Withers who mumbled away now like a man sometimes does in his sleep.

Withers continued to make slow progress. He opened his eyes, and held them that way until they grew too heavy to hold open any longer, then shut them.

He mumbled gibberish. It sounded as if he was choking, but Jack saw this was not the case.

Several minutes later, Withers opened his eyes and kept them open. Jack peered into his face, shocked at what he witnessed in the sneak thief's eyes. They were as blue as a summer sky, and completely serene. They seemed to speak to Jack, and it was as if he was staring down a long, tranquil blue tunnel. Withers had found a peace known only to a precious few. Goose bumps traveled the length of his body, and it was as if he were viewing a sacred painting, rife with emotion.

The thief, Withers, had experienced some great conversion.

He saw this in the man's eyes, and by the enshrined glow that fired his face.

His face had fallen slack, and the lines and wrinkles that'd grown there over the lengthy years of his infamous cutthroat existence, disappeared—replaced by a look of mental fitness, one of total peace and submission to whatever fate might throw at him next.

Withers attempted to speak but failed to make it go. He raised a hand in a cupped motion and lifted it to his lips. Jack brought him a dipper of water and assisted him as he gulped it down. When he'd had his fill, he still couldn't speak.

"You need to see Dr. Katz?" Jack said.

Withers shook his head, and it seemed strange to see the transformation that'd come over the man. It was as if he'd died and had been reborn a new and better man.

By and by, he sat up. Jack helped to a chair and sat him down by the water bucket, where in case his thirst returned, he could drink to his heart's content.

Later, sufficiently recovered, Withers got to his feet, took up the cell keys, entered the cell across from Axel Twelvetrees, reached through the bars, locked the door, then pitched the keys out to Jack.

Murphy shook his head then in outrageous disbelief, stunned by a thing he couldn't understand.

21

At dusk, Jack fired the lamp and kicked back in his chair to await Sheriff Hyde's return. But even before he fell slack in relaxation, he was jarred to his feet by the loud hum of a large crowd outside the door. He walked to the door and peered out.

The entire circus troupe stood in front of the Sheriff's office.

But instead of performing their routines, they started chanting loudly for Twelvetrees.

Across the street, stationed once more on the porch of the hotel, Tom Easy lounged against his favorite post. Evidently, he was unaware that his boss lay sprawled out on the floor of a jail cell across the street.

Just then, one performer pushed up before Jack Mahan.

"Need to speak with Mr. Twelvetrees," he said.

"He's resting right now, unable to speak to anyone," Jack said.

The troupe's spokesperson said, "When'll he be ready to talk, you reckon?"

"That'll be up to a judge," Jack said, "after his trial. But Hyde might just have enough on him to hang him."

"You mean he's locked up?" the spokesperson said. His voice bulged with disbelief.

"He is."

The man craned his head to see over, under or around Jack Mahan, who stood huge in the doorway. The man seemed to be trying to determine if Jack might be lying.

"Don't see him, and mister. Hell, we ain't been paid."

"Oh, he's in there all right," Jack said. "Stretched out on the floor of his cell. The sheriff is gone right now. Come on back when he returns. You must talk to him if you want to see Twelvetrees about your pay. I don't have the authority to allow this."

The man looked none too sore to learn that Twelvetrees was locked up."

"Never thought I'd see the day when that unbearable bastard got tossed in jail," he said. "This might even be worth losing our pay."

The man moved back into the crowd. A large buzz of voices grew louder as the news of the great man's incarceration circulated through their ranks.

Jack looked up then. Hyde was riding slowly toward the jailhouse.

Jack Mahan felt a warm relief the man had returned. When the sheriff entered the crowd, the performers broke ranks like a herd of cattle, allowing him to pass through. They then started drifting off.

Hyde tossed the reins over the hitch rail and stepped up on the sidewalk.

"What's going on?" He jerked a thumb toward the crowd.

"They wanted to talk to Twelvetrees," Jack told him. "Claim, they haven't been paid. But since they didn't bother to speak to you, it looks like they must've figured it'd be too much trouble, and just gave up. Likely, they have to move on.

"Axel's inside right now. I caught him strangling Withers and tossed him in a cell."

Frank Hyde's mouth fell open in amazement. "Don't tell me you used that same sly stunt on him you worked on Murphy."

"Yessir, I did. But it wasn't a complete success. I knocked him to one knee all right, but feared if I hit him again I'd break my fist. So, I used my pistol butt on him."

"Now, don't shit me, Mahan. Is it true?"

"I wouldn't shit you, Hyde. You're too big a turd. Remember?"

Hyde brushed past him, walked inside, and stood before Axel's cell. "You reckon he's still alive?"

"He's been out for quite a while. But I doubt he's dead. Take considerable more than what I gave him to kill that man."

"He's plenty enough alive," Murphy said. "I saw him move 'while ago.
He was mumbling … carrying on a conversation with his mother." "My good god," Hyde said. "I don't believe what I'm looking at here." He turned to Jack, then shook his hand in congratulations.

Murphy interrupted them. "I damned sure wouldn't go off bragging so big and proud just yet. Better wait until he's dead and stinking."

Frank Hyde said, "You don't know how long I've waited to see the big ugly bastard in this cell, mister. Listen here, I fired my last deputy for downright laziness.
How's about if I hire you on in his place?"

"Can't do it, Sheriff." Jack's mind returned to the love of his life holed up in the hotel across the way. "I came here with a chore to do. Besides, I got a business to run back down home."

The circus troupe migrated back up the street. At full dark, they gathered their gear and loaded their wagons. As soon as they had it all packed up, they left town in a long cavalcade, unpaid, going on to another location, where the pay might be better.
But the hard group of men that made their daily wages working for Twelvetrees was still there, all right. They were drinking heavily, six of them, including Bill Bolt, Bobby Sikh, and the dark-haired woman, Lana, who had exchanged shots with Tillman Dead out at the compound. They were loud and obnoxious as only drunks can be, standing on the sidewalk in front of Wilfong's saloon. Axel's sister shouted and cursed as loud and crude as any man there.

Someone had informed them that Jack had tossed Twelvetrees in jail, Jack figured. Soon the unruly bunch called out for his release.

Across the street, Jack noted the orange glow of Tom Easy's cigarette.

The woman killer had taken a seat on a bench placed up against the weatherboarding of the hotel. An old man, a stopover traveler, with probably a night's layover at the hotel, sat next to him, and he appeared to be longing for conversation.

But Easy, a man not given to excessive speech, just sat there and watched over things, smoking.

"Twelvetrees burned down Tillman's dining room, Sheriff," Jack said.

"Also, he had Easy kill May. Shot her twice through the heart."

"Yeah. I met Till as he left town, when I rode back from the Peavey's.

He had May in the back of his wagon. Dolly, over at the hardware store, had cleaned her up. Put a nice dress on her.

"Till said he couldn't bear the mortician to touch her. He took her off to bury her. Said he'd be back by daylight. He means to kill that old boy in that cell there, and Easy as well. Don't know what he'll do now that Axel's in jail. He's sometimes wilder than a spooked buck."

"I've noticed." "Listen to Bobby Sikh up there, and his bunch. Him and his cronies and Axel's big sister are really getting donkey-eyed. They plan to pull some sort of mischief later on, I reckon. They jeered at me about springing Axel when I passed by. Hell, I didn't even know he was in jail."

"Think they really might try to spring him, Sheriff?"

"Yep."

"There are six of them," said the saloonkeeper. "If you count the woman."

"She might just be the meanest of the whole damned lot. But you missed the count by one. Tom Easy's still across the street, monitoring Lenore. He'll be plenty ready to lend a hand if he deems it necessary, or if the spirit moves him."

Hyde produced his pipe and filled it. "Well," he said, then lit up and puffed away while the pipe spoke to him in a squeaky voice, "let 'em try. We got lots of lead."

He pointed toward the full gun rack, "and the means to deliver it. It won't be as easy as they think." The two men stepped outside and sat down on the bench the old men used on sunny winter days to warm their bones while they batted around the breeze, and early mornings before it grew too hot in the summer.

The two men sat in silence. The stars were all a-blink in the heated sky. Up the street, Bobby Sikh's boys sounded as if they'd already made great progress toward intoxication. Loud and ponderous rolls of laughter echoed off the buildings across from where the sheriff and Jack sat. Tom Easy was sitting across the way, a dark, ominous shadow against the lighter color of the hotel wall. His cigarette glowed bright always and even brighter when he dragged deeply on it.

The old man who earlier had been determined to draw Easy into conversation, had given up and gone inside, engaging in a lively dialogue with Alfred, the night clerk. For a time, Jack watched their exaggerated arm movements through the window, lit up by the bright golden lamplight inside the hotel office.

It fell quiet for a time. Hyde's mousy pipe-speak was the only sound.

By and by, Jack broke the silence. "What sickness you suppose Twelvetrees has to make him like he is?"

"Who knows? It's best not to even ask.

You can't change the man. Me, I ain't even going to try."

Time passed. Hyde knocked dottle from his pipe and cupped its bowl in his broad hands as if he were afraid to put it away for fear he might need it in a rush and wouldn't be able to get to it fast enough to suit him.

At last, he said, "I figure he suffers from a gross lack of lead in his diet."

"You might be right."

The sheriff exhaled loudly and then shifted his weight on the bench.

"Well, we got a remedy for what ails him. If it's lead, he's in need of."

"Might be a rope he's hungry for," Jack said, drawn into the sheriff's wry humor.

"It'd have to be a ship's hawser then, I do believe. No commonplace rope would get the job done. That sonsabitch is heavy."

Later, Murphy cried out for Hyde, and both men got up and stepped back inside the jailhouse.

"Axel's waking up," said the onetime guard. "At least he rolled over on his back."

"Axel?" Hyde cried out.

Axel's eyes were open wide now.

"I'm just taking a break, Sheriff," answered Twelvetrees. "Be up and around directly."

Jack Mahan looked off for just an instant, and when he turned back, Twelvetrees loomed before them at the bars. Jack was surprised that a man of Axel's size could move with such speed, but there he stood, damned nigh as wide as a boxcar door.

The last thing I recall," Twelvetrees began, "I was dealing with that fellow over there." He pointed toward Withers, who stared back at Axel with what Jack took to be a look of absolute compassion.

Withers attempted to speak, but his words came out in hisses, and were difficult to understand.

"What did the man say, Sheriff?" Axel wanted to know.

"Says he forgives you, Axel."

The sheriff surely possessed a keen sense of hearing. Jack did not understand a word Wither's had said.

Axel laughed heartily at this revelation. "Maybe you do, Withers, but I damned sure don't forgive you. Hell, you brought trouble down on me when you lured that fellow out to the ranch. The one in that loud shirt.

"I just can't forget a thing like that and damned sure don't forgive it. I'll get to you later on. Just be ready." He turned to Hyde.

"What did you hit me with, Hyde—a crowbar?"

"It wasn't me had that pleasure, Axel." Hyde placed a hand on Mahan's shoulder. "This feller here did it. Knocked you to your knees with his fist. You wasn't quite out, though, so he clipped you right smart with the butt of his pistol."

Axel stared hard at Hyde for a time, on to Jack, then back to Hyde. "Now if that ain't the damnedest lie I ever heard. There's no man alive who can knock me to my knees with his fist."

"You're wrong there, Axel. Waverly here used to fight for purse money in St. Louis. He did the deed all right. Just ask Murphy. He saw it all." Murphy lay stretched out on the floor, arms crossed over his chest, hands clasped together like those of a dead man.

Twelvetrees chuckled like a tree toad. "Murphy's pretending to be asleep. He knows what's in store for him when I get out of here. I'll tend to him right after I fix Withers. He's first on the list, then Murphy, then…" He paused a second and raised a large finger, and pointed at Jack. "Then, I'll settle accounts with you, mister, for hitting me with your pistol."

"Nope," Frank Hyde said. "Them old roughhouse days, killing, kidnapping, murder and child abuse, rape and lawlessness of all kinds are over for you. You're going to swing. That is, if we can find a heavy enough rope to do the job proper."

Twelvetrees attempted to stare down the sheriff, but failed. Hyde didn't blink a lash.

"A man can dream, I suppose, Sheriff. So go ahead, have your fun while you can. I'll fix the lot of you … and this damned town. After all, I've done for these people, too. This just proves it never pays to be too damned liberal. I won't show any more compassion for the other fellow. Not again. Not after this."

Hyde took his turn. He laughed and did so in a near uproar.

"Hell, Axel, you're so full of shit, it's a pure wonder your eyes ain't afloat in your own sewage."

"When are you cutting me free, Hyde?"

"I don't know's you'll ever get out, Axel."

Suddenly he grew serious. "Not until we haul you into court, and maybe later on, when you walk up the gallows steps.

"We have a witness to the murder of the man you hung on the arch timbers of your gate," Hyde said on a bluff.

"Yeah, and just who might this witness be?"

"Why, the very man you tried your best to strangle before Mr. Waverly knocked you out."

A slow smile, unnerving in his ruined face, broke over Axel's mug.

"That minor problem can be taken care of, I believe."

"You're in deep enough as it is," Hyde cautioned. "The murder of Judge Lodge is bad business. When the news of his death gets out, it'll have dire consequences for you."

"Lodge was a fool, Sheriff. The man deserved what he got."

"There are certain laws even you can't break and get off free.

The murder of the judge is one of 'em. You'll hang … unless Tillman gets you first."

"Lodge crossed me. I can't allow that." He stepped closer to the bars, staring at Jack with tightly squinted eyes—eyes they were burning like live coals. "I've been thinking about you, mister. Wondering where I've seen you before. Just now Hyde called you Waverly, it dawned on me. You're the fellow who tried to steal Lenore from me.

"Your name, though, is not Waverly. You're Mahan … and if I remember right, you still owe me an eyeball. I never figured you would be dumb enough to follow me all the way to Scarlet."

Twelvetrees grasped the bars of his cell. He flexed his shoulder muscles until it looked as if the seams of his coat might rip.

"Forget it, Axel. You're in there to stay."

Then, before Jack could blink or draw another breath, Axel shot an arm out through the bars. All he saw was his huge hand streaking toward his face like the blurred strike of a snake. He couldn't move or do anything except watch the hand speeding straight for his eyes.

Frank Hyde's revolver leapt upward like a conjurer's trick. He slammed the barrel hard across Axel's wrist and drove it down to the side.

The big man's wrist popped sharply when metal met bone.

Jack stood and stared deep into Twelvetrees's wide eyes. They were overflowing with a sickness inconceivable outside the worst of the wildest nightmare.

In a voice that did not bend, Hyde said, "Nebo County is my territory, Axel.
I'm the old boy who has the final say here, despite what you might think.
Try that again, and you're just apt to wind up in hell."

He holstered his revolver. "And it'll happen damned quick when it happens."

"I need to see my lawyer, Hyde," Twelvetrees said, falling back on that final, sorry lament that all criminals use.

"Yeah … and people in hell need spring water, too," the sheriff said.

"I mean right now, Hyde. I won't allow you to stick me with a damned thing.
I mean to see Hollis. That's my right." "I hear he's gone over to Henderson. I reckon you've got plenty of time to sit and think things over like any other common criminal."

Axel continued to protest and complain about his detainment and his abused rights. Jack thought this filled with the sweetest irony. People like Axel were always the first to cry and howl, and make the heaviest weather in such cases.

Jack Mahan and Sheriff Hyde settled down at the desk with a sharp eye out in case the ruffians outside Wilfong's saloon decided they were loaded with sufficient whiskey courage to try a run on the sheriff's office.

Withers continued to hiss his snake speech at Twelvetrees, declaring his forgiveness for the brutality committed against him. Twelvetrees just laughed at first.
After twenty minutes of this, though, he'd had his fill.

"Shut your damned mouth, Withers," he roared. But Withers had suddenly found a fountain of magnanimity and continued to pardon Axel of his abuses.

Murphy kept his trap shut, lying on the floor with an arm over his eyes, as if this act alone might somehow protect him. Later, all three of them shut up and fell asleep.
Bobby Sikh and his bunch up the street were raising hell as high as possible so they could set blocks under it, growing louder and more profane every time they bent an elbow.

Hyde remained seated at his desk, in a heated contest with a game of solitaire, squeaking his noisy pipe in thought before every play.

Jack was edgy. His head pounded like a flat wheel on a railcar.

He recalled the warning by Dr. Caron, that he'd suffer headaches for the rest of his life, thanks to Bobby Sikh's heavy-handed use of his pistol butt.

Laughter, name-calling and taunts from Sikh's up-street bully ruffians, aimed at the sheriff, increased as they grew bolder. Jack glanced across the desk at Hyde to learn what his response might be. Hyde, though, kept his attention entirely on his game, showing no emotion, even though Sikh's gang had just taken up headquarters across the street, in front of Johnson's hardware store. They were sitting in perfect position to stare straight into Sheriff Hyde's office through the open door.

A few minutes later, a shot rang out, Jack leapt to his feet springing for the door for a look, but Hyde stopped him.

"Pay 'em no mind," he grunted around his pipe stem, and added, "They ain't properly fired up yet."

Jack wondered then just what the sheriff required to prod his anxiety.

He was definitely a cool head.

After a considerable amount of time passed, Jack figured he should shut the door. He was uncomfortable sitting there before an open door. He stood up, walked to the door, and was shutting it.

"Don't shut the door," Hyde said. "How'd'you keep your eye on 'em if you can't see 'em?"

Later on, one of the gang walked off down the street. Jack said, "One man just left, Hyde."

Hyde studied his cards so severely it seemed he was trying to intimidate them.

Minutes later, another man cut out. "There goes another one."

Then a third man drifted from Jack's sight. "They must break up and heading home. Another fellow just took off."

Hyde twisted up his face at this, then plotted out his next assault on Old Sol.

Suddenly, from his cell, Twelvetrees burst out in laughter, revived now by the threat his men were posing to the law of Nebo County.

"Better get ready, Hyde. They're coming to free their boss. They are loyal soldiers."

Hyde took time out from his game to throw a look over his shoulder at Twelvetrees. "If they come for you, Axel, it won't be from any kind of loyalty."

"My men are loyal, Hyde. Damned loyal. Especially Bobby Sikh.
They come no more loyal than Bobby. He and Billy Bolt and Tom Easy."

"Sikh just don't want to lose his grubstake—his cushy job.
Them boys ain't loyal to you. Ain't nobody that damned dumb ... unless maybe it's your mam."

"Leave her out of this, Frank Hyde. She's just apt to eat your liver before this deal is done."

Hyde dropped the argument, and turned back to his game, which still hadn't swung his way.

Twelvertrees grew as bold as a blue jay nested in a backyard tree. "Come on in, Bobby. Come and fetch me out of here. I'm tired of hanging around in this trap."

Later, one man called out to Hyde in the voice of a schoolyard bully. "Come on out, little Frankie Hyde. Come on out and play with us."

Axel laughed, rose on an elbow, and called out to Hyde, "They're coming in, Frank. Better get ready."

Hyde didn't even raise his head.

Axel's men continued their shrill catcalls, tossing off challenges, drunk as pigs. Jack Mahan stepped outside and stood alongside the old-timers' bench. Sikh's bunch jeered him as he stood on the sidewalk. He looked up the street at the hotel. Tom Easy still stood there, on guard duty.

The bright orange glow of the murderer's cigarette flared in the night with each drag and dimmed when it set idle between his lips. Finally, a vivid orange gemstone streaked skyward as Easy flipped away his smoke. It tumbled in the air like a bright jewel, end-over-end, reached its apex, then descended, still in a tumble.
It crashed to earth, and burst like a meteorite into a million tiny angry sparks.
They flared brightly in climax before the breeze carried them off.

22

Jack Mahan stepped back inside the jailhouse. Twelvetrees was standing at the bars like a huge ape-man, unknown even to those in the study of The Science of Savages. He seemed a new species, part man, part devil, and all bad. The sickly smile on his face looked twice as wicked in the pale yellow glow of the lamplight.

Outside, in the street, a tall, shadowy menace from a dream-horror, shrouded in black was walking across the street, heading for the jailhouse. Dust arose in slow puffs from the feet of the revenant with its every step. The hairs on the back of Jack's neck arose stiffly one at a time.

He nudged the sheriff, and Hyde glanced up.

"Well, I'll be damned," he said, and abruptly turned to. Twelvetrees. "Your momma's come for you, Axel. She figures to spring you from my jail. Damned if she don't."

"Go to hell, Hyde."

The dark, shrouded hobgoblin reached the walkway, stepped up on the sidewalk, crossed over to the doorway, and in an instant, entered the office. The hem of her long black dress swept the floor of dead match stems and cold cigarette stubs.

A black laced veil hid her face.

Her dictatorial presence dominated the room. Jack realized he stood face-to-face with a flawless representative of evil. Hyde dropped his cards onto the desktop, pushed back his chair, and stood up.

"My word," he said, "if it ain't Mrs. Twelvetrees herself. What's the occasion of your honoring us with your noble presence, madam?"

"Goddam you, Hyde. I'll rip your head off your shoulders! Show my mother the respect she deserves."

"Well, now," said Hyde, "I don't see how I could show her any more respect than I already have. I used up all the high-flown and flowery words I could dredge up."

The dark lady stood high above all the name-calling and sarcasm. She said, in a slight accent Jack had heard before in other Spanish-speaking people, "I've come for Axel, Sheriff Hyde."

"Is that so?"

She placed a roll of greenbacks on the desk.

"Ma'am, Axel's in deep trouble. You know he killed Judge Lodge, don't you?

It's going to take some doing to spring your boy from my jailhouse.

Lady Twelvetrees placed another hefty roll of bills on the desk, and waited in silent patience like a gambler for Hyde to raise, call or throw down.

Frank Hyde palmed the two wads of money, lifted them to judge their worth. He said, "Nope. It ain't enough, ma'am." He spun to Axel. "Hey, Axel, your mother's trying to run a bargain. She figures to buy you out on the cheap."

The big, scarred man mumbled a mouthful of obscenities, which faded away like the image of a blown-out lamp, slow to die. He then stood by and watched as Hyde turned back to the woman. The expression on Hyde's face declared plainly that no amount of money would buy Axel out of his jail.

Jack attempted to catch a glimpse of the woman behind the veil. The material was just too dark, though. He caught only a hazy glimpse.

Hyde set the two rolls of bills back on the desk, and said, "Nope, sorry, ma'am. A wagon filled with gold won't spring your boy … not this time. He's in too deep. He's going to swing."

Without another word, she turned, stepped outside, and walked swiftly back across the street, reached the far side, and proceeded up the far sidewalk toward the railroad depot.

At last, she entered the telegrapher's shack, and Jack turned away.

"Now," said Hyde to Jack, "you can shut the door."

He fired his dead pipe, and in a self-assured voice, added, "You better screw down your hat tight as you can. Make your ears bend. I figure we're in for one hell of a rank-assed ride."

They waited expecting at any second Bobby Sikh and his roughnecks would charge the jailhouse. Hyde forgot all about his card game. He threw back in his chair and extended his heels to the edge of the desk.

They waited.

An hour passed. No assault. Eventually, Hyde stood up, walked over and opened the door. He stood in the doorway and stared outside. This act offered him up as a fine target, back-lit like a cutout figure by the light of the lamp glowing brightly behind him in the small room.

"By god," he announced in a voice of disbelief. He stepped outside and sauntered off down the walkway, boot heels loud upon the boards beneath him.

It grew quiet in Scarlet. No drunks were about. No catcalls. Nothing moved. All the business places were closed down for the night, which included Wilfong's saloon. This seemed damned curious. It was only eleven o'clock.

Jack figured everyone on Front Street had grown afraid of what seemed about to happen. Soon, he heard Hyde's booted footfalls on the sidewalk, headed back inside.

I think them boys of yours are gone, Axel," he announced as he stood before the great man.

Strangely, Axel kept his mouth shut, but continued to stare malignantly at the sheriff. His hands clutched the bars of his cell, knuckle-pads white from tension.

Hyde said, "You've been abandoned, all right. By your mob, and by your momma as well."

At midnight, Hyde fell off to sleep in his chair. But Jack was too wound up for sleep. He caught up Hyde's deck of cards and dealt out a game of Old Sol.

Finally, at three o'clock in the morning, he dropped the cards in an untidy pile, kicked back in his chair, closed his eyes and soon fell asleep.

At first light, Hyde started rooting around in the tiny stove in one corner at the rear of the room, and this woke Jack. The sheriff built a small fire of wood chips and made coffee.

Jack Mahan sat up, pushed back his hat, and stretched. Just as his muscles relaxed, Hyde set a cup of coffee in front of him. Its odor was like the brightest promise ever made to a favorite child. He sipped cautiously and regarded the sheriff over the rim of his cup. After the first sip, Jack placed the cup on the desk. "What happened to that bunch of roughnecks last night?"

Hyde sat down in his chair, fired his pipe, and blew smoke ceiling-ward, then noisily slurped his coffee. "Who knows? If I could figure out the criminal mind, I suppose I could save a lot of people a lot of grief."

"You're an insincere bastard, Hyde," Axel said.

"Good morning, Axel," Hyde said, but didn't bother to turn to face him. "Glad you're still with us."

"Go to hell, Frank Hyde." After this, Twelvetrees rolled over and fell back to sleep.

At a quarter to six, Jack heard the early passenger train chugging to a stop before the depot. At six sharp, a team and wagon drew up outside the jail, followed by the squeak of seat springs as they returned to their normal shape. Footsteps scuffed faintly upon the boardwalk. The door swung inward, and Tillman Dead entered. His cheeks were deeply sunken, and this forced the bony protrusions of his cheekbones to stand out greater than usual.

Jack reckoned the old man hadn't slept in quite some time, for his youthful manner had fled him.

Dead trudged across the floor, boot heels in a slow drag. He paused, and with a lazy flash of his eyes, glanced to the cell where Twelvetrees lay asleep, and then allowed them to drop away.

"Pull up a chair, Till," the sheriff said. "Have a sit."

Tillman Dead removed his beaver hat, held it in hand, took to his chair, placed the hat atop the desk upside down, and ran his dark fingers through his gray hair.

His fingernails flashed white as the inside of a mussel shell against the darker skin of the backs of his hands.

Hyde fetched a cup of coffee, slid it before Dead, and sat again on his own chair.

Dead drew the heavy, white crockery mug close. Steam issued upward from it in a fine mist.

He sipped his coffee, then said, "Good coffee, but I can make it better."

He reached and caught up a bottle of whiskey from an inner pocket of his vest, and spilled half of the coffee onto the floor. "Settling the dust," he added, and replaced the spilled coffee with whiskey. He bent his head, then slurped his coffee royal.

"Much better," he muttered, drying his lips with a quick swipe of a backhand as he spoke.

Hyde said, "Make a long trip?"

"Yessir, and a sad one. But it's over and done with. I've got other chores I need to tend to now." The sheriff gestured with a nod toward Twelvetrees's cell.

"We got him, Till. He's going to hang, hear? No thoughts of revenge. There are others in this area wants to see the man hang. That way there won't be no questions.

Do it out in the open, so all will witness it."

"How'd'you manage to jail him, Frank?" Dead said, as he rolled a smoke with the skill and ease of many thousands of repetitions.

"Wasn't me. This old boy here did it." Hyde jutted his chin toward Jack. "Knocked him to his knees with his fist—followed that with a right fine rap on the head with the weighty end of his pistol."

Dead fired his cigarette, then passed the saloon owner a look from his black eyes—dark and unemotional, which revealed unearthly calm, as he stared through the flame of his match.

"I wouldn't have believed it if anyone but you said it, Frank."

"Murphy witnessed it, Tillman."

Tillman shook out the match, dropped it, then turned again to Jack. "I sort of looked forward to doing the deed, my damned self."

"The man was strangling Withers when I came in on 'em, Tillman. So I didn't do it for you alone."

"Good. I hate to be beholden to any man. But under the circumstances, I guess I don't have a beef.

"You must be damned good with your dukes," the old man added. He then dragged strongly on his cigarette.

Sheriff Hyde inherited the tale. He revealed all that had occurred in the old man's absence, and then said, "Don't know just why them cutthroats left right after the grand lady left us last night. The minute she stepped off the street, we were primed for war. But nothing happened. I can't figure it."

"I can," Tillman said. "She plans on her lawyer, Hollis, setting him free, and I 'spect she's 'bout right."

"I hear Hollis has gone off to Henderson."

"Was gone. I just saw the man step down off the train and get into his carriage, when I drove past the depot. She wired him, probably. Told him to get home, fast."

Hyde swore.

"Axel will be out by noon," Tillman added. "I reckon that's good far as I'm concerned. I figure he's not yet done with his devious tricks. This'll give me the chance to put a good-sized nugget of lead in his fat gut. Then I'll deal with Easy."

"If you do it," the sheriff warned, "do it legal. He needs to hang to pay for all his crimes." "I don't think I'd get the same satisfaction seeing him hang, Frank. After all the dirty sonsabitch has done to me."

"It'd be the same, man. Hell, he'd still be dead."

"Yeah, but it wouldn't be personal … if you know what I mean. I'll try not to go awry of the law, though…. Take note, I did say try."

At ten o'clock, B. A. Hollis appeared at the jailhouse, all smiles and overt politics. He shook hands and slapped shoulders as if it were election day and he was in a tight contest for the governor's office. He beat the old man's predicted time by two hours.

Hyde cut Twelvetrees loose, and the man looked like a kid gone straight from church to the playground where he'd ruined his best clothes.

His white suit was black from lying on the dirty cell floor, ugly crusted bloodstains adorned the coat front, and his coat collar was turned up. He'd cast off his tie earlier, and the tail of his shirt hung outside his trousers.

Hollis attempted to rush him outside and away, but Axel was much too vindictive for this.

He told Withers, "Be ready, Withers. Your time's coming."

Withers merely stared back from tranquil, spiritually enlightened eyes. In his close brush with death, he seemed to have received a path that led to deep eternal peace. No verbal retaliation broke his lips. He'd recovered some small portion of his voice though, for when he forgave Axel again, everyone there understood him.

Murphy still lay sprawled out on his back, forearms over his eyes.

"You be ready, too, Murphy," Twelvetrees said. He banged on the bars of the hairy man's cell when he passed by.

Murphy gave no sign he'd heard him. Next, Twelvetrees stood before Jack Mahan.

Axel looked like a hobo in his ruined suit of clothes. Jack forced back a smile.

"And you barkeep, still owe me an eyeball. I mean to collect it right shortly."

Hollis, ever the politician, slapped the big man on his broad back, guided him toward the door, and smiled at Jack Mahan, who was standing slouched against the wall by the doorway. The lawyer's teeth gleamed like buttons of mother-of-pearl.

"Come along now, Mr. Twelvetrees," he said. He then pushed a fat cigar in Jack's face. "We've important matters to discuss."

Jack didn't snatch up the cigar, as the lawyer expected. Hollis blanched and struggled to find the proper words to prosecute Jack's slur. This must've been the first time this little trick of magic failed to pay the man top dividends, Jack figured.

"I don't smoke, mister."

The lawyer returned the cigar to its ornate tortoiseshell case, lined in lime green silk. His teeth gleamed brightly in an attempt to put a positive face on Jack's affront.

"Keep what I said in mind, Mahan," Twelvetrees cautioned.

Hollis guided him on outside, where the generous rays of the sun shone down on the blessed and the damned with equal magnificence.

Jack remained in the doorway with his eyes following them.

Finally, he turned away as they fell from sight. Hyde hailed a boy with bright red hair, freckled of face like an egg from the nest of the great speckled bird. He hired the boy to run over to his house to have Rose, his wife, prepare five plates of food and bring them back to them at the jailhouse.

An hour later, the redhead returned with a large wicker basket of food, and the men made a wonderful meal of fried eggs, thick steaks and cornbread, which they washed down with more of the sheriff's coffee.

Later, Tillman Dead stood up, adjusted his gun belt, donned his hat, and headed for the door.

"You going to eat and run, Till?"

"Yep. Thought I'd go down to the saloon. I figure if Axel decides to torch it like he did the diner, it'd be better if I were there to see what I could do to prevent it.

"I've given Axel to you, Frank. Hang his low ass if you like. I'll take Easy for my damn self. I got that right, I figure … since he killed May. Jail me later, if that's what it takes."

The wind blew strong, lifting dust high off the street, dropping it back to the ground, then tearing off again in a scurry down the street, creating hellish dust devils, heavy with grit.

"We'll watch out for you the best way we can," Hyde said.

Tillman Dead smiled a spiritless smile. His face was drawn, and this showed his true age. "Better watch out for yourself … and that old big boy alongside you there."

He turned and left the office.

His forlorn footsteps upon the boardwalk were the echoes of the pain he was probably experiencing. "Tillman's hurting," said Hyde. He pondered the inside of the bowl of his pipe a moment. "I was afraid he might do something rash."

Finished with the inspection of his pipe bowl, he filled it, tamped, filled again and then fired up. "With his wife and son gone, he probably feels he ain't got nothing left to hold on to.

"But I'm glad to see him thinking straight, leaving Twelvetrees to the law.

He's always been pretty damn wild. He'll be a real hellion now, I 'spect."

"Drinks some too, I noticed," said Jack Mahan.

Just then, a long roll of thunder broke over the town.

"Yeah, he does. But, you know, I ain't never seen the man too drunk to perform.

And I damned sure ain't never seen him completely drunk."

Jack kicked back and listened to the steady, lazy drone of red wasps as they hovered about their nest in the rafters of the porch. Then, with a gut full of steak and eggs, he fell asleep.

23

CR—ACK! CR—ACK!
CR—ACK!
CR—ACK! CR—ACK!

Jack Mahan jerked awake. The five gunshots receded slowly in his lethargic mind. Those shots sounded as if the great earth itself had suddenly burst the restraints that bound it steadily in its track across the measureless heavens.

He leapt to his feet, grabbed for his revolver, and ran for the door.

"Hold it, mister," Hyde said. He caught him by the arm. "You're apt to get your head blown off. Let's go with care."

Together, they stepped outside.

"Came from Dead's saloon," Hyde said as they hurried up the street.

When they neared the saloon, three more shots rang out.

Bobby Sikh, all leather and wool, with iron in his fist, smoking hot, reeled backward out of the saloon like a drunk. He dropped his revolver. It thumped loudly on the steps like a slow thumb down a washboard. He clawed at his stomach, soaked in crimson blood. His face flushed red with doomed surprise when he realized he'd just been gut-shot.

By the free flow of blood from the gunman's innards, Jack realized that Sikh's wounds were beyond earthly repair. Sikh's shirt from mid-chest down had already soaked through with the stain of his blood. His trousers all the way to the knees were heavily soaked as well. Bobby Sikh was spouting blood like water from a well pump, with no way to stop the flow.

Bobby Sikh, for the dire shape he was in, backed with extreme care, across the boardwalk in front of Tillman Dead's saloon. Further trouble struck him when the slick leather of the toe of one boot slipped on the first step that led down to the street.

The bad man nearly fell, but because of his lithe, athletic, youthful vitality, he regained his balance long enough to reach the street. His eyes bulged, awestricken.

He'd fallen in deep shock, and this alone kept him on his feet. He cast anxious eyes back into the dimness of the saloon, as if any second the commissioner of his gut wound might come in a run to finish the job.

The sheriff stepped up closer to the dying man.

Jack followed. Sikh staggered to his gelding—the bright sorrel of fable, white-stockings, mane and all. The walking dead man unhitched the creature from the rail, and set a toe in a stirrup to swing up into the saddle, but finally gave it up as if it were too big a chore.

He turned to Hyde, then shifted once more to the patient animal. Still unable to mount, he sank slowly directly beneath the belly of his animal, and took refuge in its skinny line of shade. That tiny streak of shade offered him a bit of relief, perhaps, but nothing had stopped the blood flow from his guts, and there was no way for him to hide.

He dug out the makings to roll a smoke with hands so blood-gory it looked as if he'd just finished butchering a hog. The blood clung much too heavily to his fingers. As a result, he could not separate the cigarette papers.

Slim ropes of guts from four closely placed slugs started a slow slide through the loops of his shirt, between the buttons, unstoppable.

Frank Hyde bent to the man.

Sikh stared up at him with eyes fixing to glaze over. He fought against unconsciousness, against the fast approach of his death.

Hyde said, "Need some help with that cigarette, Bobby?"

Bobby had lost his hat, and his long black curls had fallen down over his face onto his thin, straight European nose. The carefully cultivated tuft of hair beneath his lower lip trembled. He smiled a weak smile, filled with forced humor.

"No. I reckon not, Frank. I probably ain't got time left to smoke it no-how."

Death tapped him on the shoulder. He turned to it. It beckoned with a bent finger, and Bobby Sikh answered its call. He fell in upon himself, rolled over onto his side, and lightly brushed one of the hooves of his patient mount. The good animal moved with caution, so as not to step on the man-creature beneath its belly, dead now upon the main street of Scarlet, Kansas.

Frank Hyde checked for a pulse to see if Sikh was truly dead. He rose, satisfied, and climbed the steps and pushed on into the saloon.

Tillman Dead was sitting at a table in the center of the room. Two revolvers and a ten-gauge shotgun lay upon it in easy reach. A full quart of whiskey stood between one of the pistols and the shotgun. He reached out and fetched up the quart of whiskey. Hyde and Mahan strode across the room toward him. He thumbed out the cork, and it popped loudly in the quiet room. Dead stared for a second at the stopper. Then he licked off the whiskey, tossed the cork into his mouth for a second as if to savor the corn and barley from which the whiskey had been created and the sweetish taste of the charcoal from the bowels of the barrel that'd aged it. When he'd extracted all its essence, he spat the cork onto the floor. Blood, in a slow fall, a drop at a time, plopped to the floor from the left sleeve of Tillman's shirt. Sikh had put one into the old man high up on his shoulder.

"Hurting, Tillman?"

In a rough, raspy voice, the old man said, "What man ain't hurting—that ain't a liar?" He took a quick sip from his bottle.

"What was the row with Sikh all about?"

Dead smiled, as if he were aware of a hilarious joke that only he'd caught.

"Twlevetrees sent Bobby Sikh up here to gun me down—but more than a distraction."

"Distraction?"

"That's right—to get you away from the jailhouse.

"I'm going to sit here now and wait for Tom Easy. I must trust you to take care of Axel, Frank.

"Too damned bad you had to fall for his little gambit. I reckon he already has your prisoners."

Hyde swung to Jack Mahan, and they both recognized their mistake at the same instant. Tillman's face broke slowly in a sorrowful smile. There was no need for more words.

Hyde jumped for the door in a run—Jack right behind him. Jack's eyes had become acclimated to the dim interior of the saloon, and the light blinded him when he burst onto the sidewalk that way, the sun full in his face.

He blinked like a turkey in a hailstorm and ran back toward the jail to catch up with Hyde.

Twelvetrees had indeed taken control of Hyde's two witnesses, and they were crossing to the center of Main Street. Bill Bolt and six other owl hoots accompanied Twelvetrees.

Withers went along as peacefully as a sacrificial lamb. His face shone as bright as that of a sun-touched mystic too long alone in the desert, guided along by Axel's heavy hand.

Murphy, though, was a different tale. He was going nowhere peacefully.

He screamed loudly, kicked viciously, and forced the rough louts attempting to drag him across the street, to work for their pay. The man likely realized Twelvetrees would kill him right after he strangled Withers to death, and he in no way seemed ready for it.

He tossed one of his oppressors away from him like a sack of rubbish. The man fell in an unruly lump in the dust. This freed an arm. He pummeled the man nearest him so viciously that when the man had taken all of it, he could bear, he drew his revolver and struck him across the left temple. Murphy fell to his knees. Now, in a daze, he shook his head back and forth. Blood flew in all directions like a breeding-quality bull that has torn the ring from its nose in the heat of its fervor, led too slowly to accommodate its heated zeal, to a cow ready in her time to conceive.

Twelvetrees stopped in the center of the street when he saw the approach of Hyde and Jack Mahan. He placed a hand flat upon the sneak thief's shoulder the way a preacher might lead a convert to the baptismal stream. Axel had cleaned up, dressed now in a lightweight suit of tan broadcloth, brocaded vest, and a wide-brimmed, crème-colored beaver hat. Still, he looked tremendously ugly, despite his splendid apparel.

The three men, engaged in the sweaty enterprise of restraining the Irishman, finally sidelined him with a rope, where if he tried to move suddenly, he'd fall to the ground.

"Aha!" announced Twelvetrees. "Just as well stand back, Hyde. You can watch while I deal with Withers."

Jack stopped sixty feet from the gang of reprobates. Hyde said to the saloon-owner, "Stand here." He stepped forward to face Twelvetrees alone.

"No need to get yourself killed, Hyde," boomed Axel.

Hyde disregarded him, and continued to walk straight at Twelvetrees, slow and calm as the lazy flow of a stream in summer.

Axel cackled his peculiar, nervous laughter. "Better stop where you are, Hyde. Go on over there. Sit on the sidewalk. I see the start of a good shade on your bench."

Hyde continued his advance on the grand degenerate, not at all interested in the shade.

"I've given fair warning, Sheriff. You really don't think you can get by Billy Bolt, and all my other fine fellows, do you … alone as you are?"

Hyde halted.

"And just suppose you were to get by these boys here," Twelvetrees droned on. "I'm sure Tom Easy can fry up your bacon for you quick enough. He's right close at hand."

Frank Hyde stood fifteen feet from the big, ugly man. It was obvious Axel didn't know Dead was bird-dogging Easy.

"If you're wise, Axel, you'll return these men to their cells. I mean for them to testify again' you in an honest court of law.

"You'll go down right here on the street of Scarlet … or you can hang. I'll leave that up to you."

Frank Hyde had told Jack to remain where he stood, but being a man capable of independent thought, he took his own advice, fair or foul, and stepped up and stood next to him. Strangely, he felt a good deal more confident alongside the sheriff.

He briefly wondered where Lana and Axel's mother were.

To top off the entire crazy shambles, Mr. and Mrs. Peavey and the girl, Nancy, stepped out of Johnson's store and rushed toward their wagon. Nothing could have been worse than for these good people to expose themselves to danger in this way.

Twelvetrees saw Nancy Peavey mount the wagon seat, and his eyes grew wide. His lower jaw fell.

"Grab that girl. I want her," he cried out.

One of the bolder men in Twelvetrees's pay rushed toward Nancy Peavey.

But the man made it to less than ten feet of his goal, when Sheriff Hyde dropped his gun hand, and his pistol reared upward. He fired all in one pure, silky motion, fast as the fall of an eyelash. He shot the man through the ankle. Blood and pulverized leather flew skyward.

The sudden jolt knocked the man for a quick cartwheel roll like a loop thrown around the forelegs of a running calf. He struck the ground on his back. Dust boiled upward in a heavy, murky cloud, and this was all it took to start the gun battle.

Bill Bolt fired twice at Hyde in retaliation. Both shots missed their mark. Hyde swung his pistol on Bolt and squeezed off a round that caught the man neatly in the ribcage. Bolt, though, continued his assault on Sheriff Hyde, unaware, it appeared, that the bullet had caught him.

A tall man with a wild shock of frizzed up hair that snaked in all directions from beneath his filthy hat, took a wild shot at Jack and missed.

Jack drew his revolver, and without thought pulled the trigger. He felt the good buck and heard the roar of the revolver in his fist. His shot knocked the fellow in a catawampus tumble. The man rolled around in the street, cried out, and grabbed his shattered hipbone.

The brave men who held Murphy must've realized there was far too much lead in the air for good health. They cut out in a dead run back across the street.

They reached the sidewalk and lit out up the alleyway between Dead's millinery and the barbershop.

Immediately, hot slugs of lead kicked up great divots of turf alongside Jack. Gun smoke filled his eyes. He blinked back tears. By the time he could see clearly again, he found that Twelvetrees had released Withers, and started in a run toward Nancy Peavey as fast as his bulk allowed him.

Withers found the proper path. He hurried to Murphy's side and untied him. When the hairy Irishman stood up, set free, he pulled foot, in a rush to put himself in the clear of all the loose lead that was turning the air blue. Withers, though, was not a man to run. He picked up a fallen gun and closed his fist around it.

The thunderstorm that'd threatened Scarlet for the past two days grew noisier.

A tremendous cloud of dust rose from the street, soared skyward and hid the sun. Jack noticed the Peavey team drawing its empty wagon down the street in a gallop, chased along by the dust cloud.

The team passed from sight around a corner. Jack then saw the reason the wagon was empty. Mr. and Mrs. Peavey were lying upon the street. Evidently, they'd gotten in the way of errant slugs, or Twelvetrees had shot them both down. Jack allowed the latter the more probable.

The missus lay upon her back, motionless, with only the hem of her dress rippling in the strong gusting wind. The mister lay sprawled out face down, both hands spread far apart, as if he had thrust them out before him to break his fall. Jack was sure the man was dead. Abruptly, the roar of gunfire ceased. It grew stone quiet upon the street except for the pitiful sobs of the man Jack had shot down made crawling in the direction of the sidewalk in front of the jailhouse. He whimpered softly in the sad way humans do when under terrible duress. At last, he reached the sidewalk, then dragged himself upon it. Reaching the loafers' bench, he slithered beneath it like a rattlesnake in cover. Arcs of brilliant arterial blood spurted high from the entry wound of the slug that struck him down.

Frank Hyde had killed three men. One of the men was Bill Bolt.

Three other ruffians had fled, and the man Jack shot was out of action without question.

The hard cases had come out the worst in that quick tempest of lead. Twelvetrees was now standing with his enormous hands clamped around Nancy Peavey's thin, delicate neck. The sound of her muffled sobbing broke loud upon the suddenly quiet street. The wind blew dust down the street in a large whirlwind until it finally crashed against the side of the livery stable and broke up. By then, two more had joined in a race down the street, locked in a fierce, side-by-side competition.

Lana Twelvetrees stepped down onto the street then, and with a gun in her hand, she was a formidable force.

"Kill her, Axel," she screamed. "Break her neck. Make it snap like a whiplash."

Frank Hyde was still on his feet, despite a wound in his chest, and the blood flow darkened his shirt and vest. He still held his gun trained on Axel. The gun didn't even waver, but stood incredibly steady even for his obvious pain. "Turn Nancy loose, Axel," he commanded. "Turn her loose, or it all ends for you right now."

Twelvetrees swung the frightened girl in front of him as a shield from Hyde's gun. Lana smiled smugly, and held her revolver trained on the sheriff.

They had a standoff.

"Kill her, Axel. Do as I say!"

The great man's hands, his tremendously strong fingers, inched tighter around Nancy's thin, vulnerable neck.

"Don't listen to her, Axel," Hyde warned. "If you do ... I'll snuff your candle right now. There won't be no waiting 'round for a court trial. No gallows walk.

You'll be dead and your sorry carcass will be stinking up Scarlet before the sun goes down."

"I'll blow your head off, Sheriff," Lana warned.

"If I have to shoot Axel, shoot Lana," Hyde said to Jack. "She'll kill us both if you pause. Heed me now."

"I'm ready, Sheriff." Just then, the sneak thief spoke up. "Don't worry about Lana, Hyde. I've got my gun on her too. It ain't no way out for her with both of us again' her."

Hyde took a step toward Twelvetrees. The big man drew Nancy even closer.

Axel said, "Hold it, Hyde. By god, you'll kill the girl. Her blood will be on your hands!"

Lana Twelvetrees's finger tightened on the trigger of her weapon. Jack was still worried over where the mother was. The last thing they needed right then was another gun against them.

Sweat spilled down Lana's face. She cursed Withers's interference in a long string of obscenities, for she realized, without a doubt, if she pulled the trigger, she'd likely die in instant retaliation, and she'd take her brother with her. The compulsion to kill stood out clearly on her drawn, haggard face. The powerful lust to kill had struck her hard and deep, and she didn't lower her gun. Not even an inch.

"I knew you were bad news, Axel," Hyde said, "the first day you showed your ugly face in Scarlet. If it'd been legal, I would've shot you dead. But the law protects the bad along with the good. It might not be right, but it's the way of it."

Then, just as Jack feared, Axel's mother made her dreaded reappearance.

She stood there, revolver in hand. An unearthly flow of foam ran from the corners of her mouth. She raised her index finger and the little finger of her hand in a display of the horns of the goat ... the ancient sign of the carnuta.

"Kill the girl, Axel," she commanded. "Lana and I will protect you. Go on now. Do what I say!"

Jack Mahan could no longer hold himself in check. He rushed forward, placing himself in a position to put a chunk of lead into Twelvetrees's worthless hide.

He squeezed off a round. The revolver bucked in his hand.

The strong, overpowering odor of gunpowder smoke, from his own weapon, and from those of all the other combatants on the street clogged his nostrils.

He rushed his shot and missed. He squeezed off another round. Twelvetrees moved just as he fired. Jack Mahan missed the headshot he'd aimed for. His slug instead struck Axel in the upper right side. Dust spouted from the material of Axel's suit coat where the slug struck him. He flinched insignificantly, as if a bee had just stung him.

He swung toward Mahan, Nancy still held in front of him.

A bright line of jagged fire rippled across the sky, followed by a tremendous rolling explosion. It shook the earth with a magnitude that could've originated from nowhere else except the parting of the satanic portals of hell. The soles of Jack's feet tingled from the concussion.

The thunderstorm had finally broken its leash. It sounded more than an ordinary earthly storm, roaring with the intensity of a fearsome, supernatural power, and fit perfectly in the midst of the gun battle.

24

"Axel!" screamed his mother.

Jack fired off another round, but missed, and then felt a slight burn stir to life on his shoulder. Through and through, the bullet coursed.

He fell to a knee to present a smaller target. As he did so, the sheriff caught another round. Jack grimaced as Hyde toppled forward.

The enormous veins in Axel's hands grew larger as he gripped Nancy's neck tighter, and still he held her in Jack's line of fire.

He fired at Lana Twelvetrees instead. The dust and gunpowder from the rush and scuttle of so many feet hindered his aim, and he missed her.

The next time he attempted to squeeze one off, the hammer struck on a dead cartridge. He then stood there, defenseless.

"Don't kill the barkeep," Axel yelled out. "He owes me."

Twelvetrees shoved Nancy into Lana's arms and latched onto Jack Mahan.

"Where's my razor?" Axel called out. "Where's my razor?"

He'd forgotten everything in his rapture. His mind filled with thoughts of victory and revenge.

With Sheriff Hyde down, Jack faced Axel all alone and empty-handed.

Twelvetrees had won.

They'd tried Jack Mahan and the sheriff, but had fallen a little short of their goal.

Axel couldn't locate his razor, and despite the gunshot wound, he grabbed Jack around the neck, and started squeezing, slowly and powerfully.

Jack attempted to break Axel's terrific grip, straining with every grain of his strength to part one of Axel's fingers. He needed to dislocate one of them to stand free.

It was not to be, though. The man was berserk with his strength.

Jack failed to part one of Axel's fingers. He wasted all his energy and reserves of air. He sank slowly. Once down, he wouldn't be able to climb back to the surface … not in this world.

Then in spite of his weakness, just as Jack started to fade away and call it quits, Axel's razor pressed against his chest in a pocket of his vest. The razor sang out to him in a pure, sweet voice.

He reached for it, found it, and flashed it forth. His fingers groped for the mechanism to spring the blade. The razor clicked smoothly and finely from its perfect and clever creation. In Jack Mahan's hands it no longer felt like an instrument of evil, but became instead a quick and sharp, deadly weapon of justice and salvation.

He swung it upward, searching for Axel's jugular. But just then, the grand dame cried out in her full, deep voice.

"Axel! He has a knife."

Jack struck swiftly. But because of the woman's warning, Axel sprang backward, and he missed the large vein that transports the power of life throughout the body. Instead, he hit him high on his right cheekbone. The slow grate of the blade, slicing sweetly downward across Axel's lower jawbone, felt wonderful to him even though he missed the vital target.

Axel freed him instantly.

Air rushed back into Jack's lungs. His heart pumped life throughout his body, and with this new burst of energy, he felt a powerful surge of hope.

Twelvetrees yelped like a startled dog, standing, staring in amazed surprise.

Jack saw, though, the man didn't fear him … razor or not. He circled him and looked for an opportunity to strike him again.

Then, before he even had time to blink, Axel leapt forward in his unnatural quickness. He caught Jack by the wrist, squeezed him so hard, Jack's hand fell limp.

He heard the soft, sad plop as the razor struck the thick dust.

His final hope fell with it.

"Now, by god!" Axel said.

Just then, a rifle cracked loud upon the street, and the big man fell. A shot from behind him had cut him down.

Axel struggled to his knees. He looked about as if to ponder what had struck him, and where the authority he'd commanded over everything had suddenly gone.

His lips moved slowly. Blood in a gelatinous roll oozed from his mouth.

"What's happening to me?" he said, blood spurting from his mouth.

"What's wrong?"

He'd uttered both questions with no hope of an answer, it appeared. There'd never been answers to such questions, and Axel Twelvetrees was not the first man to express them.

The rifle cracked again from the sidewalk. Axel pitched forward from his knees onto his face, thrashed about, and then lay silent. Stilled for all time.

Jack Mahan looked about him, searching for the person who'd saved his life.

Carla Daws was standing on the sidewalk, rifle still at her shoulder, face chiseled deeply with dedication and purpose.

"Carla," Jack cried out, then watched helplessly as Lana Twelvetrees thrust Nancy Peavey down onto the street, and swung her gun on Carla.

In a swift blur of motion, Carla shifted her own rifle toward Lana Twelvetrees.

The two women fired at the same moment.

The sharp, double report of both weapons cracked loudly.

It seemed at first that each woman had missed. Both remained standing.

Then in a flash, Lana Twelvetrees's soul fled her, and she pitched forward on her face, as her brother had done earlier. Axel's mother—the family matriarch—swung her own revolver to shoot down Carla Daws. Jack felt a sick sensation of helplessness.

But before Axel's mother could pull the trigger, a shot from off to the side rang out, loud and unexpected.

Jack Mahan struggled forward to aid Carla Daws. Just as he did so, a few drops of rain fell in loud plops onto the deep dust of the street. The mother of Lana and Axel Twelvetrees crumpled to the sidewalk. She sighed once and then gave up the ghost.

Jack swiveled to the sounds of the shots that'd killed her.

Withers stood there. "I hated I had to kill her," he said in his ruined voice. "But that woman had taken up the wrong cause ... and lost out."

Just then, someone crashed against Jack, and two arms encircled his chest in a tight grip. He returned the embrace and suddenly felt an urge to weep for joy.

Carla Daws stood in his arms, crying low against his chest.

"I was afraid she'd killed you," he told her.

Carla looked up at him through her tears, unable to speak.

He swung her about with the thought of thanking Withers. But Withers had already dropped his gun, and Jack and Carla watched him stride quickly toward the livery stable. Later, he emerged from the stable astride a bay with a blaze face.

The re-born man stared down at Jack Mahan. "I owe a woman in Military Springs a deep debt, Mahan. That money won't never replace her son, but it'll help her survive. Tell Hyde I'll be back."

"I will, Withers." Withers got up from his mount then and galloped out of Scarlet.

Jack recalled the money hidden beneath the lone tree alongside Shippen Creek, and the debt Withers owed Willis's mother.

He guided Carla toward the hardware store. Dolly Johnson met them on the sidewalk. She nuzzled him aside.

In a tender voice, she said, "Go on. You're still needed. I'll clean her up and tend her until Doc Katz has a chance to look at her."

Lana Twelvetrees had hit Carla with one slug from her weapon. Fortunately, like his, hers too, was minor.

"I got to go help," he told Carla. "There are dead that need to be carried in off the street."

Sheriff Hyde was standing on his feet as Jack approached him. Hyde's knees were wobbling as if at any moment he might pitch forward onto his face. Jack assisted him over to the jail, where he sat at his desk, trembling in pain. Jack filled the bowl of his pipe, lit it, and passed it to him.

"You hit, too, Jack?"

"Passed on through. Didn't hit a bone. I'll live, Sheriff."

"We couldn't have made it without your help," said Hyde.

"You right sure I can't interest you in a deputy's job?"

Jack smiled a wilted smile, but didn't respond.

Dr. Katz came in off the street. Jack backed out of the man's way and allowed him to tend to the sheriff. There would be time later for Dr. Katz to look at his own wound.

Jack Mahan stepped back onto the street, in the midst of the men carrying off the dead. The thunderstorm continued to blow. It rattled windows still, but the rain had stopped, and precious little it'd been at that. Perhaps later on it might rain more. But there would be no great downpour, not in this rain-deprived country.

Jack noticed Tillman Dead standing upon his porch, with a bottle of whiskey in hand. Jack didn't see Tom Easy anywhere about. Bobby Sikh still lay where he'd fallen. His horse was still standing there, as if on guard.

He crossed to the other side of the street with the intention of cutting up the boardwalk to join Tillman. But just then, he heard someone call out to him. He turned. Nancy Peavey rushed into his arms as if he'd been sent to her for her protection.

She was a short girl. Her head struck Jack mid-chest. She sobbed in a choked, ragged manner, as if unable to release her full emotions.

Nancy had lost her mother and father, and now she'd latched onto him in an attempt to find solace, comfort, perhaps some meaning, and certainly she longed for stability and security. Jack did everything in his power to help her.

He raised a hand to the back of her head, and the moment he did so, she released all her pent-up emotions in a torrent of tears.

There he stood, Jack Mahan, thirty-three years old, owner of a saloon, ex-prizefighter with a grossly disfigured mug. He'd arrived in Nebo County on a quest to locate Carla Daws, to carry her back with him to Sweet Home. Now he found himself with an abused child on his hands. A child who'd gone through more grief in her brief life than anyone should endure in an entire lifetime.

"It's all right, Nancy."

His voice sounded peaceful, in a way he hadn't known it could. This compelled the girl to dig in closer, cry harder, and cling to him with even more ferocity.

Nancy Peavey had staked her claim on him as her refuge and sanctuary.

Jack already had one stray child in Bridget McReynolds to care for, and while older than Nancy, she too, was only a child. Suddenly it became clear this was his opportunity to raise a family, which was exactly what he'd longed for all his life.

If what he'd learned a few days earlier about the prohibition of liquor being proposed were true, he saw then that he might need to find a new line of work.

He was a grown man.

He felt he'd have little trouble providing for a family. He intended to do his best and to claim them all as his own. This strong decision made him feel much better.

He escorted Nancy back to the hardware store, where he'd left Carla. Before Mrs. Johnson met them. She'd watched their reunion on the street. The gentle old woman took Nancy to her side.

"I'll watch after her, sir," she said.

However, when Nancy saw him about to leave, she reached out for him.

"I have a few things left to do. But I'll be back for you. And believe me … I promise no one will mistreat you ever again."

Carla Daws appeared just then. Without uttering a word, she coupled hands with Dolly Johnson, and together they formed a warm circle of protection around Nancy Peavey. Carla smiled softly at Jack over Nancy's head. "Go on, Jack. She'll be fine now with us."

Nancy Peavey allowed Carla and Mrs. Johnson to draw her inside the store and off the street.

Jack approached Tillman Dead, and heard the old man whistling a tune he recalled hearing as a youngster in St. Louis, played on a fiddle by a blind man outside the door of his uncle's saloon. Because he admired the song, he learned that the title of the tune when translated from Gaelic was, "Give Me Your Hand."

Now the sweet, sad memory of the tune and of a time long gone just about stopped his heart.

Tillman ceased whistling. "Got rid of Axel, I noticed. Had my eye on you all the time."

Jack nodded. "Sheriff Hyde got shot up some as well, but Doc Katz says he'll be just fine."

"Tom Easy just went inside the livery barn, Jack. He figures he'll skip town."

"The law won't touch him, Till. The crimes he committed will all be laid at Axel's feet."

"I figure he needs a damn good killing, and I reckon I'm just the kid to do the deed."

The old man slugged back another drink, the bottle nearly empty.

When he lowered it from his lips, he said, "Men like Easy make a habit of shaming the law. That's their art. I've seen it happen all my life. If we're going to have laws, then I say they shouldn't be allowed to tip too heavy. Give all a fair shake.

"If Tom Easy leaves Scarlet, it won't be until after he kills me ... and I don't think he's man enough. I've had my eye on that scurrilous runagate for a good long time. I won't let him off after he killed May. No damned way."

Dead set his bottle on the floor alongside his shotgun, fetched forth tobacco and a paper, and rolled a smoke. Done, he fired up and smoked with his thoughts to himself. He stood with his eyes trained on the livery stable while he smoked. By and by, the cigarette turned to ash. Dead ground out the stub, took up his shotgun, leaned it against one of the porch supports. His nerves seemed on edge.

He hefted the whiskey bottle, drank off the spider, and set it empty back on the floor next to the door of his saloon.

He straightened up just as Tom Easy stepped from the deep shadows of the livery barn.

Easy led his horse until he reached the edge of the street, turned the creature to the side, and stuck a toe in the stirrup.

Tillman snatched up his shotgun and blew off a round skyward.

The explosion bounced off the building directly across the street from the porch where Dead stood. The report of the ten-gauge roared in echo so loud that Jack's ears rung like a dinner bell. The heavy shot tore up the earth all about Tom Easy and his horse. The frightened animal rolled its eyes, threw its head high in panic, and ripped the reins from the hands of the cold killer, then fled back into the safety of the barn. A thick cloud of dust hid Easy briefly, then fell back to the ground, exposing him. He stood there isolated, abandoned, and all alone, at last.

Tom Easy searched with wide, anxious eyes for the source of the explosion.

"Up here, Tom. I'm the one let off that round." Tillman bent and leaned his shotgun against a roof post.

Easy still hadn't spoken a single word. Dead whistled that old Irish tune again, softer this time, born of habit. He glanced with a regretful eye at the empty whiskey bottle, then stepped off the porch, crossed the sidewalk, put both feet on the street, and stood there to face the bad man, Easy. Bobby Sikh, growing cold, lay nearby.

The wind had laid a trifle, but still had enough energy to lift sheets from a castaway newspaper high into the sky where they danced about like excited schoolboys.

Dead stepped to the center of the street. He stopped whistling, and the final strains of his sad tune lived past their time echoing off the buildings.

Presently, he said, "Where you figure you're going, Tom?"

Tom Easy's eyes dogged the old-timer. They were cold and intense with the strength of his observations. The man didn't blink. Didn't speak.

Dead said plenty. His voice boomed off the walls of the buildings on the far side of the street like that of a trained orator.

"You shouldn't have killed May, Easy. Now's time you paid up."

Dead allowed his gun, in hand, to fall to his side.

Tom Easy's tiny, cold eyes continued to track Dead's every move. Tillman spoke again, louder, "You do your best work behind a man's back, I know.

But you'll have to look me in the eye, mister. You'll not beat this rap, Easy."

Tom Easy stood firm to his ground, as if he'd taken root in the soil of Scarlet's main street.

The old man was attempting to push him to the embankment that slides over into hell itself, and then shove him on in the way it appeared.

He said, "You mean to yank that piece, Tom, you better go ahead on.

The kind lord knows I ain't getting no younger."

Easy made as if to swing about to return to the stable, but on reaching a quarter turn, he snatched in desperation for his weapon. He flung himself to the side, all in one swift, puma-like move, landing on his knees in the street. His revolver sprang up, thumped twice, like a churn dasher at work inside an empty churn.

Easy might as well have saved the lead and powder. He missed his mark.

The old man raised his own pistol, and with great care, squeezed off a round.

Dust puffed from Tom Easy's shirtfront.

Easy dropped his revolver and fell atop it.

Tillman Dead approached the hard case. Suspicion stood out plainly on his dark, weathered face. He reached him, and turned to Jack, back to Easy, then kicked him hard in the ribs. Easy didn't flinch a muscle. Tillman holstered his weapon, spun on a heel, and walked back toward Jack.

"Is he dead, Tillman?"

"Yeah. That man's as dead as a turd in a whore's pisspot, Jack."

Then, behind the old man, Easy whipped up his gun.

Jack drew his as well. But Easy was faster. He fired from his knees and drove a slug deep into Tillman Dead's back.

Jack Mahan squeezed one off. Dust sprang from the murderer's shirtfront.
He fired again and hit the merciless man in the heart. Easy wouldn't rise again.
Not from the way he crumpled like waste rags.

Jack stepped forward, curious. Tom Easy's revolver lay on the ground two feet from him. He picked it up, stuck it behind his belt buckle, and then rolled Easy over on his back.

The low coward attempted to speak. Spates of blood streamed from his mouth.
Jack couldn't make out a single word, and since he'd never heard Easy speak, he knelt alongside him with the thought he might have something important to relate, a message he wanted passed on. He felt, though that any words from him would be nonsense. Nevertheless, he felt compelled to remain with him until he died, in much the way a vulture sits atop a dying animal. He was determined not to allow him to play sly with him, as he had Tillman Dead.

Easy spoke, garbled and unintelligent.

"Once more, Easy. Go slow, so I can make it out."

Easy's lips flapped up and down, and bowed like a fish thrown high up on the bank to die. Blood gushed even more intensely from his mouth from the horrible wound—one that could never be repaired, not in Scarlet, Kansas, or in Paris, France, for that matter. The flow trickled off to nothing in time.

"It's hot, mister," said Easy at last. Jack felt a keen disappointment. The man would've been better served had he but held his tongue a few minutes longer.

"Well, it'll soon get a lot hotter where you're bound, Tom Easy."

Easy's heart stopped beating by and by, and Jack turned from him and knelt alongside Dead.

"Get that reprobate?" The old man's voice wavered like telegraph wires in the wind.

"He's dead, Tillman."

Oily sweat beaded up on Tillman's forehead. Jack vowed then never to show his back to a coward, even if the man happened to be dead and lying in a box in his own parlor.

Just as Jack thought Tillman had died, Dead said, "Tell Frank to take me to Smoky Hill. Have him bury me alongside May and Raymond."

"I'll tell him, Tillman."

Shortly after conveying this message, Tillman fell silent. Jack bent his ear to the old man's chest.

Tillman Dead's courageous heart had fallen silent.

Jack Mahan picked him up and carried him off the street.

At the door to the saloon, he pivoted and looked back at Tom Easy.

The green flies were already at work on his face ... in his open mouth, his nose cavity.

He stared down at Tillman Dead.

He held in his arms a man born with nothing but a skin shelter upon a hostile prairie. His family roamed constantly for subsistence, but given the proper shove, he'd made out right fine. Tom Easy, through the lottery of birth, had had a foot up to start with, but had done absolutely nothing with his advantage. Somehow, it didn't make a whole lot of sense to Jack Mahan.

"Let the green flies have Tom Easy," he muttered, and shoved on inside.

"They'll play hell getting you, old man."

He placed Dead on his bar top, walked behind the counter, found the towel drawer, selected a couple of clean bar rags, took them and wrapped them tightly around Tillman's head and face.

The flies were busy. The cloths would prevent them from crawling into his mouth and nose. Tillman Dead had earned much more respect than had a man like Tom Easy.

23

Sheriff Frank Hyde had caught four slugs in the gun battle. Later Jack stepped inside the sheriff's office, told him of Tillman's final request, and was flat out surprised to see the sheriff already back at work. He sat there shirtless, bandages wrapped tightly around his chest. Frank's wife, Rose stood at his side with a twisted look of concern on her face and of love as well as pride for her husband.

Jack said, "You should be in bed, Frank."

"He wouldn't hear of it," Rose Hyde said. "A horse fell on him once. I reckoned, well, Frank Hyde, old boy, you've met your match this time. What'd he do? Stayed in bed four whole days. The fifth day he got up and went to work before I could stop him. Afterwards, I figured there was no sense trying to make him go gentle. He's too stubborn for his own good."

"I'm the law in Nebo County," Hyde said. He fired his pipe. "Who'll keep the peace, if not me?"

"You need help, Frank," Jack told him. "A man you can trust to guard your back trail."

"I know. Right now, though, I'm more interested in hiring a couple of men to go with me to dig Till's grave. I ain't in no shape to do, it seems to me, and Till ain't going to keep much longer.

"What did you do with Withers, Jack?"

"He cut out right after he shot down the Twelvetrees woman.
He's a changed man, Sheriff. I don't think he'll go crosswise of the law ever again."

"Too many people died here, Jack. There'll be a big investigation when this gets out. I'll run him down later, I 'spect."

"You won't have to run very fast, Frank. What about Murphy?"

"He dropped in after all the dust laid. Said he heard Twelvetrees was dead.
Felt he ought to check in with me.

"Told him to go on about his business. I'll call him when it's time for his testimony."

The mortician became the busiest man in the county, hauling off the dead, preparing them for the grave.

Two days after the gun battle, they buried them all—the good along with the bad.

Jack sold off his mule. The creature hadn't been much use to him, and he would've given him to any man who needed one. As it turned out, he went to the livery stable for his horse, to settle his bill, to purchase a team and wagon, and the stable owner offered to buy the animal, which thrilled Jack to the soles of his feet.

He loaded his wagon and went with Nancy Peavey back to her home to retrieve her possessions. They were now stored away in the back of Jack's wagon. Emotionally, she vowed never to return to Scarlet, but young people, he knew, often suffered from peculiar unaccountable changes of mind. He asked Frank Hyde to keep his eye on the Peavey house.

If Nancy still felt the same way in a few years, he'd have A. Ray Leavitt, a lawyer from Sweet Home, come up and dispose of her property. Nancy might as well have some little nest egg to rely on. She'd want to get married one day, unless he missed his guess. She was hurt right now. She probably would be hurt for some time, but he intended to do everything possible to bring her back into the thick of life. He hoped someday she'd realize just how good life really could be. That it wasn't all drudgery, pain and disappointment. The town of Sweet Home would help her. Those same citizens had taken him in when he'd been weary, filled with doubts and heartsick. Sweet Home had brought him back into the fold of caring, wanting and needing again. Nancy would heal as well, with the aid of the town's wellspring of love, of this, Jack was certain.

He collected Carla Daws, and they were ready to leave for home.

Jack drew rein at the sheriff's office to bid goodbye to Frank Hyde, and to wish him well. Another wagon stood just outside the office. A handsome fawn-colored milk cow, with calf, was tied on behind it, working on its cud.

Jack stepped to the ground with Carla and Nancy, and all three entered the office together.

A tall man stood at Hyde's desk. He held his hat in one hand, and in the crook of the other arm, a baby lay crying at peak volume. Its blankets were filthy where the infant had been colicky and had spit up many times. An unmistakable odor arose in a thick, humid wave that rolled upward from the heavily swaddled infant.

The tall man talked in a voice pitched high. Jack could feel his unease. "I was all over this town and entire county, Sheriff. I got to find someone to take this baby. I got a ranch to run. But I ain't had time for nothing but tending this child.

"This baby needs a woman. I can't find a soul to take him in.

"I knew you had children of your own, Frank. I thought maybe you might be interested in one more."

Frank Hyde had revealed to Jack that he had two children of his own already and was rearing three of his dead sister's youngsters as well. The last thing he and Rose needed now was another one—especially not an infant.

Hyde removed his pipe, exhaled, and lifted his hand in a defensive posture. "Can't help you, Exeter. I've already got more sprouts than I know what to do with."

The man, Exeter, Jack recalled from Dr. Katz's sad tale, had lost his wife in childbirth. Now here he was, hoping to find someone to take the baby.

Exeter shifted on his feet the way a man does when the plans he'd hung all his hopes on had just slid to a halt like a runaway team and wagon, and toppled over in the ditch. He looked about ready to give up, but there didn't even seem to be an easy way for him to do that.

Jack felt his heart going out to him. His own father had been in the same sorry jackpot years ago when Jack's mother had died. His father too had a ranch to run, and a motherless child in need of attention. Jack wondered what he might do to help.

While he mulled the problem over, Carla Daws stepped forward, shoulder in bandages, and took the child from Exeter. Right away, the two females left the office. The men went to the doorway and watched them cross the street toward the hardware store.

The puzzled father said, "I already tried the Johnson's. They ain't got time for him."

Jack said, "Somehow, I don't think that's what they have in mind, Mr. Exeter."

Suddenly fate slapped Jack full in the face. A cold blast from a winter wind straight out of the north came hurtling toward him. "Well, what do you make of it then?" mumbled Exeter.

Carla and Nancy stepped from sight into the hardware store, and Exeter revealed his sad tale to Hyde and Jack. After the death of his wife, he'd hated the baby, for he was left all alone with the noisy, helpless creature. His wife had been more to him than just someone to share his bed. She'd been his partner on the ranch. She did the wash for them all, help included. She kept the books and cooked the meals. So it was little wonder Exeter got bowled over when fate played him the cruelest of jokes, taking from him a wonderful, independent, warm person, and leaving him shackled to a wet, hopelessly dependent child.

He told them that after Dr. Katz's departure, he seriously considered taking the baby out and disposing of it. His better senses prevailed, though, and, instead, he started scouring the county for a family in need of a child.

Still, his run of bad luck hadn't ended, for no one seemed to want his child.

Jack drew one of the longest, deepest breaths of his life, as he studied the fine milk cow tied on behind the Exeter wagon. The cow looked young and healthy. It was fresh, with a full bag of milk.

At last, he said, "That cow there go with the infant, Exeter?"

Exeter grunted, coughed a couple of times, then said, "Why, yessir." His face flushed a bright color. "A pail and a holding crock too … as well as a new cloth to strain the milk through … that there calf too. A calf can't be separated from its mam, now can it? Them creatures are full Jersey blood, sir."

They stood beneath the roof of the porch, waiting. Exeter seemed to be bursting with hope, and that hope had changed the man's entire personality.

He rocked to-and-fro, heel to toe and back again. His chest expanded with what appeared to Jack to be wondrous expectations. His face glowed with new vigor.

At length, Nancy and Carla returned. They'd bathed the child, wrapped it in a fresh blanket, and oiled its tiny head right handsomely. Above all, the constant, infernal crying had ceased.

Nancy, in the role of nurse, had a large bag slung over a shoulder that probably held all the items needed in the proper care of a newborn.

Exeter smiled a wide smile. He rocked fore and aft even more vigorously.

They all stepped out onto the boardwalk. Carla mounted to the wagon seat.

Nancy held the child up to her from the ground, and she took it from her while the girl climbed aboard. Carla settled down on the seat and cooed now and then to the little boy. Nancy sat on the outside, waiting her chance to hold the infant. A few tears sprang from Exeter's eyes like the remnants of a spring shower. Jack wondered if the man's tears were because he'd just given up the boy, or if they were born of the joy of handing over his responsibilities to someone else. By and by, because he didn't want to think the worst of the man, he decided they were of the former.

The affair was over—done with, Jack knew, and he hadn't had a word to say in the entire matter.

He turned to the sheriff. "Send me a wire, Frank, if you need me for the hearing."

"It'll be some time now, I guess. But I will, Jack. I'll send for you." Jack shook Exeter's hand, and told him if he ever wanted to see the boy, he'd be more than welcome to do so. But it appeared Exeter hadn't completely forgiven the child for the death of his mate.

He said, "Naw. I don't think so. It'd probably be best if he never even hears my name."

Jack thought this much too harsh. "Whatever you think is best."

He tied the Jersey milk cow on behind his wagon, alongside his saddle horse, climbed aboard, lifted the lines over the backs of his animals, and snapped them lightly onto their rumps.

Later that night, he sat with the infant in his arms, while Nancy and Carla cooked supper.

He said, "Ever been to a wedding, Nancy?"

Nancy shook her head, then turned back to her chores.

"Friends of mine and Carla's are getting married. Maybe, if we're in time, we can attend. Would you like that?"

A tiny smile broke out upon her face. "Yessir, Mr. Mahan. I think that would be nice."

Nancy Peavey had been through so much, he knew. But if her bright smile just now was any indication, he saw that she was back on the right path. It'd take time, he knew. Time and the love of people who cared for her.

Carla Daws looked at Jack. She smiled coyly. "You might just get the chance to attend another wedding soon," she said to Nancy, but holding Mahan's eyes under her spell. "That is if a certain barkeep decides it's time to settle down." J

ack Mahan, orphaned at an early age, had never known the warmth of a close family. He figured to get his chance now. What with Carla, Bridget McReynolds, Nancy Peavey and the little boy, he suddenly had a full-fledged family.

He'd heard that Ben Short's widow was moving back to St. Joe to live with her sister. He planned to buy the big house from her. With a large family, he needed such a house. A wave of joy lifted from his chest and surged high above him, and left him weak-kneed.

He clutched the child closer to his chest.

He said, "I know one barkeep that is more than ready to settle down."

Just then, the baby burped. It was a good wet burp, which settled the matter, and they all laughed with abandonment.

END

Lightning Source UK Ltd.
Milton Keynes UK
UKHW020159090223
416651UK00003B/743

9 781990 089077